Anasazi Quest

To Dick,

Happy Reading!

[illegible]

9 February 2005

Anasazi Quest

James Gibson

Pentacles Press

This novel is a work of fiction. References to real people, events, establishments, and locales are intended only to give the fiction a sense of reality and authenticity. All of the main characters, organizations, events, and incidents in this novel are creations of the author's imagination, and their resemblance, if any, to actual persons, living or dead, or to organizations or events, is entirely coincidental.

DISCLAIMER

The author and publisher of this material are **NOT RESPONSIBLE** in any manner whatsoever for any injury that may result from reading and/or following the self-defense and combat techniques described in this work of fiction. These techniques can result in serious injury or death, and must only be attempted under the supervision of a qualified instructor after appropriate training.

Published by:
Pentacles Press
Division of James N. Gibson Enterprises, LLC.
340 N. Main Street, Suite 301B
Plymouth, MI 48170
www.pentaclespress.com

In conjunction with:
Old Mountain Press, Inc.
2542 S. Edgewater Dr.
Fayetteville, NC 28303

www.oldmountainpress.com

Digital photo work by Mark Gibson
ISBN: 0-9721351-1-1
Library of Congress Control Number: 2003093603

Anasazi Quest.

First Edition
Manufactured in the United States of America
1 2 3 4 5 6 7 8 9 10

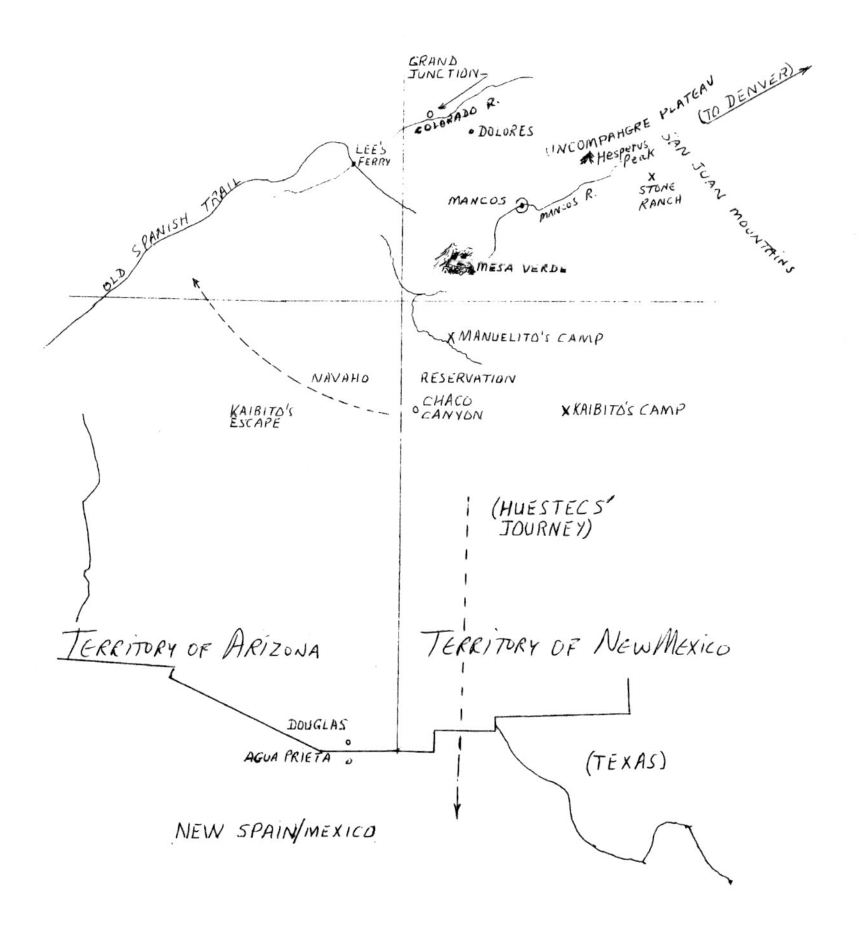

Territories

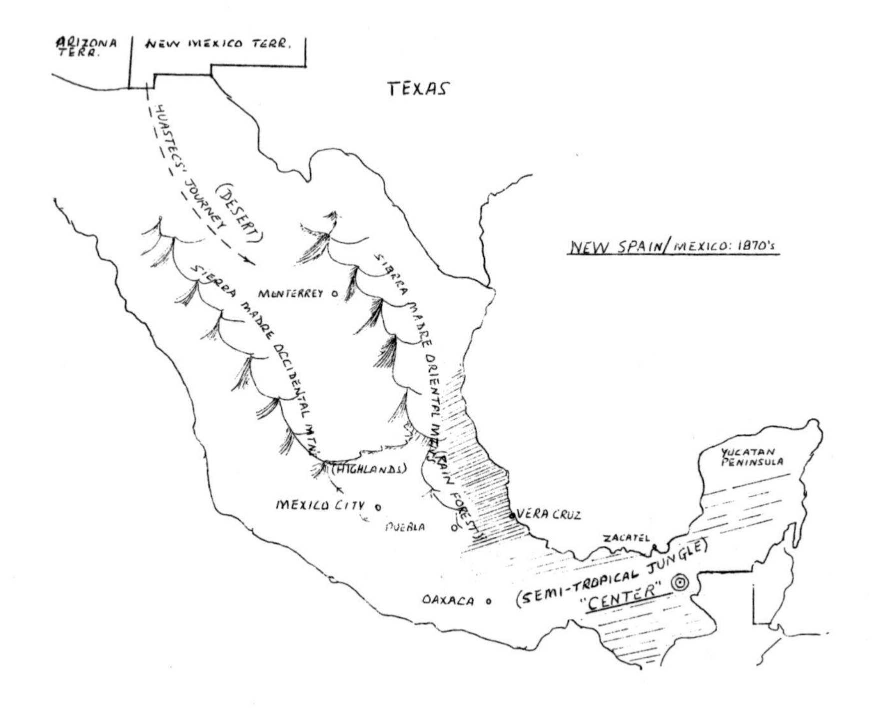

New Spain/Mexico

In Memory of
Henry Anthony ("Tony") Gibson,
(December 27, 1946 - August 18,1980)
The cousin who was more like a brother.
We rode horses together,
And he died too soon.

Acknowledgments

I AM GRATEFUL FOR the reader feedback and new friends I have made through my books. I started with a vision, and soon found there is an enormous learning curve in the writing and marketing of books. While errors and omissions are my own, many people have come to my aid with expertise, encouragement and support. Tom Davis, of Old Mountain Press, was one of my first contacts. He soon realized he had a total novice on his hands. With the patience of Job, he led me through the steps and kept my spirits up until at last *Anasazi Princess* came off the press. I cannot say enough to express my gratitude for his help and support. In addition, he writes interesting books which I enjoy reading when I need a boost.

Chris Day, Ph.D. is a long-time supporter who sets an example for what one can accomplish with boundless energy and whose insights are incisive and valuable.. Julie Keating graciously proofread *Anasazi Journey*, and made it immensely more readable (I wasn't smart enough to have her proof *Anasazi Princess*, which I now regret.) I also appreciate her valuable insights and suggestions for *Anasazi Quest*. Ralph and Mary Gillum shared their interest and knowledge of similar books, and gave helpful suggestions for improving mine. They brought the books of Sharyn McCrumb to my attention. These books helped me in incorporating the "second Sight" concept into *Anasazi Quest*. Alan Stuart attended one of my book signings, and related his experiences in the 1940s during a three month sojourn in Mesa Verde. He provided documentation of Dark Canyon, a hidden enclave with water that validated my premise that the Huastecs could have remained in Mesa Verde until the 1870s. Dale Eckerty, a friend and former business associate, utilizes his unique talents to proof my books and point out any inconsistencies, as well as providing encouragement that my books can be of interest to readers of various genres. Our son Mark is particularly helpful in providing technical support, keeping my computers running, and handling the digitalization of photos and maps. Lee Flamard provides visual arts expertise and creative ideas that help me to visualize new and better opportunities to improve my books. To Betty, Chris and others at the "Little Book Shoppe on the Park", special thanks for being the first to stock my books, and support my book signings. I also acknowledge and appreciate the support of family and friends whom I will not attempt to name for fear of leaving someone out.

And to you, the reader, thank you for your continued support. I feel we are in a partnership, on a journey together through the characters in my books. I hope you find the journey stimulating and rewarding.

James Gibson
Northville, Michigan
March 28, 2003

Author's Note

READER FEEDBACK HELPS a writer validate his or her effectiveness (or ineffectiveness!)in communicating believable protagonists in plausible events that make up an engaging story. While a writer has wider latitude in fiction than in nonfiction, the reader will suspend belief only up to the point where he or she perceives the story has become so implausible or outrageous as to become fantasy. Feedback from some readers indicated that, in their judgement, I had crossed the line!

In my defense, I propose that the *Anasazi Princess* series of books may be fantastic, but they are not fantasy. The character Tonah's shamanism is true to a long tradition that goes back some 15,000 years, as depicted in cave art in France (*Shamanism: An Introductory Guide*, Nevill Drury, p. 13). Shamanism continues to be a tradition in indigenous societies throughout the world up to the present time (Drury, p. 25). A key feature of the shaman's art is controlling the flow of energies in other worlds (*The Truth About Shamanism*, Amber Wolfe, p. 2).

Shamans in many societies have adapted "sacred plants" to their use as hallucinogenic drugs (e.g., peyote, U.S. and Mexico) as well as numerous healing agents. I read widely on this subject, and often incorporate actual rituals and/or insights into my fiction. I found a wealth of information and ideas on plants and their uses in *Oaxaca Journal* (Oliver Sacks), such as the fact that fireflies, when ingested, are lethal due to a digitalis-like substance in their chemical makeup (p. 112). The shaman Chinto imparts this knowledge to Caleb in *Anasazi Quest.* In his classic *The Way of the Shaman*, Michael Harner describes the effects of ingesting *ayahuasca,* a hallucinogenic drink made from the extract of a certain vine, while among the Amazonian Indians. The administration of frog poison by an Amazonian shaman using the burning end of a twig is described in graphic detail in Mark Plotkin's *Medicine Quest* (pp. 117-19). A recent survey by Daniel Pinchbeck (*Breaking Open the Head*) indicates that shamanism and psychedelic journeying continue to be alive and well, and active throughout the world.

Students of the Bible, particularly the Old Testament, will see many parallels and analogies in the saga of the Huastecs, a "lost tribe" seeking its homeland in a strange and unfamiliar world. Throughout the Old Testament, religious leaders and wise men of the emerging Judaism engaged in what we would now refer to as shamanistic practices, if not sorcery (Samuel, Daniel, Moses, among others). Caleb's journey to knowledge is allegorical in that his journey is that of all human beings who are forced to confront challenges to basic values and as a result to change their world view.

Caleb's experiences during his spirit quest incorporate some of the conclusions of modern quantum physics, with the case being made in the classic *The Tao of Physics* by Fritjof Capra that Eastern mysticism and quantum physics are merging in their respective explanations of existence at the subatomic particle/energy level. While the mystics claim that some enlightened people can actually face Creation, they assert that the experience is so profound and otherworldly that words cannot describe it. In the intriguing *Stalking the Wild Pendulum*, Itzhak Bentov uses quantum mechanics to explain how any oscillating system, including our bodies and that of other entities, have mathematical points of "zero velocity" and "infinite time" which would permit unlimited time in altered states of consciousness while only minute amounts of time passed in the world of ordinary reality. This conclusion could at least theoretically permit the "jogs" of time utilized by Tonah and explained to his apprentice Aurel, which Aurel later used in his own vision quest. This concept could also explain the phenomenon of Chinese students with "Exceptional Human Functions" (*China's Super Psychics*, Paul Dong & Thomas E. Rafill) who are said to be able to manipulate objects with their minds, including removing pills from sealed medicine bottles (p. 170).

To finish making the point, a native from a Stone Age society could sit in an airliner at 30,000 feet and have no sense that he was moving. He would look out the window at a jet engine and have no concept of the power it was generating, or even that the engine was operating. When he returned to his people and related his experience, they would look upon it as magic, or worse – a fabrication, for nothing in their culture would explain how such an event could be possible.

Perhaps we consider Tonah's world implausible and fantastic because we do not yet understand how things work in states of nonordinary reality. That is why I choose to write what I call "plausible fiction", for as our knowledge increases, the lines between strange and incredible fact, and strange but plausible fiction, may blur and merge. To me, the joy of writing lies in exploring the possibilities.

James Gibson
Northville, Michigan
March 28, 2003

Prologue

"Even though I walk through the valley of the shadow of death, I will fear no evil, for you are with me; your rod and your staff, they comfort me." (Psalm 23:4, Bible, NIV.)

❖

TONAH, THE HUASTEC shaman and spiritual leader of the Huastecs, approached the lodge of Shanni, his granddaughter. Shanni had reached young womanhood when circumstances forced the Huastecs to leave their home in the hidden canyons of Mesa Verde. The Huastecs found refuge with the Navaho people while Shanni recovered from her attack by the renegade, Kaibito. Tonah welcomed the respite offered by the hospitality of the Navaho leader, Manuelito.

Shanni was sitting quietly in the late afternoon sun, gazing across the Navaho camp.

"Greetings, Granddaughter," Tonah smiled. "It is good to see you up and around. You are recovering rapidly."

"Hello. Yes, I'm feeling much better and growing impatient to get on with my duties."

"And what might they be?"

"I intend to train with the Huastec men, learning the fighting skills that Manuelito's warriors will be teaching us."

"That is quite an undertaking. Are you sure you will be strong enough?"

"The training will help me to recover my strength. Eventually I will be as strong as the men."

"As you wish, but it will certainly be a change of custom. You must find a way to get the men to accept you in that role."

"I know, and I've been thinking about how to do it. They will be more receptive when they realize the need. There are too few of us Huastecs to waste even one warrior, whether man or woman. I've spoken with Ambria. She and many of the women also intend to train."

"Will the training interfere with your Gift?"

"No. I believe it will make it stronger. Already I am able to stabilize my ability to see the probabilities for the future, and I'm hopeful it will help me to look farther ahead in avoiding danger for our people."

"That is good," Tonah agreed. "We are so early into our journey, and already we have faced near-disaster."

"But maybe to a good purpose," Shanni interjected. "Now all of our people have a better understanding of the obstacles we face."

"They know of the physical obstacles, but they do not yet know of the evil forces arrayed against us in the spirit world. These we must fight alone."

" 'We?' Must you and I alone face the evil ones?" Shanni's eyes reflected her concern.

"I believe that Power has given us a new and powerful ally in Caleb Stone."

"Do you think you can train him in the art of sorcery?"

"Yes. He has at least suspended disbelief, although he has a strong will and we have little time in which to train."

"Maybe even less time than we thought," Shanni interjected. "My prescience is warning that our time here is growing short. Some threat is moving toward us in the physical world, forcing us to act."

Tonah looked away with misgiving. Shanni's gift was never wrong. Something ominous was about to happen and there was little time to prepare.

THE CAMPFIRES OF the Navaho flickered across the camp as Shanni and Tonah finished their evening meal. They sat in silence, enjoying the quiet time as the sun set and the darkness of evening settled over the land. The night was clear, and the canopy of stars slowly emerged, seeming close enough to reach out and touch. Shanni's thoughts turned to Caleb. Had they been wrong to yield to duty and postpone their marriage? Who knew when this journey would be over? Were they tempting Fate when so much could happen to separate them again? Shanni sighed, disturbed by the turn of her thoughts. Why was she in such an apprehensive mood tonight? Tonah sensed her thoughts, and felt her agitation.

"You are thinking of Caleb?" he asked quietly.

"Is it wrong to long for our happiness instead of my duty to my people?"

"No, it is to be expected. When two people give their hearts to one another, they are forever bound across time and space. Even death does not part them. It is both the grandest beauty, and the most terrible burden of this mysterious world in which we live."

"Yes, it is a mysterious world, when one stops to think. I believe one is happier focusing on everyday things."

Tonah nodded agreement. "That is why most people fill their days with activities. That way they do not have to reflect on their life and their real purpose for being born into this world."

"Purpose? Do we ever really know why we are born? Does each person have a divine purpose for his life? And if so, how does each person find it?"

"Those are deep questions, my dear," Tonah chuckled, reaching to pat Shanni gently on the shoulder as he rose. "And the answer is, that Purpose finds you at the right time and place. One can neither anticipate it nor hurry it. One can only hope to be ready, and to recognize when the time has come."

"Rest now," Tonah added, turning to leave. "I must go work with Aurel. After many years as my apprentice, he is reaching the end of the knowledge I can impart to him. He must begin his spirit quest soon, and there will be no more I can do for him. We will be needing his youth and strength when we next engage the evil beings in the spirit world."

Shanni gazed, unseeing, at Tonah's back as he disappeared into the shadows. She hugged her knees and watched the flickering firelight, trying to calm her misgivings. She realized now, more than ever, how beautiful it would be to be married to Caleb Stone, bearing his children and living a quiet life on his ranch. Was it so wrong to want contentment? Must one always sacrifice personal desires for duty? Why must there be this mysterious Purpose? Wasn't living one's life enough?

Shanni gazed up at the stars twinkling overhead. So many, and so silent, she thought, as a sense of timelessness, of eternity, settled over her. A silent song of life formed unbidden in her mind:

I raise my head up high
Gazing at the starlit sky
And again I wonder why
So much is hidden from us.

For life is such a mystery
We open our eyes but cannot see
Where or what is the key
To all that we behold.

Are we doomed to wonder why
Striving, failing, until with a sigh
We at last lay down and die
Still without understanding?

Are we only here by chance;
An accidental cosmic happenstance
Too trivial to merit a glance
From a universe expanding?

Or are we put here by design
Equipped with a questing mind
So that at last we may unwind
The mysteries before us?

I myself may never know
For mankind still has too far to go
To know the Truth, even so
We'll push on untiring.

For I believe there'll come a time
When we will know the Grand Design
And I am just grateful that I'm
Somehow a part of it.

Shanni felt calmness replacing her agitation as she rose silently to enter her lodge. Somehow things would work out for her and Caleb. She had to believe that. How could a Universe permit love to exist and not nurture it? Finding peace, she settled under the blankets and fell into a deep sleep.

Chapter 1

CALEB LOOKED OUT across the San Juan River at the dust thrown up by approaching riders. Manuelito heard the hoof beats and came out of his tent to watch. As they drew closer, Caleb recognized Lieutenant Porter at the head of a squad of soldiers. Porter had become a friend to the Navaho and the Huastecs during their recent troubles with the renegade Kaibito and his band. Porter halted and dismounted near the river. He strode forward while his men watered the horses.

"Howdy," Porter said, extending a hand to Caleb, and nodding to Manuelito. "Heard you were preparing to continue your journey."

"We plan to accept Manuelito's hospitality a few more weeks while we train the Huastec men to use rifles, and Manuelito's men will teach them hand-to-hand combat skills. When they're ready, we'll move on."

"Ahuh. Well, that's why I'm here. Being peaceful, the Huastecs aren't a problem for the military. I'm happy to leave things as they are. But we've got a new Indian Agent coming in, and he's already sent word that he'll be visiting all the tribes and making a census. If you're here, he'll count the Huastecs and you won't be able to leave."

Caleb glanced at Manuelito. Porter was being a friend, letting them know, but this was bad news for the Huastecs. They'd have to face the wasteland to the south in haste and unprepared.

"How much time do we have?" Caleb asked.

"He's due by the end of the week, and sounds like he wants to get started pronto. I'd say he'll need another week to get settled, and then he'll be riding out with his escort, which will likely be my troopers."

"We're obliged to you for giving us some warning. I'll have to discuss this with Tonah and the others, and then see what we can do."

"Least I could do after all we went through together fighting Kaibito."

Porter turned and walked back to rejoin his troops. With a wave he mounted and they spurred their horses across the river.

Caleb turned to Manuelito. "There are more than two hundred of the Huastecs, and we have less than two weeks. I'd better tell Tonah and the others."

Manuelito nodded his assent as Caleb hurried across the compound to find Tonah.

Tonah was sitting with Shanni outside her lodge. Shanni was regaining her strength from the attack by Kaibito that had nearly taken her life.

Tonah sensed Caleb's agitation and rose to meet him.

"I'm afraid I have bad news," Caleb said. "Lieutenant Porter stopped by to warn us that a new Indian Agent is arriving within a week. He proposes to conduct a census as soon as he arrives. If the Huastecs are still in camp, they will be counted and kept on the reservation. After that, if you leave to complete your journey, you will be hunted down by the soldiers."

Tonah turned to Shanni. "This is grave news. We have little time to prepare."

Shanni stood up. Determination burned in her eyes as she spoke. "We must discuss this development with Matal and the others, and find a course of action. We cannot be trapped here. Our journey has just begun!"

Tonah nodded in assent. "Caleb, could I ask you to seek out Matal and give him this news? Ask him to spread the word to the other warriors, and meet tonight in my lodge. We must develop a plan quickly to avoid panic among our people."

Caleb nodded, rising, to walk among the tents scattered along the river, looking for Matal.

THE FLAMES FROM torches lighted the way for the warriors assembling in Tonah's lodge. Matal and more than a dozen of the Huastec warriors gathered with Manuelito, Shanni, and Caleb as Tonah opened the meeting.

"You all heard the news about the new Agent. We thought we had time to train in the fighting skills needed to defend ourselves before we left camp and resumed our journey to the Center. Now time is running out. All the Huastecs must leave within the week or we will become prisoners of the Anglo government. This meeting is to develop a plan."

Matal rose to speak. "We have discussed this among ourselves," he waved a hand to include the other Huastec warriors. "We have enough silver to buy repeating rifles and revolvers. We must purchase them soon, and learn how to use them. Manuelito's warriors can teach us all the skills we need to survive the journey, but we must have time to train."

"Time is what we do not have," Tonah replied.

"Unless you can find a temporary refuge," Manuelito broke in quietly.

Matal turned to Manuelito. "Yes, that would buy us the time we need. What do you have in mind?"

"Kaibito's camp."

Caleb looked at Tonah for a reaction, but Tonah remained silent, pondering. The Huastecs had suffered in the desert. They would fear leaving the security of Manuelito's camp and returning to a journey into the unknown. Commitment to the chosen course of action would require the consensus of the people. If the Huastec warriors agreed, maybe the people would follow them.

Matal frowned, reviewing the suggestion. "It's big enough, and has water, but there is no source of food."

"It is isolated," Manuelito continued. "The Indian Agent would have no knowledge of it since there is no permanent settlement there. Wild game, mostly deer, is available two days' ride to the west, near Betatakin. I'd estimate a large group like the Huastecs could live there one, maybe two months before the game was depleted."

"Alternatives?" Tonah interjected.

Shanni spoke up. "We cannot return to Mesa Verde, and now we cannot stay here. We agree we are unprepared to resume our journey. I suggest we pack in supplies to the camp and supplement them with game. This will extend our stay and offset our dependence on hunting for our food."

"I agree," Caleb added. "But the more supplies we try to carry with us, the greater the need for horses and carts. With over two hundred people to move and care for, it will be difficult to travel without discovery."

"My trackers can help," Manuelito said. "They know the route, and can guide your travel. I suggest that the caravan travel at night, and hold up in hidden spots during the day. You should be able to reach the camp in five days."

Matal nodded. "It sounds like we have the beginning of a plan. Now we'll need to work out the details."

"But first we must bring all the others into the discussion," Tonah interjected. "We must get their suggestions and address their concerns. We will need the commitment of everyone for the hardships ahead."

"Well spoken," Manuelito agreed. "People will resist if they feel you are already committed to this course of action without having their say in it."

"We could divide up the families among us as temporary leaders," Matal suggested, his glance including the Huastecs in the circle. "Each of us could brief his group and start the process of getting everyone's agreement."

Matal was a natural leader, Caleb thought with approval. How quickly Matal had matured during the recent trials of the Huastecs! The other Huastec warriors already followed him willingly, and the challenges were only beginning.

"Is everyone in agreement with this approach?" Tonah asked.

Murmurs and nods of assent went around the assemblage.

"Then we must make haste. We will reconvene tomorrow night. If we have everyone's agreement, we must begin planning for the move to Kaibito's camp."

"What about the supplies; guns, ammunition, horses, carts?" Caleb added. "We have a lot to do to get ready."

"Leave that to us," Manuelito spoke up. "My men can use some of your silver to purchase guns and ammunition in Mexico. We will secure the carts and horses quietly among villages near our reservation."

Caleb frowned to himself. Somehow they must secure supplies and move nearly two hundred people over fifty miles through the desert without being discovered. And they must do it all in little more than a week! It would take a miracle to pull it off.

Shanni stood up and faced the men. "Many changes to our customary ways will be required. Anyone capable of fighting, man or woman, must be trained and equipped. We cannot anticipate all the dangers we will face, so all of the Huastecs must be ready to do their part. Be sure the families understand, for there can be no turning back. We must reach the Center of our ancestors or we will all die."

The men nodded, agreeing with Shanni's words. Their mood was somber as they got up to carry out their duties.

A WEEK LATER, Lieutenant Porter and his soldier escort arrived with the Indian Agent at the edge of the San Juan River. They halted their horses to gaze across at the lodges of the Navaho camp, scattered peacefully along the bank of the stream. Porter blinked, not believing his eyes. Nearly a hundred Huastec tents had disappeared as if they had never existed. Porter let out his breath and held his peace.

Chapter 2

THE FIRST NIGHT, the caravan traveled swiftly and quietly, the people recognizing the need to put distance between themselves and the Navaho camp. A number of Huastec men walked behind the other travelers with wooden rakes and crude brushes to erase signs of their passage. Cart wheel tracks and hoof prints were carefully eliminated, leaving no marks on the hard, gravelly soil.

Near dawn, the Navaho trackers led the caravan toward the low hills and found a hidden canyon suitable for temporary day camp. The tired travelers ate and then put up temporary shelters from the sun. Soon they settled down to sleep under the watchful eyes of sentries.

Tonah awakened early in the afternoon and ate. He rose and walked to the shade of a boulder to sit quietly, thinking. He sensed Shanni's presence and turned as she walked through the crowded camp toward him.

"I saw that you had awakened," Shanni said as she paused in front of him. "I hope I am not disturbing you. I know sometimes you like to meditate alone."

"No, please join me. I slept deeply, but awakened with a troubled mind. I have not yet determined what is causing it."

"I, too, am troubled, although our travel to Kaibito's camp seems to be going well."

"It is not the physical world which weighs on us; it is the spirit world. I suggest that we travel together in the spirit world to determine what is the cause of our misgivings. The travel should require less strength, since we will seek allies and not have to combat enemies. Do you feel strong enough to try?"

"Yes. I need to eat, and then I will return."

"Please ask Aurel to join us. We will need his support."

Shanni nodded her agreement. "We will return soon."

Aurel stretched a blanket on four poles, creating a shelter in the shade of the canyon wall. Using coals from the camp, he kindled a small fire nestled in a bed of stones. Tonah and Shanni sat comfortably on a blanket spread under the awning and stared into the flames.

Tonah cast about with his eyes, searching. A pebble caught his eye and he moved to grasp it in his left hand. The stone felt smooth, comfortable in his hand. He peered at it, appreciating the striations of color embedded over millennia. The pebble would anchor him to this "time" and "place" in the manifestation of the physical universe.

Without being told, Shanni gazed with her eyes unfocused, until a glint of light caught her awareness and she looked at the source, a glass-like stone that lay among the gravel. She picked it up and cupped it in her hand as she sat back down beside Tonah.

"Look at the flame, and then close your eyes," Tonah said. "After a moment, you will continue to see the flame. Follow me up the flame into a higher vibration. On that plane we will seek knowledge."

Shanni did as he suggested, and felt calmness settle over her as she watched the flame. She felt Tonah's awareness touch her and then move up the heat from the flame, moving skyward. And then she was floating effortlessly, moving "up" through the darkness, weightless. She felt temporary disorientation and a sensation of falling.

"Steady," Tonah's voice reached her. "Soon we will reach a signpost."

Shanni's perception detected a glimmering in the distance, a silvery presence that glistened like light on a dewdrop. She felt a sensation of movement toward it, and became aware of Tonah's hand on her shoulder.

The dewdrop began to expand, and she was looking inside it into a world of snow-capped peaks with green valleys and sparkling rivers. Near the center a low peak rose from the valley floor supporting a white structure of many windows looking out over the surrounding plain.

She saw Tonah out of the corner of her eye as he soared downward, leading her into an open doorway. She perceived the immensity of the building as they stood, dwarfed by the entrance that led into a long hallway. At the end of the hallway the wall was filled with strange statues, lit by innumerable candles set in wooden shelves.

They walked forward, and a solitary figure dressed in a long robe rose from a kneeling position and turned to look at them. Shanni had the distinct feeling that the figure was expecting them. Without a word, he gestured for them to follow and entered a dimly lit room. He bowed and moved behind them out of the doorway, closing it behind him.

Shanni stood beside Tonah as her eyes adjusted to the dim light and she perceived the form of an ancient man, sitting quietly, meditating. A feeling of kindness and compassion flowed out from the figure to envelop them. Shanni felt her apprehension draining away to be replaced by a feeling of warmth and well-being.

The man opened his eyes and smiled impishly, like a small boy who is delighted in a new toy.

"Greetings, my friends. I am honored by your visit. What brings you to my humble dwelling?"

"We come seeking answers," Tonah said. "We have discovered unknown enemies in the spirit world. We must learn how to withstand them."

"Your choice of words is not lost on me," the man said with approval. "If you sought to meet confrontation with confrontation, I could not help you."

"We seek only to resist the spirits that seek to do us harm. Already they have threatened our lives in the physical world."

"Then we must have a look. I will join my perception with yours while you remember your contact with the beings."

Shanni felt a tickle as the man's awareness expanded, enveloping them in a sentient bubble. Instantly, like a runaway dream, Tonah's memory replayed the events he had experienced in the dream-catcher and later in the stone temple. Shanni saw herself trapped in the cocoon and her feelings of fear and dread resurfaced, to be gone as quickly as Tonah's awareness returned to the room.

"Somehow you have created a disturbance in one of the innumerable spirit worlds. These worlds are far removed from the physical place we call 'earth'. Each world has its own self-importance. Seldom do beings from one world even acknowledge the existence of other worlds, let alone concern themselves with them. This is most unusual. What could be their motive?"

"Our people, the Huastecs, are forced by circumstances to attempt to journey back to the ancient Center of our civilization," Tonah said. "We seek to reconnect with our people. The trouble began when we started the journey."

"Ah, I recall your memory about the disturbance in the node of causality. Without being aware of it, you are threatening something long hidden."

"How can we find out what it is, and how to address it?"

"The answer is not immediately apparent. You may have to journey to the center of the spirit world, and wrest the answer from the very beings that threaten you."

"That means a battle of wills. We would have to overcome their resistance to divulging the secrets which we threaten."

"I'm afraid so. I see no other way. We may be able to provide support at a critical juncture, but we are unable to interfere."

"The battle is ours to fight," Tonah *replied. "It is our fate and our responsibility. It would help if we knew how to proceed."*

"You must build the strength of your resolve, and train others with you to join in your awareness when you engage the beings. Your collective strength multiplies your power. But you must have a strong leader to focus this energy. You will need a champion."

"A person of strong stamina in the physical world," Tonah *agreed.*

"And of indomitable will," *the man added.*

"A person who would die before he would yield," Tonah *replied.*

"Precisely."

Tonah bowed in thanks, and Shanni felt the presence fading into the darkness. Again, a feeling of benevolence and compassion surrounded her as the room disappeared.

She felt Tonah's hand gently touch her shoulder and they were rising effortlessly into the void. They left the world as it turned into a dewdrop, glistening with the snow-capped mountains and the white structure in its center. It seemed to zoom away at great speed and disappeared completely. Shanni felt disoriented, as if she were falling through space.

"Steady," she felt Tonah's voice inside her mind. "Remember the stone."

Her perception centered on the stone she had picked up from the gravel and it came into view, floating in the darkness like an unlit star. As she focused, it became larger and she again saw the striations that made it unique and pleasurable to hold. As she grasped it, the void shimmered with light. She felt queasiness in her stomach and a sensation of disorientation.

Without volition, her eyes opened and the camp of the Huastecs came into view. Wet with perspiration, she breathed deeply and lifted her hand to gaze at the stone.

Chapter 3

Continuum
How large is large, how small is small?
We may never know.
I've spent my lifetime seeking the truth
And I've still too far to go.

How insignificant is Man: On a minor planet,
Near a meager sun, in an unimposing galaxy,
in an unbounded universe?
It can be said that Man is small.

Yet Man is made up of organs and cells;
Composed of molecules and atoms as well.
And if smaller we go, to sub-atoms and below
We do not know
What is there.
So one can tell, equally well, that Man is large.

The point of all this is that Man exists
Standing between the outstretched arms of God.
Without ending or beginning
In an eternal ring,
A marvelous thing,
Continuing.

(Tonah's explanation of the universe to Aurel, the apprentice.)

CALEB RODE TO the rear of the travelers and nodded with satisfaction. Several of the Huastec men were using their horses to drag brush back and forth across their trail. A careful tracker could find signs of their passage, but sweeping the trail obliterated obvious marks and hid the size of the group. The normal desert winds would remove any remaining indications of their travel in a few days.

He turned and rode to the head of the column. He saw the caravan strung out for nearly a mile as the Huastecs, some leading the horses pulling carts, trekked toward Kaibito's abandoned camp. Hardship awaited the Huastecs at the camp, Caleb knew, but being there would buy them time to prepare.

He saw Walpi, Manuelito's tracker, outlined ahead in the light of the full moon. Walpi had guided him after Kaibito, and Caleb knew Walpi to be a competent tracker of few words. Caleb rode up beside Walpi, who turned and nodded. Walpi was a stocky, barrel-chested Navaho of immense strength and unassuming manner. He was one of Manuelito's most experienced men and Manuelito placed great confidence in his judgment. His knowledge of battle tactics and hand-to-hand combat were key to the training of the Huastec warriors.

"The journey goes well," Caleb noted. "We can expect to reach camp the day after tomorrow."

"It will be good to arrive. The camp can be defended. Out here, in open country, the Huastecs are vulnerable to bandits," Walpi replied.

"Where are the other trackers?"

"I sent them far ahead, an hour or more. If they spot trouble, there will be time for one to ride back and warn us, and for us to prepare."

Caleb nodded his approval. Manuelito had said that Walpi was more than a tracker. He was also a thinker.

"Did Manuelito speak to you of the need to provide combat training for the Huastec warriors?"

"Yes."

Caleb smiled to himself. Sometimes he wished that Walpi were not so reticent. If you found out what Walpi was thinking, you had to drag it out of him.

"And what do you think of that?"

"I will do it." Walpi seemed puzzled at the question.

"The Huastec men are few," Caleb continued. "The Huastecs wish for both women and men to train, to increase their fighting force. Did Manuelito discuss this?"

"Yes."

"Will that be a problem for you and your men?"

"No."

Caleb rode in silence. Maybe he was wrong to ask. Had he insulted Walpi by implying that the Navaho might have a problem with training women fighters?

Walpi pulled his horse to a stop. "I have lived a long time, and survived many battles. A warrior is a warrior. The training is difficult, as it must be to prepare for life or death struggle. I have great respect for anyone who is willing to accept the training. Do not concern yourself with me. Life brings changes. I adapt and I survive, and I enjoy each day."

For Walpi, that amounted to an oration, and Caleb's surprise showed. Walpi could not suppress a smile. Caleb realized Walpi had been toying with him.

Caleb returned the smile. "Guess I underestimated you. That was quite a speech!"

"Before the training is over, I'm afraid your charges will be complaining to you to shut me up!" Walpi laughed.

Caleb waved his thanks and rode back toward the column. He was glad he'd broached the subject with Walpi. Something had passed between them. Now Walpi seemed less distant and more human. With his natural reserve, he had waited for Caleb to break the ice. Caleb looked forward to beginning the training.

THE JOURNEY WENT well and the tired travelers reached Kaibito's abandoned camp near noon of the sixth day. They set about erecting tents and preparing for a long stay. Water was brought from the small stream and food set to cooking on the campfires. Then the people settled down to sleep after the long night's travel. Tomorrow they could look forward to returning to their normal schedule of sleeping, instead of travel, during the night.

The Huastecs took over sentry duty, freeing Walpi and the other trackers to begin preparation for combat training. Matal and the group leaders were responsible for identifying all who were to participate in the training from among the Huastec families.

Walpi asked the Huastecs to bind bundles of straw together into mats and stack them in an open area outside camp. He and the trackers swept the ground, clearing off an area large enough for all the trainees to assemble together. They erected sun screens, and set water containers inside. Posts set into the hard earth were wrapped with padding. The posts would be used, Walpi explained, for the trainees to perfect the striking and kicking techniques essential to hand-to-hand fighting.

Time passed as the camp settled into a routine and the day came for the training to start. Caleb, Matal, and Shanni joined the trainees assembled in the cool of the early morning.

Caleb looked around, surveying the group. Nearly fifty men and women stood conversing quietly, waiting. Not all would complete the training, Caleb knew. Accidents and illness would take their inevitable toll. But it was a good beginning.

Walpi, followed by the other three trackers, walked to the front of the assembly and turned to face the group. An expectant hush fell over the participants. Knowing Walpi's reticence, Caleb wondered what he would find to say.

"You all know why you are here, and I welcome you. This is a serious undertaking. What we will teach has been learned in battle. Much of it was learned at the cost of good warriors' lives. By applying yourselves to train well, we will assure that you can fight effectively and not die needlessly.

"Never forget that combat is a dirty business. It consists of sweat, blood and terror. Combat is not to be sought lightly, but when it is inevitable, you must be prepared. Does anyone have a question?"

Everyone remained silent, watching attentively.

"Very well. There are four key principles you must know and consciously apply. Forget them, and you will lose focus to your peril. First, always remember that the aggressor has the advantage. We will teach you to defend yourself by attacking. Overcoming an opponent before he can get set is critical. Second, you must clear your mind and be focused only on your attack. There is no time for anger, fear, or other distraction. This you will learn. Third, only a body that has trained hard is in physical condition to carry out maximum effort with minimum damage to itself. You must push yourself past what you think are your limits. The body has an amazing depth of reserves, but you must reach deep to find it. Do not expect it to be easy. Fourth, you must continue, despite the temptation to quit. That is how your body learns stamina, and your will is strengthened. Success in battle is as much about mental toughness as physical ability. Only you determine if you fail or succeed, and in battle the penalty for failure is death.

"Now we will begin."

Walpi motioned to the other trackers. "Manteh, Nantan, and Antay will assist me. Manteh, please continue."

Manteh, a tall warrior with piercing eyes and muscular arms, stepped forward and began speaking.

"Note the way we are clad. The hair should be worn long, to the shoulders, for protection from the elements as well as to protect the neck. A broad headband holds the hair in place and helps keep perspiration out of the eyes. Straps for rifles or water bags should never be worn over the neck. They can entangle you. Wear the strap over the shoulder only and you can drop it with a shrug, or let it pull away. Leather boots with leggings are supple and quiet, yet protect against cactus and snakebite. Now Nantan will lead you in the first exercise."

Nantan was shorter, nearer Walpi's height, and had a slender frame. But he was wiry, with determination on his face, and he could move swiftly. "Sit down cross-legged, in place. Close your eyes and take deep, slow breaths. Concentrate on your breathing in and out. Think of nothing else. This will clear your mind to focus on the training, and prepare you to go into combat."

Following directions, Caleb joined Shanni, Matal and the others in sitting and doing the breathing exercise. Walpi had made an astounding speech, he thought. And Walpi obviously had given thought to what he would say, knowing the importance of getting the group focused. But there was so much to do, and so little time. Even now, they should be planning...

"Quiet!" Nantan's command broke the stillness. "All of you are letting your minds wander. Stop it and concentrate on your breathing!"

How did he know? Caleb thought, and then he realized that Nantan knew what they would do until they learned to quiet their minds. The mind raced along until it became a habit. As a result, one was always thinking of other things, and never centered in the "now". Caleb began to appreciate the real meaning of focus.

Sheepishly, he concentrated on his breathing, in and out, feeling his agitation melt away. He felt his pulse beating, slowly and steadily, and heard his breaths, long and unhurried. He began to relax and a feeling of serenity and well being engulfed him. So this was what it felt like to be centered. He felt alert and ready, unhurried and confident. His total focus was on the training. He was ready to begin.

Tonah watched the training with interest from his vantage point on a ledge overlooking the camp. The sight of the Huastecs doing drills in unison under the direction of Walpi was gratifying. At last they were implementing a plan essential to the success of their quest to travel to the Center, and to their survival as they faced untold dangers.

He watched as individuals stopped to wipe perspiration. Some were already going to the shelter for water. They had never worked out like this, and the test would be how many could continue when sore muscles and fatigue began to set in. But somehow they must find a way through it. As Walpi had said, this was no game. Failure in games meant second-best, and perhaps loss of face. Failure in combat meant death, there was no second-best, and they would all face many battles before their quest was achieved.

He saw Aurel climbing up the narrow path toward him. Aurel sat down and joined Tonah in watching the men and women working on the training field.

"Tonah, have I failed you?" Aurel opened, a troubled look on his face.

"Why, no. Why do you ask?" Tonah replied, surprised.

"In your battles in the spirit world, you relied on Caleb Stone, Matal and even Shanni. As your apprentice, I do not understand why you did not use me."

"Put your mind at rest. Those were not training exercises. Even I faced evil I had not met before. To defeat them, I needed the strength developed by experienced adults. In adversity some develop strong wills, and that was what I needed to prevail. You have the skills but not yet the years to develop a strong resolve."

"What about Matal? He's only a few years older than me."

"It is not about years. Matal is blessed with a strong personality and natural leadership. But even his lack of testing was almost our undoing."

"Then I must get the experience if I am to grow," Aurel said. "Skill in sorcery is not enough, and yet you forbade me to train with the warriors."

"You have great natural ability in the arts, and I have invested a great deal of training in you," Tonah replied. "Your greatest contribution to the Huastecs will be in sorcery. As a warrior, you would be exposed to the danger of a premature death. All your potential would be lost to us."

"But my full potential as a sorcerer requires me to develop resolve. I can only do that if I am actively engaged in the Huastecs' struggle. I must ask you to reconsider."

Tonah pondered before answering. Was he being too cautious and jeopardizing the very talent he sought to protect? Aurel was young, in his early teens, and already he sought to train with the adults.

"Ah, I wish the correct path would show itself," he said finally. "When I am in doubt, I cast about for a sign."

"In the meantime, what could it hurt? I could train and build both physical and mental strength. Maybe by then we would both know if that is the path I should follow."

"I cannot argue with your logic, but so much of life cannot be addressed with logic. Despite my misgivings, if you want to participate so badly, you have my blessing, but it must not interfere with our sorcery training."

Aurel jumped up, smiling. "It won't, and thank you, Tonah! This is the right path for me. I know it, and you will come to see it is so!"

"Already I feel better about it," Tonah replied, responding to Aurel's enthusiasm. "But for now it is on a trial basis. We will see how things develop before we fully commit to it."

"I understand. Now please excuse me, I must go. Already they have started without me!"

"But you are young," Tonah laughed at the retreating figure. "You will catch up!"

Chapter 4

CALEB SAT DOWN gingerly to eat his meal. They had completed the first week of training, and he'd never felt so many aches and pains. He had always been active, and thought he was in good physical condition, but the drills and exercises by Walpi and his men had moved them to a new level!

He looked up as Shanni approached. While they had seen each other every day, there had been no time to be alone. They had been so close to being married in Manuelito's camp, but Kaibito's attack had spoiled it, and made them both realize they were caught up in a battle much bigger than themselves.

Their happiness would have to wait. He smiled his welcome as she sat down beside him.

"If I ever mention being a woman warrior again, please dunk my head into the stream until you clear my senses!" she said ruefully, rubbing her tired muscles.

"If it makes you feel any better, I'm a basket case myself. I'm surprised half the people haven't dropped out already."

"It's a matter of pride. No one wants to be the first to quit. It'll take illness or a real injury to force someone out. Until then, everyone just keeps hoping somehow it'll get better."

"It will," Caleb replied. "Look at Walpi and his men. They do everything they ask us to do and don't show any ill effects."

"It is amazing. I shudder at the life they must have lived to reach their level of fitness." Shanni shook her head wonderingly.

"I'm sure you've noticed the scars on Walpi's arms," Caleb added. "He got his experience at a price. He's been there, and he knows the penalty for second-best. That drives him."

"That's what we're missing, the Huastecs I mean. We never had to live a life of constant battle. We have to move up to a higher level of intensity."

"That will come, all too soon," Caleb nodded. "Let's hope we're ready."

Shanni looked dreamily at the fire. "If only we could be together on your ranch. Life would be so simple. Now look what I've gotten you into."

"It was my choice. We'll see it through together."

"I almost forgot," Shanni said, sitting up straight to look across the camp. "Matal's called a meeting of the group leaders at Tonah's lodge. I understand the people are starting to complain."

"About what? We've hardly gotten settled!"

"He didn't say, but it must be serious. Let's go. We'll know soon enough."

Matal and the group leaders had assembled outside Tonah's tent when Shanni and Caleb arrived. They exchanged greetings and Matal got down to business.

"As you suggested, Tonah, we have established group leaders over the families to keep everyone informed and to get consensus on matters affecting us all. Overall it has worked well. But all the changes, and living in a new environment, are taking a toll. People are bringing their complaints to us and so far we have been able to resolve them. We don't bother you with day-to-day disputes, but now we are getting bigger problems."

"What are the people's complaints?" Tonah asked.

"They're complaining about the food. They're tired of eating game and grain, the same food every day. And depending on the hunting, sometimes we must make the stews last several days. The people miss their vegetable gardens, fruit and melons."

"As do we all," Tonah agreed. "What do they suggest?"

"Some families are revolting, saying that we should never have left Mesa Verde, and that we're being led to our doom. They want to take what they need and pull out."

"We would not have left Mesa Verde if we could have continued to live there," Tonah's voice was sad. "The water is failing and already the Anglos are closing in to put us on reservations. Splitting up now would jeopardize us all."

"I know," Matal agreed. "But some people are confused and angry, and not thinking straight."

It wasn't fair, Caleb thought. Since he had known the Huastecs, they had relied on Tonah's wisdom to lead them. In many ways Tonah had been too strong, creating dependence none of them recognized. Well, they were in a new world now and Tonah didn't have all the answers. Like it or not, the Huastecs would have to grow up. They had to learn to take responsibility for their lives.

Caleb felt his indignation rising. He was part of it now, like it or not. He'd say his piece.

"It's not for the people to whine to Tonah to solve every hardship," he said. "Why do they think we're training? The Huastecs are fighting for their very existence, and it's time for every one to shoulder the load and get on with it!"

Some of the men looked at Caleb with shock. They'd never heard him speak so bluntly.

Matal considered a moment. "Maybe I would not spoken so forcefully," he said. "But Caleb's right. We've got to get everyone toughened to the task we face."

"But how do we do it?" Shanni broke in. "Some of the people are already near to revolting. Bringing more pressure now will surely split us apart."

"Maybe not," Caleb responded, his eyes flashing. "Now is the time we show leadership. We'll assemble all the Huastecs. We will all stand together and lay it on the line. When they see we're committed, a lot of naysayers will fall in line!"

"How do we go about it?" Shanni asked.

"The people are used to following Tonah," Caleb continued. "I defer to Tonah's wishes, but I suggest we make it clear that Tonah is the spiritual adviser, and that the rest of us are assuming leadership for the journey and the people's well-being."

"I like the way you express it," Matal replied. "Would you be willing to address the assemblage and repeat that?"

"I'd be willing, but I'm not a Huastec. Like it or not, the Huastecs are not going to follow an Anglo. I'm tolerated at best, by many of the Huastec families."

"Caleb's right," Tonah broke in. "It has to be one of us, and the time is overdue for me to shift some of my burden to new leadership. We must choose a new leader."

"There is only one among us that all the people would follow," one of the group captains said. "And that is Matal."

The others nodded agreement as Matal gazed around the group. He took a deep breath and let it out.

Caleb could guess Matal's feelings. He was hardly twenty-four years upon the earth, and he was being handed this burden in a time of crisis. He had it in him, Caleb thought. He could grow into a great leader, but taking leadership of the Huastecs at this time would make him or it would destroy him.

"We will put it to the people when we assemble," Matal finally said. "If I am their choice, so be it."

The full moon lit the camp as the Huastecs assembled in the open area used during the day for training. Families grouped together in clusters, and the buzz of conversation filled the plaza. Everyone knew why the meeting was called, and concern for their future rippled through the mind of each participant. Caleb and Matal had erected a temporary platform so that they could be seen and heard over the crowd. The flames from torches lighted the platform, giving it a surreal quality as Tonah mounted the stage to call the assembly to order. At the sight of Tonah, a hush settled over the crowd.

"You know why we are here. We are at a critical juncture for the Huastecs. Many of you have expressed concern about the course we should take. Tonight we will address your concerns and ask for your commitment to what is decided."

Matal stepped forward as Tonah moved to the side of the platform. "We all know why we left Mesa Verde. Caleb Stone spent hours discussing the challenges of the journey, and even counseled against it. But we spent days discussing our alternatives, and realized we had no choice but to go. Each of you was part of that decision. Now we are committed, and now we must be resolute." A buzz of conversation rippled through the throng.

An old patriarch, Toshni, shouted from the crowd, "That was before we found that we would starve in this wilderness! We must have food for our families and milk for the babies. At least at Mesa Verde we could live!"

Murmurs of approval greeted Toshni's words. Shouts of "He's right", and "Something must change," floated up from the crowd.

Matal's visage hardened, and Caleb saw his jaw muscles working. Matal was fighting back his anger; he knew the need to persuade and to swing the crowd to his thinking.

"Then we must sit down together and determine how we meet those needs," Matal continued. "I firmly believe that trying to return to Mesa Verde solves nothing. We would face the dangers of the journey and then have to start over. At best we would wind up on a reservation. No, we knew we would face obstacles. I say we face them and overcome them!"

"Words!" Toshni spat out. "We cannot eat words. We need food and a place where we can settle, sow and harvest."

Shanni stepped up beside Matal. "That time will come, if we remain resolute. We will find that place, but now is a time of respite. We have enough experience to know our new reality and we must react to the changes we face. Each of us must contribute. Now is not the time for whining or second-guessing. We are fighting for the survival of the Huastecs."

"What does Caleb Stone suggest?" Toshni asked. "He claims to know this country. He hasn't been much help so far!"

Sarcasm tinged Toshni's voice as he spoke. Caleb stood near the front of the crowd, next to the stage. He had planned to stay out of the fray. Whatever was decided, it must be the Huastecs' decision and they must commit to it.

"Yes, let us hear from Caleb Stone!" another shouted from the crowd. A murmur of assent followed the words. Caleb climbed to the platform and looked out over the assemblage. He could feel the undercurrent of hostility. When people were angry, they looked for a scapegoat. Even Tonah could not save him if the crowd turned on him.

"I understand your concerns and frustration. You have families to support, and you're living in hardship and uncertainty. I lived that uncertainty when I rode this country as an outcast. I knew that you would face terrible trials if you undertook this journey, and I counseled against it until I came to understand that you had no choice. Now you are committed and you are here. I suggest you elect a strong leader who can take you successfully through the unknown dangers ahead."

Caleb stepped back and Tonah moved to the center of the stage. "I have been your spiritual leader for many years, and I have done my best to counsel you, but now we're in a different time and a different place. Success will depend on strength in numbers, strength in battle, and resolve in meeting dangers beyond our experience. We are in a time of war, a battle for survival that may continue for years. We must transform ourselves, and to do so we need a person of strength to lead us."

One of the group leaders in the crowd shouted, "We want Matal! Matal is the man to lead us!" A murmur of approval ran through the crowd. Tonah sensed that the mood of the crowd was changing. The people wanted reassurance and a plan of action. Tonah seized the opportunity.

"Matal has been suggested. Are there others we should consider?"

Tonah waited as the people murmured, conversing among themselves. A hush settled over the crowd and the people's eyes returned to the platform expectantly.

Tonah looked at Matal and nodded. Matal stepped forward and spoke. "We face the challenge of our lives, and none can know the outcome. With your support, I will do my best to lead us to our new home to the south. But we cannot be divided against ourselves. I need to know where Toshni stands, and those who side with him."

The crowd turned to see how Toshni would respond. He glanced around defiantly.

"I just want to feed my family. It will take more than strong words to do that. If Matal can lead in changing our condition, he has my support."

"Well said," Matal responded quickly. "Every person must be provided for, but we must do it together. We must forget about turning back; our only future is forward. Toshni, I need your commitment there will be no more talk of splitting up. Divided we will surely fail."

"All right," Toshni said after a moment of hesitation. He was still not convinced, Matal thought. "I am with you, but I will speak up again if our conditions do not improve!"

Tonah stepped in, grasping Matal's arm to hoist his hand aloft in a fist. "We have elected our new leader. Let us hear your voices of affirmation!"

A roar of approval rose up from the Huastecs, a tiny nation lost in the wilderness.

Early the next morning, Caleb joined the other trainees in the plaza under the watchful eyes of Walpi and his men. After the group stretches and the warm-up drill, Walpi watched approvingly as Manteh stood up to introduce the day's activities.

"Observe Nantan," he commanded.

Caleb joined the others in turning to watch Nantan, who stood in an open area in front of the trainees. Nantan burst forward into a sprint, and then leaped up and forward, extending his left hand. He tucked, rolled along his arm and across his back, completing a roll and returning to his feet, in balance and ready to attack.

"Watch again," Manteh commanded.

Nantan grasped a rifle in his right hand and turned. Again he sprinted forward, leaped and tucked, turned a complete cartwheel and came to his knees ready to fire the weapon. Caleb shook his head. That kind of fall could cripple a man, but Nantan made it look effortless.

"You must never be motionless in battle," Manteh explained. "A moving target is harder to hit. This is especially important when you face an armed enemy who is out of reach. It is very difficult for even an expert marksman to hit an object rolling toward him. That may be all the edge you have to avoid being killed. Today you must master this skill."

"Kneel and place your left foot out, knee up," Manteh continued. Nantan and Antay walked among the trainees coaching and assisting in getting into the correct posture. "Now place your left hand on the ground in front of you, with the palm down and pointing back toward you."

Caleb followed the others. The position felt awkward, and his legs strained from the unaccustomed stretch.

"Push off with your back leg, and roll along the arm and across your back. Now!" Nanteh barked.

Caleb reacted without thinking at Nanteh's sharp command. He rolled and found himself back on his knees.

"Now bring your left knee up and do it again."

Caleb was surprised. Other than feeling stiff, the technique was remarkably easy. He could now see how Nantan's wiry build and natural suppleness aided him in his effortless rolls.

"A similar technique is used to fall and roll backward. You must extend your hands out, squat on your heels and roll back. With practice, you can complete the fall without injury, slap and roll back to your feet. The ability to fall backward and roll forward under control is a critical skill in close combat."

After they had practiced the rolls, forward and backward, Nantan and Antay dragged up the reed mats from the stack beside the practice area.

"Watch again," Manteh commanded.

Nantan again sprinted forward. At the edge of the mat, he launched up and over, landing on his back on the mat, and rolling off the other side onto his feet. Walpi followed, barely brushing the mat as he catapulted over and to his feet.

Manteh grasped a rifle and took his turn rolling across the mat. "With practice, this will become second nature," he said. "Now you begin."

The trainees formed a long line and each took a turn, running forward to tuck and roll, using the mat to soften their landings as they perfected the technique. Soon the participants were beginning to relax and enjoy the drill.

"Expect soreness when you get up tomorrow," Walpi interjected. "Your bodies have been used for strength, not suppleness. But you will soon find that you are developing both strength and flexibility, which are essential in combat. Knowledge of fighting skills is useless if the body cannot respond effectively."

Caleb nodded his understanding and looked down the row of trainees. He saw Aurel, dripping with perspiration, rise to take deep breaths. Aurel caught Caleb's glance and smiled, launching himself at the mat.

Walpi joined Tonah, Shanni and Caleb as they ate their evening meal by the campfire. Caleb was feeling the aches of the day's workout and hesitated as sore muscles rebelled as he reached to pour coffee.

Walpi noticed Caleb's pained expression and smiled. "Soon I'll have to eat by myself. Nobody will want to eat with the one who is the source of their pain!"

"I thought I was the only one hardly able to walk," Shanni interjected, "So I was keeping it to myself."

"My men and I have been visiting among the trainees, encouraging them. Believe me, you are not the only ones complaining!"

Tonah smiled. "That is probably my only advantage as an old man. I do not have to subject my body to such torture!"

"Soon it will be second nature, and your bodies will like the exercise," Walpi returned. "Nantan and the others were actually playing out there today."

"How are we progressing?" Caleb asked.

"Most of the trainees are doing well. A good deal of time is spent getting them into shape, and that cannot be rushed. Only when the body is ready can we teach the techniques. We will soon move to the hand-to-hand combat skills against knives and guns. After that will be practice and more practice to perfect a few key moves. That will be all we have the time for."

"Doesn't look like we'll have time to learn many techniques," Caleb observed.

"True enough," Walpi replied. "But it is better to do a few fighting techniques well than to do many poorly. One technique, masterfully applied, can save your life in battle."

A good point, Caleb thought, nodding.

"Something to think about," Walpi continued. "We Navaho are guerilla fighters, good at hitting and moving, but the pony soldiers are drilled in fighting as a unit. They are superior in battle in covering each other's advance and retreat. We must be alert to an opportunity for that training."

"I'm surprised you give the U.S. cavalry that much credit," Caleb smiled.

Walpi returned the smile. "In combat one is always learning."

Chapter 5

MATAL WAS OF medium build, tending toward muscular. His distinguishing feature was a restless intensity coupled with a young man's confidence. He had a natural grace and coordination that made him a quick study with games and physical activities. As a result, he was enjoying the combat training, and developing a level of conditioning that added to his natural energy. He hadn't asked for the position of leadership, but by the gods he would succeed at it!

The dubious honor had not come at a good time, for Matal was in love. Under the cover of darkness, he eased to the edge of camp to meet Ambria, daughter of Toshni.

"I'm here," Ambria whispered out of the darkness as he drew near.

He moved to her and they embraced, his senses burning with desire. They kissed passionately, his intensity overpowering her so that she drew back, cautious.

"Careful," she whispered. "We must not lose control of ourselves!"

Matal drew back, breathing heavily, to gaze at Ambria in the dim light. Large, dark eyes that glistened with an effervescent glow, revealing her energy, marked her even features. She had a playfulness and brashness that kept her engaged with life, enjoying every activity that filled her day. She attended training alongside Matal, and delighted in besting him in learning the new combat techniques.

Matal loved her and desired her, and he was not a man who held back easily.

"It is easy for you to say," he whispered. "I want you so badly I could devour you!"

"It is not so easy for me, either!" Ambria shot back, her quick spirit flashing. "You are not the only one who feels desire."

"What's stopping us, then?" Matal answered, reaching for her.

"We must wait until we are married. I cannot give myself until I am your wife."

"I've asked you to marry me, and you've agreed, but yet you do not set the date. What is the delay?"

"I want us to be married more than anything, but now is not the time. Look around us. We are in a temporary camp in the middle of the desert. We are engaged in combat training, and soon we will resume a journey into the unknown. Marriage and the responsibility of children would jeopardize our lives, and your responsibilities as the new leader of the Huastecs."

"But we may be journeying for months, even years!" Matal protested. "We cannot put our lives on hold forever!"

"Maybe when we resume our journey, we will find a place of refuge, a place to settle and call our own. Then we will be able to put down our roots again."

"And what if we don't?"

"At some point, the people will have to decide how they will live, and then we will be free to think of ourselves."

"I could refuse leadership and we could think of ourselves now!" Matal returned stubbornly.

"I think that is your passion speaking. Could you really think only of us at this time, when your people need you?"

Matal dropped his eyes. "No, I cannot. The people chose me, it is my duty to lead them."

Ambria embraced Matal gently. That was why she loved him so deeply, she knew. He was a man of integrity. He would do what must be done. And he would be sorely tested in the days to come. Matal returned her embrace, reveling in her closeness. With Ambria he felt totally alive and complete. With her as his wife, each day would be a delight, and the world would have meaning. Why had their world been turned upside down?

Her words had returned his thoughts to the Huastecs and he stepped back, holding her at arms length. "As their new leader, I intend to do something that will impress the people, even your father, Toshni."

"Don't be too harsh on Father. He is old and our circumstances weary him."

"Even he will have to support me after I bring fresh vegetables and melons to the camp!"

"What? Surely that is impossible. We are in a desert!"

"We have a plan. Walpi knows where we can buy them further south, nearly a hundred miles from here. Walpi and several of the group leaders will accompany me. We will take horses and carts and leave before dawn."

"But the produce would perish in this heat before you could return."

"Not if we take extra horses and travel day and night, with only brief stops for rest. It can be done."

"At great risk to yourselves, and you will be exhausted when you return. Why would you do such a thing?"

"It was my idea," Matal returned, suddenly defensive. "I intend to address the needs of the people."

Ambria smiled suddenly, her eyes flashing. It was an audacious plan, one that would appeal to a man of Matal's energy. She knew he would succeed and she almost wished she could go with them.

"Poor Father," she said. "He'll have to eat his words!"

Matal felt the release of tension and hugged her. She understood his need to make a gesture. Life with her would be a delight. He could not imagine a future without her.

Hand-in-hand, they walked back toward the camp. With the optimism of youth, they would face the world together.

Toshni was troubled as he finished his morning meal. Despite his misgivings, he had agreed with Tonah's decision to leave Mesa Verde. Without water, they could not survive there, and the drought was drying up the water. But now Toshni had experienced a strange and hostile world. This world of deserts and renegades had already cost the Huastecs lives, and Toshni was sure that if they continued, more would be lost. In fact, now that he saw the enormity of the journey they faced, he feared that all the Huastecs would perish before they reached their objective, if indeed it any longer existed.

Toshni was not a troublemaker. He was a gentle man who only wanted to live and raise his children in peace. He had noticed his daughter Ambria's attraction to Matal, and he did not disapprove. Despite the impetuosity of youth, Matal had good character and would be a good provider. With maturity he would settle into a solid leader.

Toshni was also a religious man, who had prayed all his life to the gods of the Huastecs. He had believed in the gods' benevolence and he had been rewarded for his devotion.

Now he felt that the Huastecs' predicament was a result of their failure to respect their gods. Tonah, their spiritual leader whom he had supported for many years, had grown old and had lost touch. The gods had become angry and dried up the rain. And now the Huastecs faced destruction.

As was his custom after breakfast, he walked over to visit with other family heads in his group. They were seated in the shade of an awning as he approached.

"Greetings, Toshni," Ahik the elder greeted. "We were discussing your speech at the rally last night. It is good that you spoke up. Something needs to be done to change our course."

The others nodded assent as Toshni sat down.

"My friends, you know my words were not to cause dissension, but I am deeply troubled. We have known nothing but trouble since we left Mesa Verde, and I see no reason to hope that our condition will improve."

"Maybe Matal will lead us in a new direction."

"Matal is a good man, although young and inexperienced. I support him as our leader, but I feel that he cannot address the Huastecs' real problem."

"A problem he cannot address? What is in your mind?"

"Think back. For generations, Mesa Verde provided the Huastecs with plenty. Then suddenly a severe drought comes and threatens our home. We are forced out. Surely we must have done something to offend the gods."

"But what could it be? Tonah has led us in all the rituals, and we have followed faithfully."

"I wonder myself. I turn it over and over in my mind. If we could find the answer, and appease the gods, we could return to Mesa Verde and live out our days in peace."

"It would be the best of all alternatives if we could make it so."

"The only thing that changed was that Tonah brought the Anglo into our midst," one of the men spoke up. "And now he relies on Caleb Stone's counsel. Maybe Tonah should be praying more and listening less to the Anglo."

A murmur of assent went around the circle. Toshni pondered the man's words. He did not support the Anglo, but he wanted to be fair to Tonah. Tonah had always had the best interests of the Huastecs at heart.

"Maybe it is too late for that," Toshni finally said. "Maybe we should pray to the gods ourselves."

MATAL, WALPI AND the six Huastec men reached the small village at the edge of the green valley near the evening of the third day. They had traveled fast with four carts and extra horses. Walpi had sent a rider ahead to prepare the farmers to deliver the produce the following day, so that they could load the carts and head back without delay.

The following morning, the farmers met them and the produce, including melons and fresh vegetables, was delivered as agreed. The village was upbeat, happy to sell so much produce for badly needed silver. More produce could be grown before winter, but money now permitted the purchase of much-needed supplies for the village.

The region was poor, and word traveled fast about the strangers with carts and horses who paid for food with silver. Bandits in the nearby hills paid well for such information. Soon a small group of riders left the camp and rode to inform them.

Matal was upbeat as he rode up beside Walpi, the four carts and horses strung out behind as the caravan started north.

"I was worried that we might arrive to find too little produce to take back. I didn't relish returning to the Huastecs empty-handed."

"It would've been a bad omen for you as their new leader," Walpi agreed.

"Now all we have to do is get it back before it spoils," Matal continued. "We made good time coming down."

"We will hope for the best, but remain vigilant," Walpi smiled.

"Don't you ever relax?" Matal returned. "We didn't see a soul on the trip."

"Sometimes I worry more when I don't see anything."

"We'll keep alert, then, but keep the carts moving."

That afternoon Walpi halted the caravan and looked back at the small band of horsemen that had appeared out of a side canyon. He motioned the drivers to bring the carts alongside each other, in a defensive position, and left one man to hold the horses.

Walpi, Matal, and the other men advanced on foot, away from the carts, to face the six oncoming riders. The riders slowed to a trot as they approached, and then drew up a few yards away as the leader surveyed Matal and the others.

Finally the leader spoke. "We heard you were buying produce. We thought we would see where you took it. There must be a lot of people around here somewhere."

"We have a way to go yet," Matal agreed. "And we need to get moving."

"Don't let us delay you. We thought perhaps you would like to trade horses. Yours look spent, and our horses are fresh. We would need only a small bit of silver to make up the difference in value."

"Our silver is gone. It went to the farmers for the produce."

"Maybe the carts, then, to make up the difference."

"Can't haul the produce without the carts."

"Ah, my friends, then I'm afraid we are not going to be able to help you."

The leader turned his horse and spurred into a gallop, his men following. Soon they entered the canyon and disappeared from view.

"They'll be back," Walpi stated. "They were sizing us up. They want the horses and carts."

Caleb blinked back sleep as he nudged the tired horse forward in the early morning hours. They had changed to fresh horses for the carts and continued travel all night. The horses might be fresh, but Caleb and the men were wearing out. It was good that they expected to reach the Huastec camp by late afternoon. Up ahead in the dim light he made out Walpi's silhouette, riding silently and watching the trail. Didn't he ever sleep?

Walpi became aware of Caleb's approach and pulled his horse up to wait. If he was tired, he didn't show it, Caleb thought ruefully.

"They will attack at first light," Walpi said simply. "And they will be tired and angry. That will work to our advantage."

"Why do you say that?"

"They expected us to camp for the night. When they came back to surprise us, we were not there. Then they had to find and follow our trail, so that they, too, have ridden without sleep. The difference is that they did not expect it. They will be anxious and make mistakes."

"Shouldn't we alert the others and get ready to defend ourselves?"

"I have alerted the others, and we are already ready. That was the purpose of the training. When the time comes, they will know what to do."

Caleb smiled. Walpi was always self-contained, almost gentle. But when he moved, he moved with purpose and deadly intent. Caleb had never seen a man so calm and centered.

"You've lived your whole life as a fighter," Caleb observed. "But it seems you have no history."

Walpi looked puzzled. "Everyone has a history. I do not feel mine is noteworthy, therefore I do not speak of it. It was my fate to grow up in a time of war. I fought to survive."

"Do you have a family? Children? Was there never a time to live peaceably?"

"Yes. I had a wife. She died from measles brought by the white men. Our son died trying to be a warrior too soon. He was audacious and he was killed. Our daughter is married, and has given me two grandchildren."

"It is a great gift that you chose to help the Huastecs when you could be at home with your people."

"It is my nature to be restless. Manuelito knows me well. When he asked, I told him I wished to do this. Since I was a boy, I have sought action. I do not consider helping the Huastecs to be an imposition."

"Despite the increased danger?"

"I do not dwell on it. I consider each day of my life to be a marvelous gift. When my time comes, I will do my last dance in celebration of my life on this earth and then I will let go of this world and look with expectation to the next one. All will proceed as it should."

"I'm afraid I can't be so accepting. I consider death the enemy, to be fought to the last breath."

"Do not misunderstand me. I, too, resist death, but it is a matter of perspective. We began dying the day we are born. We know our days upon this earth are numbered, but we do not know the number. So be it. My intent is to savor my life and then to go into the hereafter. The fact that I do not know the divine plan does not deter me from trusting it."

"Doesn't that make you careless in battle? Caleb asked. "When I'm fighting for my life, my whole being is focused on that moment."

"It actually makes me less careless. I go into a zone where time slows down. I anticipate what my opponent is going to do, and counter before he can start. Only later, after the battle is over, does my body feel the energy drain."

"It certainly seems to work for you," Caleb observed. "I've never seen you lose your composure."

Walpi laughed. "You never saw me when my wife disapproved. I assure you I have known fear!"

"Was she overbearing?"

Walpi was suddenly serious. "She was the love of my life. Each day with her was a day of enchantment."

"I apologize," Caleb said. "I should not have made light of your relationship."

"No need. We were both joking, to lighten up a little. After all, we've been awake all night!"

Walpi pulled his horse to a halt and looked to the east where the sky was growing light. Sunrise was approaching. Caleb looked around. They were in the middle of a long valley, with low hills away to the east. There was no place to take cover, and no place to hide. They were caught out in the open, Caleb noted with alarm.

Before he could voice his concern, Walpi grunted with satisfaction. "It is good. We are away from the canyons. Our pursuers will have to ride out into the open to approach us. "

"I can't say I see the advantage," Caleb answered. "Everything I've been taught says that men on horseback have the advantage over men caught out in the open with carts and harnessed horses."

"The secret of success is surprise," Walpi replied confidently. "You must never do what the enemy expects. We are about even in numbers. They won't have a chance!"

I hope he knows what the hell he's doing, Caleb thought. I'm not all that casual about risking the hereafter.

As the sky lightened, Caleb and Walpi sat on their horses and watched as the enemy riders, as expected, exited a canyon to the east and galloped slowly toward the caravan.

Walpi gave instructions for one of the Huastecs to remain to hold the horses. He dismounted and removed his rifle from the saddle scabbard. He led on foot away from the carts and horses with the rifle ready.

Caleb fell in to his left, and the remaining Huastecs walked a couple of paces behind. Walpi motioned for them to spread out as they walked away from the horses to face the approaching riders. The approaching riders slowed to a trot, and then stopped out of rifle range to confer. They must think we're crazy, Caleb thought, to be walking out on foot. Apparently he guessed right, for the riders suddenly spurred their horses into a run, bearing down on Caleb, Walpi and the Huastecs.

Without warning, Walpi broke forward into a run, rapidly closing the distance on the approaching horses. Caleb and the Huastecs, caught off guard, raced forward as Walpi pulled away.

Some of the enemy riders began firing, their bullets kicking up dust near Walpi. Suddenly, Walpi appeared to stumble. He rolled and came up on one knee, rifle level, and squeezed off a shot. The nearest rider flipped backward to fall limply onto the hard desert floor. Walpi fired again and a rider slumped forward. Caleb and the Huastecs rolled forward, came up to their knees, and fired a volley that broke the charge.

The leader wheeled his horse, followed by the others, and spurred back out of range. He had two riders down and one wounded. He cursed in frustration. The enemy had looked so easy that his riders had not aimed. Their bullets had sprayed out to no effect.

"Damn it!" he roared. "Aim this time! Don't fire unless you've got a target!"

One of the riders protested. "Hell, we can't aim from a running horse!"

"Just mow them down! They can't stand up to us." With a wave the leader turned and spurred forward.

They galloped forward into rifle range, and then pulled the horses to a sudden stop, swinging out of the saddle to fire at the Huastecs.

"Hit the dirt!" Walpi ordered, pitching forward to lie prone, his rifle extended in outstretched hands.

Caleb and the Huastecs followed suit, their volley rattling among the enemy horses. A man fell with a grunt, and two others cried out in pain. The remaining riders clawed back into the saddle and spurred away from the hail of bullets. The leader, suddenly alone, hooked a leg over the saddle as his horse panicked, racing away with him clinging precariously to the side.

"It's over," Walpi said, climbing to his feet and beating the dust off his clothes. "The riders are done with us and their leader won't dare attack alone. Now we need to get some distance away from their downed riders. They'll come back for them and head home."

"It worked," Caleb said grudgingly. "But I had to see it to believe it. I was all for heading back to the horses myself."

"Seeing us on foot made them overconfident," Walpi replied, "So that they did not take time to aim. That was their undoing. It is almost impossible to hit a man rolling toward you. Even an expert marksman will fire over the person. When we came up into the kneeling position, we were perfectly set for accurate return fire, to deadly effect. They learned a painful lesson. They won't try that again."

"But they compensated," Caleb returned. "In the second attack, they dismounted to aim."

"And by lying prone, we gave them too small a target from that distance. While they were trying to get set, we were firing. They were always one step behind. That is the edge, the element of surprise."

"I hope you didn't learn that fighting the soldiers!"

"The soldiers thought there were more of us than there were," Walpi smiled. "We were always outnumbered, and moved to give the appearance of overwhelming force. But those days are gone. Maybe both the Navaho and the Anglos are learning the futility of war. Now let's make haste for the Huastec camp!"

Both men and horses were near exhaustion when they cleared the valley and made their way up the canyon into the Huastec camp. The sentries had advised of their approach, and the Huastecs were out waving and celebrating as the carts pulled into their midst.

Matal was pulled from his horse and carried on the shoulders of the men in celebration, as the remaining riders began to distribute the melons and vegetables among the families. Soon pots were boiling as the produce joined the roasting meat brought in by the hunters.

Celebration filled the camp as the Huastecs applauded Matal's audacious gesture, and his success. Even the doubters agreed that the selection of Matal as leader had been a good choice.

Far to the south, the bandit leader rode into the village with his wounded men, and two dead riders slung over the saddle. The villagers rushed to their aid, and soon the men were hovering over food and recounting their misfortune.

"They were not human!" Alphonso Alvarez, the leader of the bandits insisted. "You sold your produce to demons! When we attempted to overpower them, they abandoned their horses and flew through the air, firing as they came. Even our horses panicked. We are lucky that any of us escaped!"

The villagers listened quietly, eyes averted. The beings had looked like men to them, and had paid with real silver. Let Alvarez believe what he wanted and salvage his pride. There was no gain in disputing him, for like always, Alvarez and his bandits would return to their camp in the morning and life would go on as usual in the village.

Chapter 6

AN AIR OF excitement swept through the Huastec camp in the morning air. Caleb left his dwelling to join Tonah and Matal as they followed the crowd winding around the tents to the edge of camp. Shanni came out of her tent and joined them as they passed. Smoke rose in twin columns, and they heard the sound of flutes and drums as they pressed forward through the crowd. People turned and pushed aside, recognizing Tonah's arrival and making room for him to pass.

Tonah and Matal broke free of the crowd, and paused, speechless. At the base of the canyon wall, Toshni and his helpers had built a platform of stones to serve as an altar. A stone god carved by the Ancients that Toshni had hidden and brought all the way from Mesa Verde stood on the altar. Twin fires burned in front of the god, and meat and vegetables had been set as an offering. Several of Toshni's neighbors, including their families, were kneeling and offering prayers. Others in the throng began to move forward, forming a line to offer their prayers.

"What's this?" Tonah's strong voice carried over the assembly. Toshni rose to face Tonah as the crowd turned and grew silent.

"We are repenting and returning to our gods," Toshni replied. "Our neglect brought the drought and our near ruin, but it is not too late. We will regain the favor of our gods and return to Mesa Verde to live out our days in peace."

"That is not possible," Tonah replied with emotion, his voice strong with conviction. "We know conditions at Mesa Verde are changed forever. We will never be able to go back. Splitting our forces now would jeopardize us all."

"We have respect for your leadership," Toshni replied, "And we do not wish to quarrel, but it is the deep conviction of many of us that we have failed our gods, and they have turned away from us. Perhaps we placed too much faith in the work of our own hands, and did not seek wisdom. Now we must face our failure and change, or we will all perish!"

A murmur of approval swept across the crowd at Toshni's words.

"But you have set up a stone carving, nothing more!" Tonah replied in exasperation. "It is not a god, and it can do nothing to help us!"

Toshni jerked back, startled, lifting his hand as if to block a blow. "Your words insult the gods! How can we appease them when you disavow them?"

Again the crowd reacted, frowning and gesturing at Tonah.

"The last thing we need is to defy our gods!" one of the onlookers shouted. Tonah saw that the restive crowd was backing Toshni. The Huastecs were suffering hardships and were afraid. They wanted to believe there was a way out of this nightmare. They wanted to believe they could return to Mesa Verde and live in peace.

"The gods exist in the spirit world. They do not reside in carved stones!" Tonah answered, raising his voice over the rumble of the crowd. "We must seek their spiritual guidance."

"In the days of the Ancients, the gods sent their spirits down to reside in the stone carvings," Toshni argued. "If we turn back to them, they will return again to protect us."

Tonah could feel the emotion sweeping across the crowd. The people could not be swayed with argument. He turned to Matal, who stood nearby.

Matal recognized the crisis. Never before had the Huastecs questioned Tonah's spiritual leadership. Matal had achieved great popularity and support with his daring trip to bring fresh food, but now he knew he had to tread carefully as he spoke.

"We must speak with one voice. It will take our combined strength to successfully complete our journey. You elected me your leader, but I cannot decide spiritual matters. I agree we must continually seek the gods' favor, but Toshni and Tonah must agree on how best to do that. For now, let us return to our dwellings and pray for our spiritual leaders to make the right decisions. We cannot stay here long, and we still have much to do."

A murmur of assent swept through the crowd, and Matal felt the tension easing. The people did not want a confrontation; they wanted reassurance - a reassurance he could not give them in a temporary camp in the hostile desert. Matal turned and led away, followed by Tonah and the others. Matal noticed as they passed that the crowd was dispersing. They had bought some time, but the rift in the camp was real and would have to be addressed.

Tonah, Shanni, and Caleb followed Matal to the campfire outside his tent and sat down. Matal was worried, and Tonah seemed sad.

The silence dragged on until Shanni spoke. "Toshni was always quiet and gentle. I never suspected he would lead a religious uprising!"

"He is only reflecting his fear, and that of many of the people," Tonah replied. "They now realize the enormity of our task and they seek a way out. When people are in distress, they turn for comfort to ways that worked in the past. The danger for us all is to attempt to apply old methods to changed reality."

"We must resolve the issue," Matal observed. "We need to resume training, and to continue stocking food and supplies for the journey. We knew all along that this camp was only temporary."

"How to do it is the challenge," Tonah replied. "Toshni is a good man, however misguided, with strong convictions. He has struck a favorable chord with many of the others. They want to go home and live as they did in the past. We must find a way to convince them of their error."

"What if you cannot convince them?" Caleb asked. "What if some of the families pull out and follow Toshni north?"

Matal had been asking that question himself. If Toshni left, would Ambria feel obligated to go with her family? Could he convince her to marry him and stay? Aside from their personal issues, would the remaining Huastecs be enough to complete the journey? There were a lot of new unknowns, and they already had too many.

"We are already too few," Matal answered. "If Toshni leaves with a large number of families, they will die or end up on a reservation. There would not be enough of us remaining to fight our way to the homeland to the south. It would mean the end of the Huastecs."

"I'm surprised this came up now," Caleb observed. "It seems the time to disagree was before Toshni and his followers left Mesa Verde."

"The world view of the people has changed very drastically in a short period of time," Tonah answered. "People need time to adjust, and there has been no time."

"And there is little time in which to change their minds," Caleb returned. "We'll be running short on food and supplies in another week."

"The stone god is an artifact, a relic of the past," Shanni broke in. "I could destroy it with my will in front of their eyes! Maybe that would shock them back to reality."

"I thought of that," Tonah answered, "And believe me I was tempted during my frustration with the crowd today, but if we use sorcery, they will see it as blasphemy toward the gods. We will succeed only if we can change what is in their hearts."

"How do we do that?" Matal asked.

"I do not know," Tonah answered. "I will go to the ruins across the valley and pray. Maybe the gods will show favor and point out the way."

Matal nodded and got up. He excused himself and walked across camp to the training area. He had to see Ambria tonight, as soon as the training session was over.

Tonah stared at the fire, sadness in his face. "I don't know how I could've let this happen," he said. "I must have lost touch with the people."

"Don't blame yourself," Caleb responded. "You were busy fighting battles on their behalf that they could not see."

"I'm not sure there is anything you could have done anyway," Shanni agreed. "As you said, it was an inevitable reaction to their new and frightening view of the world."

"And I fear it has only begun," Tonah sighed. "Even I find this world we've entered to be both enormous and dangerous. Already there have been times when I longed to be back in Mesa Verde."

"I went through my moment of truth many years ago when I left home," Caleb said. "I learned to fight, and sometimes to kill, in order to survive. Survival is the same for everyone, including the Huastecs."

"And we will survive!" Shanni answered with passion. "We did not come this far to fail."

Tonah smiled at her spirit, but remained silent. Already she looked like a warrior with her headband, leather shirt and cotton pants, Tonah thought. She had tanned in the afternoon training sessions, and her muscles had hardened. She looked no different than Walpi and the others. The fire of youth, Tonah saw, would be the salvation of the Huastecs. The young people had their lives yet to live, and they would fight for their future.

"It's time to go," Caleb said, rising. "The combat training will begin in a few minutes."

Walpi had slept well as he watched the Huastec warriors assemble for the afternoon's training. Word had gotten around about his fighting tactics in repulsing the bandits. He could sense a new seriousness in the trainees. Now they realized the importance of what they were training to do.

"Today we will focus on hand-to-hand combat," he opened. "Sometimes your weapon is knocked away in a pitched battle and you may face your enemy empty-handed. Without knowledge of what to do, your enemy will kill you. Watch carefully."

Walpi motioned to Manteh, who stepped out grasping a knife in his right hand. Walpi faced him and nodded. Manteh thrust the knife forward at stomach level. Walpi twisted his body and his left hand shot out to intercept Manteh's wrist. Quick as a snake striking, Walpi's right hand joined his left, grasping the knife hand, as Walpi stepped across and spun around on his right foot. Manteh's knife arm was cranked like a lever, lifting Manteh's body completely into the air, to tumble over onto his back on the straw mat. As he landed, Manteh's arm straightened and Walpi lifted the knife from the nerveless fingers. Walpi made an elaborate charade of drawing the knife across Manteh's defenseless neck.

The entire defense had been so fast that Caleb's eyes could barely follow it. A murmur of appreciation went through the group of assembled trainees. Caleb could hear some of them comparing notes in whispers.

"The key to this defense is practice," Walpi continued. "You must train until you have complete confidence in yourself. Even the least hesitation can cost you your life. Now observe with the revolver."

Manteh stepped out with a revolver held at waist level, pointed at Walpi's midriff. Manteh pulled the hammer back, ready for firing. Again Walpi's left hand snaked out. He grabbed the top of the revolver so that the pad of his hand filled the space between the hammer and the firing pin as he gripped the cylinder to prevent it from rotating. Manteh had reacted instantly, pulling the trigger, but the hammer dropped too late, stopped short against Walpi's hand. Walpi stepped through and spun, throwing Manteh in a tumble onto the mat.

Manteh got up and brushed himself off as Walpi turned to face the group. "Any questions?"

A young warrior raised his hand. "Seems to me you're risking death grabbing for a gun pointed at your stomach. Suppose you don't stop the gun hammer in time?"

Walpi smiled. "Good question. I'm pleased you are paying attention. I need a volunteer to come forward."

Caleb looked around. Eyes were suddenly looking down. Nobody knew what to expect. It was not a good time to volunteer!

Caleb stepped forward. Walpi motioned him to stand in front of Manteh. Again Manteh removed the revolver from the holster, but this time he held the weapon up for all to see and carefully removed six bullets from the chambers. Caleb glanced at the startled stares as realization sank in that Walpi had demonstrated the technique against a loaded gun!

At Walpi's nod, Caleb attempted to seize the revolver. A loud click reverberated across the training plaza as he missed and Manteh pulled the trigger. Caleb grinned weakly at Walpi whose eyes gleamed with mirth. Caleb glanced at the trainees out of the side of his eyes. Walpi now held their rapt attention.

Walpi stepped forward. "When you start this move, the first thing is to twist your body to the side as you reach out. Even if you miss and the gun fires, the bullet will go by harmlessly. Watch."

He motioned Caleb back into line, and turned to face Manteh. Again Manteh held the revolver up for all to see and inserted a bullet into the chamber. Walpi faced him as Manteh held the revolver at waist level with the hammer pulled back for firing.

Walpi's body twisted as his hand snaked out, and he deliberately grasped the revolver forward of the hammer. The weapon fired with a loud roar, but the bullet sped harmlessly past Walpi's right side, where his body had been an instant before.

"Any other questions?" Walpi asked, turning again to the trainees.

One of the trainees held up her hand. "Why can't he pull the trigger before you twist out of the way?'

"Another good question," Walpi replied. "The secret is intent. Once you make the decision to act, you have timing on your side. The enemy has to react. That split second delay is all you need to get your body out of the way, and to seize the weapon."

Another warrior held up his hand. "Do we have to practice with loaded weapons?"

Walpi joined in as laughter rippled across the group. "Not for a while. I'd like to have a few of you left to complete this course! We will practice with wooden knives, and unloaded guns. For each of you, there will come a time when you are ready, and you will make that call. Then you will complete the defense against a loaded gun. Only then will you have the confidence to act without hesitation in battle. So it is important that you train seriously."

Walpi watched the eyes of the trainees as they sobered. He was pleased. They were beginning to understand. This was not play. The penalty for failure was serious injury or death.

"Incidentally, he added. "The defense works against a rifle, but is a bit more difficult to execute. We'll work on that later. Now let's pair off and begin practice."

Wooden knives were passed out and the mats distributed across the training ground. Now Caleb understood why they had been practicing the front and back falls for weeks on the mats. Each step in the training led to the next step, and was key to developing the confidence the warriors needed in their ability to fight effectively.

Today Caleb faced Shanni, who was training with a focused intensity. Perspiration dripped as they alternated, each taking a turn in throwing the other. Despite his conditioning, getting up from the mat tired him quickly. He found himself lying several seconds after being thrown, catching a rest. Not Shanni. She was driven to build her strength and stamina. Never again would she be helpless when confronted by an enemy.

There was little talk as they practiced. Shanni became so intense, Caleb realized with surprise, that she might have been a stranger practicing with him. And she was growing stronger, much stronger.

Chapter 7

DUSK HAD FALLEN when Matal met Ambria at the edge of camp. They kissed passionately and held each other a long moment. With all the turmoil in camp, it seemed they only had seconds together.

"I thought the training would never end today," Ambria whispered, stepping back to look into Matal's eyes. "We have much to discuss."

"There is only one subject of importance. Will you stay with me if your father leaves us?"

"I pray he will come to his senses and stay. I worry for my mother and young brother. At least here they have the support of others in the camp. Traveling in a small group I would fear for their safety."

"As would I. I hope that Tonah can find a way to convince him. I would hate to keep him with us as a prisoner."

Alarm flashed across Ambria's face. "You couldn't do that. I mean surely you could not hold him here against his will!"

"If it were for the good of the majority, I would have to. In Mesa Verde, we had the luxury of permitting each family to do as it wished. With no outside stress, we could operate by consensus. Conditions have changed. We may have to dictate actions that are best for the Huastecs' survival."

"But people might rebel, and you could lose your support as their leader. You must be careful not to abuse your position of authority."

"Don't worry," Matal smiled, pulling her into his arms. "I have no desire to create more problems. I trust the majority of the people to support the tough calls that will be required."

"You've done a good job of avoiding the key question," he continued, holding her at arms length. "Will you marry me and stay if your family leaves?"

"If it comes to that, I will stay. We must look to the future, and the only future for the Huastecs is here, not back in Mesa Verde. There are several families who I could stay with."

"And our wedding?"

"I don't know where that fits in right now. There is so much else to cope with. Let's get past the rift first, and hope that my family stays."

"We cannot keep putting the decision off," Matal insisted. "Like it or not, the journey has become our life. We must adapt and find happiness as best we can."

"I know," Ambria replied. "I want to be your wife and to have a family, but we need some kind of stability. Everything is too unsettled. I fear having babies to protect when we expect to be fighting for our lives as we continue south."

Matal held her tightly and gazed up at the silent stars. His head told him she was right, but his heart yearned for happiness. When could they find a place to live and to call their own?

Tonah completed the long walk across the valley and climbed the stone steps up the face of the mesa. He reached the plaza of the natural cavern in the wall, glanced around at the dusty abandoned dwellings, and sat down to look out over the valley to the low hills on the horizon. The cavern, long abandoned, had a ghostly quality. The musty smell of disuse emanated from the fire pits and stone apartments that once had supported a people long vanished.

Tonah closed his eyes in meditation, and he felt the ghosts of the people moving about their daily lives, the women cooking over the fire pits, while children played on the polished stone of the plaza. Below, their men returned with game they had traveled far to obtain. Like Mesa Verde, it had been an energetic society that existed precariously by the full occupation and daily energy of the people. There had been no time to think of the precariousness of their existence. Only a little change in the environment would be enough to threaten their survival. A year of drought, or a decrease in game would have been enough. Something had changed and the people who remained had been forced to leave. So the Huastecs were not alone, Tonah thought with resignation. There was evidence of upheavals all across this vast and hostile land.

Tonah turned his thoughts to his present quandary. When times were good, he had enjoyed the love and support of all the Huastecs. They looked to him for spiritual leadership and followed him without question. While his highest aspiration was never to fail his people, their unquestioning devotion placed a heavy burden on him. He was still only a man, and no man had all the answers.

He had prayed with sincerity to the gods all his life, and he had felt their compassion and love surrounding and protecting himself and his people. And yet with all his powers of sorcery, he had never conversed with the gods. He had come to realize that there was a Presence throughout the universe so vast and all encompassing that man was limited in his ability to comprehend it. Each person was an inseparable part of that Presence, sensing the connection and longing to somehow reunite with it. But the description of the Presence, and people's manifestation of it in the form of gods, was limited by each person's imagination. Some saw gods in the clouds, others saw them as man-like creatures, and men like Toshni saw them in an ancient stone carving. The problem was that all were right, and all were wrong. How could man conceive of a Presence that was a part of and yet bigger than the entire universe?

Tonah quieted his mind and continued gazing across the vastness. His attention turned inward. His gaze became an unseeing stare as his mind reached across an inner reality, a multi-dimensional universe that rivaled and even surpassed the physical universe of which he and all beings were a part. Tonah's mind pictured a stone, half-buried in the ground. Half was visible and a part of the physical world that one saw; the other half was hidden, and a part of the world that one knew was there but could not see. Man was like that stone: his body existed in the physical universe, but the force that gave the body life was part of the Presence, a form of energy that permeated the universe. A rational being could not acknowledge one without the other. When a person reached that level of understanding, all of life became a miracle, an inexplicably beautiful journey.

Tonah's mind expanded, experiencing and absorbing wisdom from beings elsewhere in this world and perhaps in others. The time came when a feeling of great satisfaction came over him and his awareness returned to the plaza and the view of the valley. He felt a sense of peace and well being, and he knew what to do.

Shanni sipped her coffee, looking over the rim of the cup at Caleb who sat nearby. The training had been tiring and they were content to rest by the campfire as the afternoon waned. Caleb seemed preoccupied, his mind elsewhere, a change Shanni found unsettling.

She was used to him being in the present with his attention on her. Had she somehow offended him today?

"Too tired to talk?" she ventured.

Caleb roused from his reverie with an effort, and turned to her. "That's part of it."

Shanni waited. What was he thinking, and did she have to pull it out of him? "Well?"

"I've got a lot on my mind and I don't want to worry you."

"I guess all we've been through together doesn't mean anything."

Caleb raised his eyebrows and looked fully at her. What was that all about? "Touchy, today, are we?"

"I don't like being shut out. We've hardly seen each other lately."

"We just spent two hours training together."

"That's not what I mean. We haven't talked."

"You've got to admit, there have been distractions."

"Yes, and all the more reason for us to be together with our thinking."

"You're worried too, aren't you? That's why you're edgy."

"I suppose so. I'm worried about Tonah. He tries not to show it, but I know he takes Toshni's rebellion personally. He is tired. You can see it in his eyes."

"This journey has been hard on him, not to mention the battles in sorcery. He has more to complain about than Toshni and the others!"

"I know. I wish I knew how to help him with Toshni."

Caleb paused a moment, thinking. "This may sound harsh, but we're reaching the point to where people will have to be told what to do."

"What do you mean?"

"When life was good, back at Mesa Verde, everyone could do as he wished. Without discomfort and stress, consensus was easy. As the danger and discomfort increase, and they will if we continue south, we can expect more discontent and second-guessing. Someone will have to make the tough decisions for the welfare of all."

"It would be a big change for the Huastecs. Autocratic leadership, I mean. At the least, it would add to their stress."

"Nevertheless, we won't have time to debate every move and to consider everyone's opinion. Matal must become a strong leader. He'll have to make decisions and make them stick."

"It seems that every day we get farther away from what made our way of life superior," Shanni sighed..

"I'm not saying I like it," Caleb continued. "But we're in a different world now, and it is not going to change. The Huastecs have to meet it on its own terms, or perish."

"I hate to think that we become like the savages we detest in order to live."

"I'm not talking about savagery, but the Huastecs must have a system of rules, 'laws' if you will, with judges and enforcers. People who do not follow the rules can jeopardize the survival of the whole group. Matal must have people reporting to him who can settle disputes and enforce laws. He cannot do it alone. Think about it."

"What about Tonah?"

"I think this dispute with Toshni points out the need. It has already gone too far with others beginning to follow Toshni's lead. Now I'm afraid Tonah has to find a way to get past it. There cannot be a next time. Such dissent must be stopped, and not allowed to fester. I plan to bring this up with Matal at our next meeting."

"So that's why you were quiet. You do have a lot on your mind!"

"I'm either with the Huastecs or I'm out. My life is at stake, as well as yours. I'll have my say in what I think is best for us to succeed. I cannot stand idly by while we all wander about, jeopardizing our lives. I think you see that, and that's why you are training so hard."

"Yes, I've sensed the need for more organization and more focus. All of us have to be committed to the task. It is just that many of our people are confused and don't have a personal sense of how to proceed."

"That's what's missing," Caleb agreed. "And that's what we've got to have before we set out from this camp."

Shanni looked up to see Tonah making his way up the canyon. He walked purposefully, his stride light as always. He did not look tired or worried as he approached to accept the coffee and sit down.

"How did it go, grandfather?" Shanni asked.

"Well," Tonah replied. "I will speak with Matal, and then tomorrow we will bring Toshni back into the fold!"

The camp of the Huastecs was stirring in preparation for the day's activities. Breakfast was past as Tonah led Matal and the others across the camp toward the altar of the stone god. As Toshni's influence had spread, more and more of the Huastecs had begun to place offerings in front of the god. The presence of the stone god brought introspection, and with introspection came guilt. More and more of the Huastecs were turning to Toshni's view that their tribulations resulted from their failures to their gods.

Toshni and several of his followers had on blue vests, giving them a priest-like appearance as they tended the twin fires of the altar, and arranged the offerings around the area. Toshni looked up and recognized Tonah as he emerged from the crowd.

"Welcome, Tonah," Toshni greeted. "I hope you have come to join us today as we seek the gods' favor."

The people looked expectantly toward Tonah as he stepped away from Matal, Caleb and Shanni. "I have always sought the gods' favor," Tonah replied.

"Good, then you will join us!" Toshni was obviously pleased. He did not relish confrontation with Tonah.

"My experience has been that spiritual leadership is based on an understanding of what the gods require of us humans," Tonah replied. "Do you not agree?"

Toshni was caught off guard. He hadn't anticipated a debate with Tonah. Toshni was a straightforward man. He felt at a disadvantage in a public discussion with Tonah.

"Yes, I suppose so." Toshni was hesitant in his reply. He glanced around at his helpers for support. They, too, seemed uncertain where Tonah was leading.

"Then we all need to understand what the gods are seeking from us," Tonah continued. "Has the stone god told us what he requires?"

Toshni sensed a trap, but he could not refuse to answer. "Of course not. The stone god is a representation. The gods are spirits. The stone god is to focus our attention on the true god."

"So the stone god that sits on the altar is not the true god. Has the true god spoken and told us what he requires?"

"Not yet. We have not done enough to appease him and bring his presence to us, but we have humbled ourselves and we are trying, are we not?" Toshni raised a hand to his followers. A murmur of assent rippled through the crowd.

"Do we know when we may expect him to respond?"

Toshni was becoming agitated. "As I said, that is up to the god. He will determine when we have done enough. That is why we are increasing the offerings."

"So it could be days, even weeks?"

"We expect an answer soon."

"And then you will return to Mesa Verde?"

"Yes. When we regain the god's favor, we will return with his protection."

"What if he does not want you to go?"

Toshni looked stunned. He had not considered that possibility. The crowd hushed, waiting.

"I don't understand," Toshni replied. "Of course he wants us to go. He has been one of our gods for hundreds of years at Mesa Verde. We will return him to his place of honor in the temple."

"The stone god is hundreds of years old," Tonah pressed. "It was carved by the Ancients, who left Mesa Verde. Maybe the god told them to leave, and now wishes us to leave. Maybe the drought was not a punishment. Maybe the gods are encouraging us to find a new and better land."

"A caring god would not send us to our deaths." Toshni continued stubbornly.

"I think he is helping us to avoid death," Tonah responded. "The Anglos are taking over our lands. We have seen what is happening to other native peoples. Is it a coincidence that our source of water failed so that we would leave before we were discovered and sent away? The evidence is that the gods are favoring us, and helping us to return to our homeland where we can live in peace and prosper."

"But look at how we are living!" Toshni protested. "Our lives are in constant danger, and we have little food. Already some of us have perished."

"For each hardship we've faced, the gods have presented an answer. We were provided silver to pay for weapons and supplies. We have been provided with allies to teach us how to fight, and now we have even been provided with melons and produce in the middle of a desert! Cannot the gods expect us to do our part?"

A murmur ran through the crowd. Even Toshni seemed to recognize the plausibility of Tonah's words.

"What if you are wrong?" Toshni replied, putting the onus back on Tonah. "What if we follow you to our deaths?"

"We are all men, not gods. I do not speak for the gods, either. The gods speak to each of us individually in our hearts, and we would do well to follow their guidance."

"But what if he speaks to us and tells us to return to Mesa Verde?"

"Since he speaks to all of us, all of us will hear and we will heed. In the meantime, it is clear that we should continue in the course the gods have laid out for us."

The crowd looked expectantly at Toshni. He seemed uncertain how to proceed. He was a sincere man and he was beginning to feel foolish. Tonah's perception picked up Toshni's discomfort, and his heart went out to him.

"You have done well to bring our attention back to our gods," Tonah continued. "Through your efforts, we are finding favor and committing together to our new path. I suggest we continue to give the stone god a place of honor to focus our spirits and that you continue to lead us in that effort. When the time comes to depart from this camp, we will set up an altar in one of the carts and carry the stone god with us as a reminder of our trust."

Without waiting for a reply, Tonah turned to the crowd and raised his voice. "You have heard! What do you think?"

Tonah stepped forward to raise Toshni's arm to the people. Matal stepped beside Tonah as Caleb and Shanni moved next to Toshni. A roar of approval rose from the crowd as they saw their leaders united. The conflict was resolved for the time being. They would go forth together.

Chapter 8

JUAN ZEGARRA WAS not a bad man but he had grown up in a bad time. Orphaned at age eight, he was taken in by his destitute aunt who was trying to raise six children of her own. Juan learned early about hunger, and about misery. He found school such as it was a waste of time, and preferred to spend his days around the cantinas, running errands for pesos and gleaning information that he could sell. He had lived like an animal, and had been treated like a dog. As a result, he became impervious to insult and to pain.

To Juan Zegarra, the world was a hostile place. One did what was necessary to survive. As a result of his ruthlessness and cunning, he had worked his way up to superintendent of the Zocala silver mines in Chihuahua province. The country had been in a state of chaos since Maximillian's execution. Benito Juarez was provisional president, but his rival, Porfirio Diaz, was vying to overthrow him. Who knew how the power struggle would play out? But one thing Zegarra knew: Whoever held power needed to keep the silver shipments flowing in order to fund the new government.

Juan was gazing out the window of his office at the verdant foothills of the Sierra Madre Mountains when the clatter of hooves broke his reverie. He stepped out on the low porch to see two riders dismounting. One wore the uniform of Juarez's guards. The other wore cotton pants, a linen shirt, and a sombrero. Obviously he was a local hired as a guide. A messenger from Mexico City was never good news. What outrageous demand would he bring this time?

"Welcome. Welcome, my friends," Juan greeted, flashing his best smile and bowing. "Come in out of the sun. Here, let me help with your horses."

"That won't be necessary," the guard growled. "My man will see to that. I have little time, and we must talk."

"But of course. Please come in. To what do I owe this honor?"

The guard paused on the porch to slap the dust from his clothes, and then led into the office. Juan followed, motioning to a seat by the desk.

"I am Jesus DeVila. I represent Esteban Cordilleras, who manages the Government's financial resources. Senor Cordilleras is concerned that the silver shipments have lessened over the past several months. He sent me to correct it."

"There have been problems," Juan started to explain. "The Indian workers are dying of disease and we have trouble capturing replacements..."

Jesus raised his hand imperiously, annoyance crossing his face. "I did not come to hear excuses. I came to deliver a message. Effective the end of this month, the shipments will return to the previous level, and by the end of the year, the shortfall is to be made up. Is that clear?"

Juan took a deep breath. The silver vein in the mine was running out, and the workers were dying. Unless they found more silver, and got more workers, what Jesus demanded was impossible, but he knew better than to say it. They hated bad news, and they shot the messenger.

"That is very clear," Juan replied. "We will not fail."

"See that you don't. It is a long, hot ride. I do not wish to be sent up here again."

"You won't be," Juan reassured him. "We have a dining hall across the street. You will need refreshment before you leave. Here, I will show you."

"That won't be necessary," Jesus returned. "I prefer to dine alone. I suggest you spend your time correcting your problems."

Juan ignored the insult, his face impassive. "As you wish. Of course I will do as you suggest."

Jesus turned on his heel and walked out the door, leaving it ajar. Juan followed and watched as Jesus strode across the roadway to the dining building.

He closed the door and returned to gaze out the window at the mountains. After years of poverty, he had finally found a way to make his fortune, and he must not lose it now. The superintendent's position paid steady wages, but the real money was in the percentage of the silver he had been diverting for himself. A small amount was not missed as long as the silver vein was strong, but unwanted attention came when the vein began to fail.

He wondered if Jesus suspected. The government sent inspectors up on a regular basis, but the inspectors' calculations of yield were only an estimate and Juan was careful not to get greedy.

The other problem was the slave labor. In the past, his riders had been successful in rounding up the natives and forcing them to work the mines. But the Indians, used to fresh air and better food, fell ill and died quickly in the mines.

Now his riders, led by the mestizo Alphonso Alvarez, had to go farther afield to find natives, and those that they found were elusive and difficult to capture. Recently, the men had found an Apache camp, but the Apaches had fought so fiercely that his troops killed the men who would have made able-bodied workers. At least they had captured some young women, who brought a good price in the bordellos of Vera Cruz. He had split the profits with Alvarez, and the riders were out hunting with renewed interest.

Juan had not achieved his present position by being careless. As a criollo, born in Mexico of pureblood but unwed Spanish parents, he could only rise to the level of superintendent. He was allowed to do the dirty work, while the Spanish-born aristocracy ran the government and reaped the spoils. Juarez, a mestizo, was trying to change all that, if he could stay alive. But Juan couldn't wait for Juarez. He would hold on a few more months and then he would quietly leave the mine with enough wealth to live well out of sight in Vera Cruz the remainder of his life.

His thoughts turned to Alvarez. Alvarez and his men were bandits. They survived by living off the weak and defenseless in a harsh land. Juan didn't trust Alvarez, and Alvarez was difficult to control. But Alvarez had his uses, and now he needed Alvarez to round up more captives.

Juan turned and walked across the room to peer out at the street. Once the government messenger had gone, he would send for Alvarez.

WITH THE HELP of Matal and the group leaders, the combat trainees were divided into squads of a dozen members, each led by a group leader. The squads had been numbered, and Walpi enlisted Caleb's help in training them in group tactics.

"This week we finish the formal training," Walpi began, addressing the squad members assembled on the training plaza. "So far we have concentrated on one-to-one combat, but when you face organized troops, you must fight as a team. You must know how to fight together effectively, or you will be overrun and routed."

He paused, his eyes moving across the assembled warriors. They had come a long way, he thought with satisfaction. They were in top condition, and confident.

"I have asked Caleb Stone to assist with this part of the training," he continued. "He has observed the battle tactics of the pony soldiers."

At Walpi's nod, Caleb stepped forward to face the trainees. Out of the fifty who started, over forty remained. They were not an army, but with discipline and concentrated firepower, the Huastecs could be effective against a much larger force. They would have to be, he knew, for much was happening in Mexico, and they would enter Mexico soon en route to the Center located somewhere in the Yucatan.

"To be effective in battle, each team must know how to support and protect every other team. We start by dividing you into squads, each squad designated with a number. When it is time to advance, the even-numbered squads take a defensive position and lay down a barrage of rifle fire toward the enemy. Under cover of this fire, the odd-numbered squads advance to a defensive position and begin firing in their turn. This covers the even-numbered squads' advance. In this way, all squads move forward with the benefit of covering fire. If you are forced to retreat, you do the reverse. Even-numbered squads remain in defensive positions and fire while odd –numbered fall back and take defensive positions. The even-numbered then fall back and repeat the procedure. Any questions?"

Aurel was in the front with his squad. He had put on weight with the training. He was all hard muscle, Caleb noted, with respect. Despite his youth, Aurel had focused and applied himself with intensity and it showed. He had mastered every move in hand-to-hand combat.

Aurel raised his hand, and Caleb nodded, acknowledging his question. "How do we know how far to go before we stop and take our firing positions? We don't want to get separated from the other squads."

"A good question," Caleb answered. "You will learn to count a certain number of seconds and then stop and take the defensive position. Your teammates and the other squads will count with you, and they'll know when to act. We'll practice until the internal counting becomes second nature, and everyone develops the same sense of timing. Any other questions?"

Another trainee raised her hand. "What if the defending squad is overrun, especially by mounted troops?"

"The purpose of discipline is to remain effective. The worst thing is to attempt to run away. The enemy would ride you down and shoot you in the back. Even if you are lying prone, staying together with disciplined fire will break a mounted attack. If they ride past, you can turn and fire faster than they can. With the other squads now behind them, you would catch them in a lethal crossfire. Other questions?"

Caleb was pleased as he waited, looking out over the faces. The trainees had become confident and engaged. Now they were thinking, not just doing what they were told. They were growing into warriors, but it would take a baptism of fire to forge them into an effective fighting group. There were no more questions. It was time to start the drills.

Matal assembled the group leaders along with Tonah, Caleb, Shanni and Walpi for a council as they ate their evening meal.

"The training is about finished," Matal began, "And we've preserved as much food as we have available beyond our daily needs. The time is approaching when we must resume our journey."

"I agree," Tonah nodded. "Delay now will only increase the people's unrest and add to our problems."

"We have organized ourselves to have the families pull together," Matal continued. "Our trainees have become fighting teams."

"And Tonah has given us all a lesson in statesmanship!" Caleb interjected.

Matal smiled, looking at Tonah. "I was prepared to command Toshni to fall in line, but I'm glad it didn't come to that."

"It is not always possible, but always more desirable if one can get a detractor on your side," Tonah continued. "With pressure, there is only acquiescence, not commitment. Without commitment, people will abandon you when their help is most critical."

"Anyway, it's past and we should prepare to depart. Nothing to keep us here now."

"Before we go, we need to get information on what is happening in Mexico," Caleb suggested. "We only have a few hundred miles before we'll enter Mexico and things have been in turmoil there since the War with the United States. In Mexico, we become illegal aliens without protection of our government."

"That is a point of confusion to me, and to the Huastecs," Matal responded. "The earth belongs to the spirit that created it. We are a part of it. How can there be boundaries set upon it, and what do they look like?"

"Governments divide the land, and sometimes go to war to settle who has jurisdiction over the land and its inhabitants. The inhabitants, the people, are known as citizens and the government seeks to rule and protect them. The boundaries are on paper, on a map. Unless there is a marker, you can cross into Mexico without knowing it. The land looks the same."

"So what is the difference to us?"

"The difference is that the government can use soldiers against us, to capture us and put us into prison, and we have no rights, no one to intercede on our behalf."

"How does that differ from our plight in the United States?"

"Maybe not much," Caleb admitted. "But at least there is an acceptance that you belong in the United States, since you were born here. The government attempts to provide for you to live here."

"On a reservation, with our only means of support the handouts from your government!"

"That's not fair to Caleb," Shanni broke in, reproving Matal. "He's helping us to see realities that we would otherwise overlook to our peril. He doesn't set the government's policy."

"You're right," Matal responded. "I apologize, Caleb. I'm afraid I become frustrated at all the hidden obstacles that keep surfacing. Don't we have enough to face just defending and feeding ourselves?"

"More than enough," Caleb agreed. "And I wish that was all we faced, but it isn't and I have to make sure we address these other issues before they overcome us."

"What do you suggest?"

"That we ride to the nearest town and see if we can find out what's going on in Mexico City, the capital of their government, and along the border with the United States. Maybe it will help us to know what to expect."

The clatter of hoof beats interrupted their discussion as one of the sentries reached camp from down the canyon. He dismounted hurriedly and conferred with Matal, who had walked out to meet him.

Moments later the sentry nodded and remounted to spur his horse back down the canyon.

"That ride may not be necessary," Matal opened as he returned to the council. "Porter has arrived with his troops to camp in the valley. He's asked to see us right away. Says he has news that can't wait."

Chapter 9

PORTER'S MEN HAD the campfires going and their evening meal started when Matal and the others arrived. Porter stood up, offering coffee as they dismounted.

"Thanks, but we've just finished eating," Matal answered as Caleb, Shanni, Tonah and Walpi took seats around the fire.

"Sorry to roust you out like that, but time is short." Porter responded, agitated. "Reckon you haven't access to the news?"

"No, we've been isolated here a few weeks, training and getting ready to ride south." Caleb answered.

"Well, the Apaches, led by Geronimo have declared war on all whites. They've been raiding and killing all across the territories of Arizona and New Mexico. As a result, the U.S. government has the troops on the move from all the forts along the line from Texas. The country is swarming with soldiers. It is only a matter of time until you're found."

"We'll need to leave at once?" Matal's voice was a question.

"The sooner the better!"

"What's the situation across the border?" Caleb asked.

"No better," Porter continued. "Geronimo has been using the Sierra Madres as a refuge for his people and his warriors. The U.S. has told the Mexican government it wants to pursue Geronimo into Mexico to run him down. Politically, Juarez can't allow it with Diaz leading an insurrection against him. That means that Juarez will be sending soldiers north to watch out for illegal incursions by U. S. troops that Diaz could use against him to overthrow his government. Summing it up, both countries will be crawling with troops and confusion."

"And we'll be traveling right through the middle of it," Caleb observed.

"There is no way to hide a group this big," Porter added. "You'll be spotted by any soldiers, or bandits for that matter, that cross your path."

"We cannot outrun them," Matal added. "Our only choice is to hide, or to fight."

"Or find a way to avoid them," Tonah interjected.

Matal and the others looked askance at Tonah.

"Large groups of riders are easy to detect, and they tend to travel in predictable ways," Tonah continued. "Maybe we can use the confusion to our advantage. After all, do we really have a choice?"

"So be it," Matal decided, standing up. "We'll go back and get preparations started. We'll leave tomorrow."

There had been little time to pause as the Huastec camp dismantled lodges and loaded carts for the journey. Caleb prepared his packs and gear so that he could load his packhorse quickly when the time came to depart. He strode across camp to see if he could help Shanni. He found her tent folded and packed on a cart with Tonah's belongings. All that was needed to depart was to hitch up the horses. Clearly they had been prepared for a hasty departure, which had aided the packing.

Shanni saw Caleb approaching and rose to greet him with a kiss. Arm in arm they walked away from the bustle of the camp.

"We've had little time to talk lately," Caleb opened. "There has been so much to do."

"I've felt it too," Shanni replied. "Although we see each other every day, there is no time to ourselves. We're like strangers."

"Now that we're traveling again, it will become worse. Every day will be a new challenge."

"We must not let it keep us apart. We must find time for each other."

Shanni moved to him in the darkness. He felt her strong body and thrilled at her closeness. Desire burned in him as he kissed her hungrily. Shanni was a woman now, filled with a woman's desire. She returned his kiss and clung to him, savoring the feel of his body.

They paused and Caleb looked into her eyes. "We cannot go on like this," he said simply. "No one has any idea how long this journey may take, even if we live to see it end. We have thousands of miles to cover. It could take years!"

"Years?" Shanni was incredulous. "How can it possibly be that far?"

"There was an ancient civilization called the Mayas centered in the south of Mexico. If the Center that Tonah seeks is there, we might have a chance to reach it. There is another whole continent south of that. If the Center is there, who would know where to find it?"

"We never knew that the world was so big."

"And very difficult to travel. We have deserts and mountains to cross, and likely even seas."

"What are 'seas'?"

"Large bodies of water, so big that you must go out on a boat and you cannot see land."

"I cannot imagine such a thing."

"Not now, but you will. All the Huastecs will learn to view the world in a different way."

"And we will be changed forever."

"In many ways, yes."

"And you are afraid for us? That's why you speak of such things now?"

"I feel the pressure of time. We should not keep putting off our marriage. We cannot keep living as if we have all the time in the world for ourselves. Tomorrow is promised to no one, and we do not know if or when we'll be able to return to my ranch and settle down. This is our life now and we should not live apart."

"Perhaps you are right," Shanni agreed. "I, too, have felt the ache of wanting you and not having you. Let me have some time to think. So much is going on now."

"Yes," Caleb agreed, holding her tightly as he gazed into the darkness. "A lot is going on, out of our control."

He felt a chill along his spine. So many things could go wrong, he thought, remembering his travels in a hostile land before he met Shanni. And it could go wrong so fast.

Caleb pulled his horse to a halt on a knoll and looked back along the Huastec caravan. The entire Huastec nation and their possessions were strung out for nearly a mile along the broad valley that fell away to the Rio Grande River. The families rode carts while the men and women warriors, no longer trainees, spread out on their horses on both sides of the column. It was an impressive sight, and the caravan had made remarkable time for the past week as they bore south toward the Mexican border. Caleb saw Walpi glance up and rein his horse around to gallop up the steep grade where Caleb waited.

"Quite a sight, isn't it?" Walpi said. "Reminds me of my people, the Navaho, when they made the trek from Bosque Redondo."

"Seems a long time ago that we camped among your people. We've been off the Navaho reservation for some time now." Caleb nodded, recalling the recognition dinner for Manteh, Nantan, and Antay before they left the Huastecs to return to Manuelito. Walpi had elected to stay for a few more days.

"In a day or so we'll cross into Mexico," Walpi agreed. "And then things will be different."

"Better, I hope?" Caleb answered.

"I do not know, and I have a personal quandary. Already I am in violation for leaving the reservation. If they became aware, the soldiers could arrest me."

"I'd forgotten all about that," Caleb admitted. "What was Manuelito's mandate when he let you come with us?"

"I was to train the people to fight, and help out where I could. How and where he left up to me."

"And now?"

"I must decide whether to return to the reservation or continue with you into Mexico."

"We would hate to see you go. I'm afraid the trainees all lean on you for support. They do not yet have the confidence gained in battle. Yet it would be an imposition to keep you longer and cause you trouble."

"If I return, I return to a life of quiet and dependency. It is difficult after a lifetime of freedom. At least with the Huastecs I am free."

Caleb remained silent, thinking. A man's life revolved around the choices he made, and often at the time he did not recognize their import. If Walpi chose to remain with the Huastecs the odds were he'd never return to his home among the Navaho. And Caleb knew Walpi well enough to know that Walpi would make his decision with full knowledge of the irrevocability of his choice. Caleb could not help. It was up to Walpi.

"When will you decide?" Caleb asked. Walpi looked across the valley, to the horizon, and he laughed, a quiet, deep laugh of delight, like a child who holds his first fish up to the sunlight.

"I have already decided," Walpi replied, " And today is a good day!" He turned his horse and galloped down the slope to resume his position in front of the caravan.

Aurel reined his horse in beside Shanni as they rode along the side of the caravan. Aurel's shoulders had broadened and his body had put on muscle from the training. He was rapidly growing into a man.

He spoke with the confidence of youth. "I am pleased that Tonah permitted me to take the training. I feel much better helping to guard our people."

"You did well with the training, and I believe you have grown. You seem stronger as well as more mature."

"Do I?" Aurel returned with pride. "I worked hard and I'm glad that it shows."

"Have you continued your sorcery training with Tonah?"

"No, there hasn't been time, and I've been distracted."

"Have you practiced stacking stones lately?"

"How did you know?" Aurel turned, surprise on his face. "I tried but failed. It just seemed to take too much effort!"

"It was a guess. I too have had difficulty, and I recall when you said you would soon surpass me."

Aurel blushed. "Maybe I was overconfident. But it does seem more difficult now."

"Tonah warned us that as we became more grounded in this world, the higher powers became more difficult and finally disappeared. It would appear that we both are regressing."

Aurel thought a moment. "You're suggesting that as we focus on becoming warriors, we are becoming grounded and losing our powers."

"Yes."

"Where is the greater need?" Aurel protested. "We could not sit around meditating when our people's lives are at stake. I feel much better now that I've been trained to fight."

"But you and I know that our battles take place in more than one dimension. What will happen when there is no one left to defend us in the spirit world?"

"What are you suggesting?"

"Now that we know how to fight in the physical world, we must return our attention to the spirit world."

"Before it turns its attention to us?"

"Even so."

Tonah changed his position in the cart, trying to get comfortable. Despite the padding and blankets, he still found the jarring rattle of the cart to be nerve-wracking. It was a constant distraction that he had to live with, for he could no longer ride a horse all day, and he could not stop until the caravan stopped. He could not practice his sorcery, but he could think, and his mind was busy. The evil beings from the world of nonordinary reality had attacked before Kaibito was killed. There was still much to do, and he did not know how much time he had before they resumed their threat.

In fact, he was surprised initially that the priests that had supported Jorge Tupac until his death had not reasserted themselves. Tonah sensed that Jorge had launched his attack from a location between the Huastecs and the Center. He had felt the ghosts of past civilizations that inhabited the temple complex, but it had not been the Center, and there was not yet a way to locate the Center in the vortices of the spirit world. He needed to finalize the sorcery training for Shanni and Aurel, but there was no way at this pace of travel. Yet they were losing valuable time that could not be made up when the battle was rejoined.

And then there was Caleb Stone. He possessed latent powers, unknown to himself, that made him a target of the spirit beings. They had already tried to kill him. To learn to defend himself in the sorcerer's world, Caleb would have to leave the caravan and set out on his spirit quest. In the spirit quest, Caleb would have to risk his life in the ordinary world to learn how to save it in the world of nonordinary reality. It would be the most important undertaking of his life, and he didn't even know about it. Tonah had to find a way to explain the need to Caleb, and convince him to do it.

Tonah sighed and looked up at the sun rising toward its zenith for the day. Soon they would find a place to halt and rest from the heat of midday. In midafternoon, they would resume travel until dark. Somewhere during those stops he must find the time to reconnect with Aurel and Shanni and refocus them on their sorcery training. Then he would find the way to bring Caleb into their world.

Chapter 10

THE BEINGS LIVED in a higher plane of existence, freed from the enormous energy drain of gravity on the earth level. If a human could see the beings, he would be terrified, for they appeared as bundles of pure light too intensely bright to look upon. A roar like a blast furnace rent the air as they moved their amorphous appendages in the atmosphere of the earth, dissipating heat through their multi-colored aura. They were perfectly formed for their dimension, where there was neither mass nor gravity, but not for the earth. Returning through the dimensions to appear on earth required a great deal of energy compression, a use of energy that was not undertaken without a compelling reason. After all, they had spent lifetimes working their way up to the higher level of their present existence. Returning to earth was retrogressive action that distracted them from their work and wasted their energy. Nevertheless, a few sorcerers remained on earth with the knowledge of how to contact them and seek their help. To these sorcerers, the beings were known as 'Guardians', although the beings themselves had no need for names. But even if a sorcerer were successful in making an appeal, only the beings could choose whether to respond.

There was a niggling in the complex worlds of potentiality, a disturbance in the nodes. The disturbance was an annoyance, a change in the ether that tended to distract the Guardians' attention, and sorcerers in the earthly dimension initiated it.

There were sorcerers in the earthly dimension whose knowledge went back a thousand years to the founding of the Center, and the priesthood that developed to preserve the knowledge. In the earthly dimension, the sorcerer was known as Choctyl, and he had watched as Jorge Tupac unsuccessfully engaged the Huastecs and paid with his life. Tupac had underestimated the Huastecs. Not for hundreds of years had the priests encountered anyone outside their circle who could resist an attack based on the ancient knowledge.

Now there was Tonah, who had resisted Tupac's attack, using the ancient knowledge against them, and he was training others. Tonah was powerful, as Tupac had learned, and his power was growing through the shamans, including an Anglo, he was introducing to the world of nonordinary reality. Tonah must be defeated before he could gather further power. To accomplish his defeat, Choctyl and the other priests needed the help of the Guardians, and only the sage known as Agora knew how to contact them.

Agora's body was ancient as he sat in an open-aired courtyard of the temple and basked in the heat of the morning sun. In his youth, he had traveled far and learned much of the history and geography of the earth, but as he gained in knowledge, he increasingly used astral projection to travel at will throughout the earth as well as into other dimensions. This method was a more optimal use of energy that leveraged his power while prolonging the days his body could exist upon the earth.

Agora expanded his awareness and sensed the approaching party along the side of the mountain. He recognized the priests who had supported Jorge Tupac's attempt to stop Tonah. He could sense their agitation, for they had remained unchallenged for hundreds of years. Tupac's defeat and resulting death had shaken them. Agora remained in a state of repose, waiting for the temple acolytes to show the priests in, and followed their progress with his thoughts as they walked to the courtyard.

They stopped, caught by surprise at the sight of Agora levitating in the lotus position several feet above the stone floor of the courtyard. They exchanged glances and then the priest known as Choctyl stepped forward and bowed deeply. He waited for Agora to open his eyes. As Choctyl waited, his gaze was trapped by the image of Agora as it appeared to shimmer in the morning air. He saw an ancient man, clothed in robes, whose body appeared to float in the air without substance. The face was lined and the skull was bald. It could be a dead body he was looking upon. Choctyl caught himself, and reined in his thoughts. Agora was a legend; who could know his thoughts? Even now he could be reading Choctyl's mind!

As Choctyl stared in fascination, Agora's eyes slowly opened. A chill ran through Choctyl, for instead of eyes he saw dark pools of blue-black luminescence that swirled slowly like the murky waters of a dark stream. Points of luminescence swam in the pools, making slow patterns of rotation. With a start, Choctyl recognized the luminescence as reflections of the stars and galaxies of the night sky.

"Speak!"

Agora's voice was a silent command that reverberated inside Choctyl's head as he choked back fear and tried to organize his thoughts.

"We're here to seek your help in contacting the Guardians. . ." Choctyl stammered. "Only they have the power to assist us in overcoming the strength of the strangers who destroyed Tupac."

"You do not need to speak in words," Agora interrupted. "Simply remember the events and I will read your thoughts as you recall."

Choctyl's memory flashed back to Jorge Tupac and their duel with the stranger known as Tonah. As the thoughts flashed through his mind, he was aware of the presence of Agora, reliving the events with him. He had a sensation of dizziness, and felt nausea rising. He reached out to his companion's shoulder for support. In an instant, it was over and Agora withdrew, as Choctyl tried to compose himself.

"That is all?" Agora's voice "spoke" in Choctyl's mind. "Why would the Guardians concern themselves with this matter?"

"Tupac was our leader, the most advanced of our sorcerers," Choctyl replied. "He possessed the most of the ancient knowledge."

"The affairs of men are no longer of interest to the Guardians."

"But Tupac feared the one called Tonah. He not only has the ancient knowledge, he applies it with integrity. Tupac believed that if he were allowed to reach the Center, he would destroy the duality set up by the ancients in the node of the matrix that created their worlds. This, as you know, could threaten the Guardians."

Agora remained silent, assimilating the information. The Guardians had spent a thousand earth years achieving their present level of power overseeing the creation of numerous worlds in higher dimensions. Their accumulated power was based on the potentialities that they had set in motion a thousand years ago. To achieve that power, they had taken steps to eliminate any other potential outcomes, and that had required ruthless decisions, and ruthless actions. To achieve power over galaxies of sentient beings had, in their minds, justified the means. But a man of integrity might question those means and rip apart the whole matrix that was so carefully crafted.

Agora reached his decision. It was not up to him to decide. He would not withhold the information from the Guardians. He would contact them, and get their attention, and then they would decide.

"Go now," Agora communicated. "I will communicate this information to the Guardians and they will decide."

Choctyl and the other priest bowed and backed away as the figure of Agora began to change, becoming opaque. They could see the background of the plaza and the distant mountains through his outlined form as he dissipated, like a fog, into thin air.

Frightened, they turned and fled out of the plaza. Only when they reached the horses did they stop to catch their breaths.

"How could Agora do that with his body?" The priest asked, turning to Choctyl. "It defies all the natural laws."

"That was not his body," Choctyl replied, wiping his brow. "It was a projection. His real person could be anywhere on earth, or even not of the earth."

"He must be of the earth. Only the dead can leave the earth!"

"Death takes on a very different meaning to those who can move between the worlds," Choctyl replied softly

He looked around apprehensively and spurred away down the dusty path from the temple.

ALPHONSO ALVAREZ GAZED impassively across the desert valley and rubbed his eyes in the shimmering heat. He looked again from his perch high in the mountains of the Sierra Madre and the apparition was still there! Out of nowhere had appeared a caravan of horses and carts, traveling purposefully south, without a sound. Even the pace of march was such as to minimize the dust of passage. In the rear, sweepers obliterated signs of passage. In his experience, only soldiers could field such a massive force in this hostile environment, but these were not soldiers. These were women and children, and men, and along the vanguard, warriors. It was an entire nation, on wheels, traveling his way. What could it mean?

Taking out his spyglass, he scanned the advance riders and recognized the ones who had been with the carts when he had attacked. So they had returned! And this time with women and children. That would slow them down, and he would have his revenge! But not now. There were too many of them. He would need more men and that meant he needed more money.

Hurriedly he climbed down the steep bank and approached his waiting men. Mounting, they spurred away to the south.

"I COULDN'T BELIEVE my eyes at first! Why, it was a whole army of people out in the desert! I had never seen the like!" Alphonso's eyes were wide as he described the vision to Juan Zegarra. One of his riders, Juh, had accompanied him into Juan's office, and he turned to him for confirmation. Juh nodded silently as Juan turned from the window to face the two riders.

"The government wants more silver to fund its fight against the revolution. They're pushing us to increase production. We need more captives to work the mines, and we need them now."

"That's a tall order," Alphonso replied. "We've pretty well cleaned out the region, having to kill those who resisted capture."

"You'll have to range wider. You've got to bring me more workers. I don't want to tell the government man, DeVila, that you're the holdup."

Alphonso ignored the threat, thinking quickly. He sensed the urgency in Zegarra's voice. Maybe he could squeeze Juan for the funds he needed, and take on the caravan. "I've got an idea that'll get us all the workers we need, but I'll need to hire more men, and they'll need supplies, horses, and rifles."

Juan's eyes narrowed. "I already gave you money. Now I want results!"

"But this is big! We saw a caravan of people, more than two hundred, with carts, horses and guns. If we could capture that, you'd have your workers and we'd have enough supplies to more than pay back your advance."

"What do you mean a caravan? Where?"

"In the desert, on our way here."

"What would that many people be doing out in the desert? Maybe you drank too much tequila and saw a mirage." Juan's face mirrored his distaste. Why had he ever teamed up with Alvarez? He was just the kind of man to fold when you needed him most.

"I saw them all right, but I don't know who they are. They weren't Apaches, and were dressed strange for these parts."

"If I advance the money, where would you find the men?"

"Every village has men who'd rather fight than farm. That's how I got most of my present riders. Regular pay, enough to eat, tequila, and they'll ride and fight where I want."

"How many more do you think you'd need?"

"I've got twenty-five now, active or on call. I'd need twice that."

"Twenty-five more!" Juan's voice rose. "Do you think I have so much money? Already you've cost me a fortune!"

"But this will be worth it," Alphonso stood his ground. "The horses alone will repay your advance. There must be nearly a hundred."

Juan was calculating rapidly. He had to have workers for the mine, and time was of the essence. He couldn't wait for Alphonso to scour the countryside, bringing in a handful of captives at a time. If Alvarez captured the caravan, Juan could maximize output overnight, rake off his "share" and leave the country. Now was the time to gamble.

"I'll advance you wages for the men, and I have rifles I will lend you, but I want it all back when you bring in the captives. You can steal the horses for the men."

Alphonso started to protest, then thought better of it. He already owed Juan a considerable sum. Now he had the chance to pay it back and net a big profit besides. He could get men who would ride cheap just for the chance to loot the caravan.

"I would've been justified in asking for more," Alphonso protested, "And now you've cut me to the quick!"

"You wouldn't of had the gall! Already I'm advancing you too much. You should've used your last payment instead of drinking it up with the men."

"But I..." Alphonso stopped as Juan raised his hand.

"That's it," Juan said sharply, cutting off argument. "Time's short. You need to ride!"

The meeting was over and Alphonso knew it. He nodded to Juh and they turned and strode out of the office.

Juan watched silently as they mounted their horses and spurred down the street. He hoped that Alphonso hadn't picked up on how desperate he was for slaves to work the mine. He was almost where he needed to be. Any delay could spoil everything.

TONAH AND AUREL walked slowly along the dry wash looking for plants. In the desert, plants clung to niches of moisture found in unlikely places. Dew collecting along a sheer rock wall could support the lichen that provided medicine for a poultice. Foxglove could cling to moist cracks in the rock, or along damp watercourses, and foxglove was useful as a heart stimulant. Tonah's apprenticeship had extended throughout his childhood, and even after becoming a shaman, his natural predilection for healing had kept him learning. He was pleased that Aurel was gifted in healing. Aurel had a natural curiosity combined with a boy-like energy. He would make a good shaman, and Tonah felt a sense of urgency in passing along his knowledge, for Tonah knew his time on the earth was growing short. Sorcery was another thing, for sorcery moved one to another level, requiring talent and skill beyond that of shamanism, although there were overlaps in practice. He would lead Aurel to the portal, but only Aurel could go through. And it was so for all who aspired to enter the sorcerer's world.

Tonah was preoccupied. The warrior training had gone well, and the men and women were in excellent physical shape from the daily workouts. But Tonah knew that the evil sorcerers who had attempted to attack them were regrouping and regaining their strength. Soon they would launch a new and more deadly attack, based on what they had learned from their prior, failed attempts. It was urgent that Tonah lead Caleb Stone into his spirit quest, but there was never a good time, and there were Shanni's feelings to consider. Shanni would know that the spirit quest could take Caleb's life.

"You are quiet, today," Aurel opened as the minutes dragged. "Am I missing something?"

Tonah paused and smiled. "You are doing very well in identifying the plants and learning their applications to shamanism. I was preoccupied with issues of sorcery."

"I have trained hard to master the physical skills needed to be a fighter," Aurel answered. "I have never felt stronger. I feel I am ready to begin my spirit quest."

"All in good time," Tonah answered. "I do not wish you to go into it too soon. I have invested much in your training, and I want you to survive."

"Surely it cannot be that dangerous for me, after all my training." Aurel replied.

"All spirit quests of necessity risk the seeker's life. Your chance will come soon," Tonah replied. "But first we must support Caleb Stone in his spirit quest."

"An Anglo?" Aurel looked puzzled. "How can he go on a spirit quest without the apprenticeship? I've spent years preparing."

"I would have preferred the ability to apprentice him, but there isn't time. He has been specifically targeted by the evil forces that seek to destroy the Huastecs."

"But you said that one faces death in the spirit quest. What if he dies?"

"Then we all lose, for Power has chosen him as the linchpin in our battle to survive."

"I'm afraid I do not understand." Aurel replied, shaking his head.

"Nor do I," Tonah replied. "Who can know the ways of Power? Come, the sun is setting and we must return to camp."

CALEB AND SHANNI looked up as Tonah and Aurel appeared at the edge of camp and joined them for the evening meal. Aurel laid the plants they had gathered aside, and followed Tonah to help themselves to food. Their plates filled, they settled comfortably by the fire to eat.

"Were you able to find useful plants in this desert?" Shanni asked.

"Yes, the day went well," Tonah answered. "Aurel learned several new species, and we've gathered lichens and foxglove. How was the training?"

"We are nearing the end of the training. Walpi has showed us all the techniques, and now we are practicing to become proficient in their application." Shanni answered.

"It's good we're finishing," Caleb added. "Game is getting scarce, requiring the hunters to go farther afield. We'll have to leave soon and resume the journey south."

"Then we must discuss a matter of urgency," Tonah said, glancing at Shanni. "I had hoped to postpone it to a more propitious time, but you need to embark on your spirit quest now."

Shanni looked up, alarmed, as Caleb answered. "I'm afraid I don't know what you mean."

"You must go alone into the desert and stay until you face Power, and Power leads you into sorcery. When you come out the other side, you will know how to exist and survive in the spirit world."

"You mean like the hallucinations we experienced to save Shanni's life?"

"Putting it in your own words, something like that."

"But Tonah," Shanni protested. "You've always told us that a person must face death in his spirit quest. How can you send Caleb without the training? Sorcerers spend years in apprenticeship before embarking on the quest."

"Something in Caleb has uniquely suited him for sorcery, although he is unaware of it. Already Power has sought him out, and evil sorcerers know it. That is why they've attacked him. His life is in greater danger without the knowledge that he can only gain in the spirit quest. That is why we must risk it, and must do it now."

"I've already faced death, more than once, when my enemies tried to kill me. What is the point of this spirit quest?"

"You have faced death in the physical world, and that is important. Without it, I would not risk your entering the quest without training. But this will be different. In the physical world, you rely on your skill with your weapons so that you face death with a certain confidence. You feel you can win. In the spirit quest, you will reach a point where you are completely terrorized and empty-handed. Only then will you plumb the depths of your inner resources, and find those hidden means of survival developed in humankind over thousands of generations. Human beings have these tremendous survival resources of which they are unaware. One can only gain the knowledge of them by facing death. Anything else is only a game."

"Why should I agree to do this?" Caleb protested. "It hasn't been easy, but I've survived on my terms. If I've got to risk my life, I'd choose to do it where it counts, fighting our enemies, not out on some spirit quest!"

"Because you already know how to survive in the physical world, you must likewise learn to survive in the spirit world. That is where your ultimate test will come."

"How can you be so sure? Can you see the future?"

"No. I am not the one who is sure. Stop, and tell me. What do you see?"

Caleb glanced at Shanni. This was unbelievable. With all they faced, it would be madness to leave the caravan and go on some sort of spiritual quest to get to know himself. He shook his head in bewilderment.

"What do you believe?" Tonah repeated.

Caleb felt a slight dizziness, as if the world were shifting. He glanced away at the campfire, and strangely a vision of his mother's face came into view. Fragments from childhood flooded his memory as he recalled her in the kitchen, talking to an unseen person as he wandered in from play.

"Who are you talking to, Mother?" he had asked. .

"Oh, one of my imaginary friends," she had replied cheerfully. "Haven't you ever talked to pretend friends?"

"No, I guess I haven't." he had replied, perplexed..

"Well, it's really quite good for you. It keeps you from being lonely, and they keep you up to date on the news. You should try it sometime!"

"Okay, I guess." He had replied, half-convinced. He'd wandered back out as she carried on with her conversation, but resolved not to mention it to his father.

Unbidden, the answer to Tonah's question came to him. Somehow he knew that Tonah was correct. There was a part of him that was hidden. Without understanding why, he had locked it away when his mother died, and tried to forget it. For he had loved his mother, and had protected her memory. As a child he had instinctively recognized her eccentricities and spoken to no one about them. His father knew, and chided her gently on occasion But his father had loved her, and accepted her child-like free spirit as part of the personality of the woman he loved. He came from a different place in his view of the world, and could never hope to understand her. But she returned his love and that was enough.

Caleb recalled the day she had come to his father in the field, sobbing. "Please ride to the Ingrams'," she said. "They need your help. Mr. Ingram has been injured."

"What? Did someone ride over?" his father had answered, alarmed.

"No, but you must go. Time is short."

His father had looked bewildered, but seeing her so upset, he began to unhitch the horses from the plow. Soon he'd saddled a fresh horse and ridden away. Late that night his father returned, saddened by the death of Mr. Ingram, whose horse, panicked by a rattlesnake, had thrown him into a patch of boulders.

Caleb returned to the present and looked around. Tonah, Shanni and Aurel were watching him intently. How long had he been preoccupied?

"You are right. I must go on the spirit quest, and soon - as soon as possible." Caleb knew with a certainty he did not understand, and could not explain, even to himself.

Tonah nodded, and turned his eyes to the fire. "So be it," he said softly. "And before you go, we must discuss your mother."

Chapter 11

DAWN WAS BREAKING when the man appeared, running at a steady gait, his moccasins brushing silently over the desert floor. His breath was unlabored, even, and the motion of his body was mechanical, like a windmill turning effortlessly in the wind. His eyes were half-closed, trance-like, as he sped over the ground. He had been running for more than twenty-four hours and he had come over a hundred miles.

Yet his senses remained alert and something out of the ordinary caught his attention. He stopped and bent down to study the ground. He was a stocky Native American, dressed in a tunic and loincloth that blended with the gray tones of the desert. He wore the long moccasins with leggings that extended to his knees, providing protection from cacti and poisonous snakes.

Black eyes burning with intensity lit an impassive face with set, down-turned mouth. Determination mixed with ruthlessness emanated like the unspoken threat of a cunning animal.

The man studied the ground for long moments, reading the signs. He glanced carelessly at his back trail, as if he already knew he had left his pursuers far behind. They could not track him at night, but with horses would gain on him during the day. He chuckled grimly, for he knew that they would never catch him.

The man named Goyathlay in the native tongue of the Bedonkohe Apache returned his attention to the curious puzzle before him in the dry wash. He discerned that a large force had passed this way within the past twelve hours. But curiously, men had walked behind, carefully sweeping away sign of their passage. Only his sharp eyes, honed in desert survival since childhood, had spotted the anomaly of the too-perfect sweep of unbroken sand.

The soldiers and the traitorous Apache trackers pursuing him were a known threat that he was prepared to handle, but the purpose and capability of the party ahead was unknown. He could not afford to be caught between two armed and hostile forces.

But now he needed rest. He rose to his feet and scanned the shadows in the low hills to the east. He resumed his steady gait, continuing south, his eyes scanning the terrain before him. Presently he stopped abruptly, allowing his moccasins to dig firmly into the soft sand. Twisting to look over his left shoulder, he began jogging backwards, careful to place his feet in the light indentations of his former trail. More than a quarter mile back he reached the gravel of the dry wash and stepped eastward, leaving no footprints on the rocky ground. An hour later he reached the low hills and the expected creosote bushes scattered in the shadows. He lay down on his side, curling into a fetal position and raked sand over his body until he blended into the base of the plant. He closed his eyes and fell into untroubled sleep.

"Damn it!" Corporal Richard Allen swore, grasping his hat by the brim and slapping the dust off his thigh. He gazed down at his Apache trackers and the footprints in the sand. Their quarry had been running hard, leaving a trail plain as day, as they gained on him with their horses. Now, right in the middle of the valley, the trail had stopped and the man had vanished!

Allen turned to sergeant Cruz, his interpreter and second-in-command, who spoke some Apache. "What're they telling you?"

"They're advising us to go back..." Cruz began.

"Back!" Allen cut in. "After we've rode hell-for-leather to catch the murderer? What in hell's gotten into them?"

"They say we're chasing a demon. If we continue, he will bring catastrophe upon us."

"Tell them that he is a man, who leaves tracks. Our job is to catch him and bring him to justice for the murders of those settlers. I'll hear no more of this nonsense!"

Allen sat his horse impatiently while Cruz conversed with the sullen trackers. The trackers responded in reluctant monosyllables to the sergeant's questions.

"Well, what did they say now?" Allen asked as Cruz turned to him.

"They're refusing to go on. They believe we are on the trail of Goyathlay, a powerful Apache sorcerer. They say that bullets bounce off of him and that he can control the elements. They are afraid to continue."

"Tell them that they must, or face a firing squad when we return to Fort Sill. Why has this Goyathlay got them so spooked?"

"Goyathlay is his Indian name, and he is the devil himself. For years, we have prayed to St. Jerome, our patron saint, for deliverance from this man's merciless raids."

"Ahuh! Well, if he's so bad, how come I've never heard of him?"

"Because you know him by the name given to him by the Mexicans."

Allen's exasperation showed. Now even Cruz was hedging. Would he have to drag it out of him? "Who, damn it! Who?"

"Geronimo."

Mist swirled in foggy wraiths around the creosote bushes as Geronimo awakened. Only his eyes moved as his senses reached out, examining his surroundings. Satisfied he was alone, he sat up and dusted himself off. He paced cautiously along the canyon wall until he found a dry wash leading eastward. He followed it until he found small plants clinging to the damp sand along a dry watercourse. He selected a plant and pulled it free, wiping the dirt away that clung to its roots. He stuffed the plant into his mouth and chewed as he resumed walking.

He climbed out of the wash, hugging the shadows of boulders, until he reached a vantage point looking over his back trail. Far in the distance, he saw mounted troopers halted, conferring with two Apache trackers on foot, holding horses. He saw the conflict of the trackers in their body language, the impatient gestures of their leaders, and grunted with satisfaction .He did not smile. He had not smiled for a long time, not since that day he had returned to camp to find his mother, his wife Alope, and their three small children slaughtered by a Mexican raiding party. His world had changed forever that day, and he had become a ruthless man.

He had no fear of the known, and he knew of the soldiers who pursued him. They could not catch him so he turned his thoughts to the unknown party ahead. He needed to bring them into the known.

Reaching inside his waistband, he pulled out the broken twig, left by one of the sweepers, that he had picked up in the valley. He sat cross-legged in the shadows and placed the twig on a flat rock in front, in the sunlight. He sat back, gazing intently at the twig, allowing his awareness to expand, seeking.

The twig expanded in his perception. He saw the splintered end, the tender bark that had been scratched and dented. As the twig grew in size, he saw irregularities where buds were beginning to appear. The twig became a log, blocking out the surroundings.

Involuntarily his focus shifted and the twig became part of a crude broom, brushing the sand. His perception had picked up the thread now and he followed as it glided along the handle to the hands that guided the broom. He saw through the eyes of the sweeper as the man turned to follow the carts, and Geronimo saw in his mind's eye the caravan of the Huastecs.

As his awareness flew along the caravan, a bubble of perception intercepted it, causing it to pause. Startled, he watched a shimmering he recognized as vibrations adjusting, and the silhouette of a man coalesced into view.

"What is it that you seek?" The form 'said'.

Geronimo was puzzled. He knew the few remaining sorcerers who could project awareness in the spirit world. Who was this stranger?

"Knowledge." he answered. "Enemies pursue me. I seek to know if you pose a threat also."

"We pose no danger to anyone who does not threaten us. We travel for our own purpose."

"As do I. Soldiers are behind me. They may catch up to you."

"Do they know of our passage? We concealed it well."

"I believe that only I detected it."

"Then, forewarned, we will see that they do not catch up. We thank you for the knowledge of their presence."

"It is nothing. We may need to communicate again."

"The laws of causality make it likely."

"Then you know of these things?"

"Yes. You have the twig as a link to us. I request a link to you."

"Look for me on the mountain. I am called 'Goyathlay' in the physical world."

"And I, 'Tonah', of the Huastecs."

Tonah reined his horse to a halt beside the passing carts as the caravan continued its progress southward. He scanned the eastern horizon broken by low hills with deep shadows. Sunlight flashed, as if from a prism, causing a rainbow of color to shimmer for an instant above a rock outcropping. The outline of a man appeared briefly, and flashed forward like a beam of light. Tonah "saw" the form in the blink of an eye and the image was gone. But it was enough, for he had met Goyathlay, and Goyathlay had met him. In the future, they would be able to link their perceptions at will.

Tonah was not alarmed. He trusted the positive potentiality of the universe. In time the significance of the encounter would be revealed. That was the true meaning of faith.

"YOU HAVE TRAINED hard and done well," Tonah opened as Aurel, Shanni and Caleb gathered around the campfire for the evening meal. "Now it is time to complete your training in the spirit world. Time is growing short for you to become ready."

"You mean the spirit quest, don't you?" Aurel replied.

Tonah nodded, pondering Aurel's development. Despite Tonah's misgivings, the physical training had been good for Aurel. He had gained weight, all hard-earned muscle, and he had learned well. With it came a quiet self-confidence and growing maturity. Aurel was ready for the next step.

Caleb looked up from his coffee. He had just returned from a tiring three-day hunting trip. He had looked forward to a few days of rest. Shanni glanced at him questioningly.

"Each of you must pursue his own quest. The path to power is different for each human being. Caleb has experience in the world of the Anglos. He has fought and killed to survive. Therefore he is further along the path to knowledge for he has faced death. But your knowledge may also be an impediment to your progress, Caleb, for your success in the past has depended on your competence in the use of your weapons. In life or death situations, you depend on your weapons. Yet there will be times when your weapons are useless."

"What about me?" Aurel interrupted. "I have trained hard but I still do not know if I will fight well in combat. How do I know that I won't panic?"

"No one can know until that moment of truth, when life or death hangs in the balance. One can prepare, but nothing can substitute for the experience."

"When do we start?" Caleb asked.

"Soon," Tonah answered. "Soon, when Power tells us to proceed."

Chapter 12

CALEB HAD NOT slept well and looked haggard as he joined Shanni and Tonah at breakfast. Shanni's face registered her concern as she poured a cup of coffee and passed it to him. Her perception registered the turmoil in his psyche and she recoiled involuntarily.

"Something is wrong," Shanni greeted. It was more a statement than a question.

"Nightmare," Caleb answered. "Don't have them often, but bad ones when I do."

"Sometimes nightmares are a way for your inner self to get your attention," Tonah offered. "Maybe we should discuss it."

"My mother told me never to discuss bad dreams before breakfast. It was bad luck and would make them come true."

"Your mother was superstitious?"

Caleb's eyes flashed, and Tonah's perception was flooded with Caleb's raw emotional reaction. Caleb stood up, coffee cup in hand, and regained control of himself with a visible effort. "Excuse me," he said and turned to walk away.

Shanni had never seen Caleb react so, and turned questioning eyes to Tonah.

"I felt much pain in him," Tonah replied. "It comes from a hidden place. Even he may not recognize it on a conscious level, but it is very powerful and it could cause him to lash out like a wounded animal."

"Shouldn't we offer to help? I mean, I've never seen him like this!"

"We must wait. The nightmare was too fresh in his mind, too raw first thing in the morning. We'll see if he responds in the quietness of the evening."

Shanni nodded, finishing her coffee and stood up. "The day's training is about to start. I'll see if he is more reasonable then."

Shanni joined the large group of trainees and took her usual place in the column. Caleb came striding from across the camp and joined the group, avoiding Shanni's eyes. He usually worked near her, but today he joined the line in the back and Shanni was hurt by the affront. Caleb had a haunted look in his eyes, but concentrated on the training, and performed with a savage intensity.

Shanni was forced to put Caleb out of her mind and concentrate on the drills. They were practicing the weapons self-defense, and there was no time for a break in focus. The hours passed swiftly as she was caught up in the training. By early afternoon, they were dismissed for the day.

Shanni and Tonah had started the evening meal when Caleb appeared out of the shadows and approached the campfire.

"Sorry about this morning," he said sheepishly, dipping stew from the simmering pot onto his plate.

"No need for apology," Tonah answered. "We were not offended."

"Not offended, maybe," Shanni interjected. "But concerned. I've never seen you act like that. You didn't speak to me all day, as if I were at fault. It would help if you could share what's put you into such a foul mood!"

"I'm not sure I can," Caleb shrugged and spooned food into his mouth. He chewed silently, preoccupied, and swallowed. "All I know is that I had a bad dream and it's fading now. If it is like the others, soon I won't remember it at all."

"Will that be a good thing?" Tonah responded quietly.

Caleb looked up, puzzled. "Why I think so. I don't like being upset by something I can't do anything about."

"Maybe, and maybe not," Tonah replied. "I'd like to capture the content of your nightmare before it fades from your memory. There may be information that we need."

Caleb hesitated, "It was just a bad dream and best forgotten. Probably caused by indigestion. It happens."

Caleb's resistance was palpable and Tonah remained silent. Something important was in that dream, he felt it, but he did not want to push Caleb. His perception reached out and he felt Caleb's agitation building.

Caleb stood up and began to pace. "I don't know what in hell has gotten into me! I'm edgy for no reason."

"There is a reason," Tonah replied softly. "And we must find it. Would you feel comfortable now discussing the dream?"

"I'm not sure I can. It is already hazy."

"Then we will need to find a power spot that will amplify the fading vibrations of the dream before they are totally lost. But you must be willing to open up to us."

Caleb shrugged, looking at Shanni. "I'll try, if you think it is that important."

"We cannot know until we review its contents. There may be no significance or great significance."

"Then let's get it over with. What do I do?"

"We will finish our meal and then go for a walk outside camp. As twilight falls, we will experience the quietness between the worlds. It will have a settling effect on you and aid your recall. I must caution you that dreams can be extremely personal. You must trust that I will neither judge you nor change my opinion of you."

"I'm not sure I understand." Caleb shook his head with misgiving.

"We all have our self-image that we project to others. We only reveal our true selves to a few trusted friends, and that's only if we have faced our true selves. Innate urges or drives that we cannot face are sublimated into our unconscious. Often a person does not even know they are there."

"That's really troublesome. I'd hate to find out that I'm a monster. What would Shanni think of me?"

"We are all monsters when we come into the world. We are capable of anything, no matter how great or how terrible. Our experiences and our acculturation as we grow up channel us toward good or evil."

"I'll stay behind if you are not comfortable with me experiencing your nightmare," Shanni interjected. She was unsettled by the turn of the conversation. Already it had become too personal and she empathized with Caleb's discomfort.

"It's not that," Caleb responded, shaking his head. "I'm uncomfortable with this focus on me and what might be inside me. I know who I am and what I have to do to survive in the world. That's what life is all about."

He took a deep breath and let it out slowly. "If I've got to do this, I want you there. I want no secrets between us."

"Well said," Tonah agreed. "The greatest courage is required to face oneself."

Caleb stopped pacing. "We'd better get going, then, before I lose my resolve. I'm already starting to waver."

Tonah rose quickly to lead the way to the edge of camp. He set a course toward the shadows in the low hills to the west. The setting sun filled the sky with a blaze of color that shifted and changed as the minutes passed.

They neared the low hills and Tonah paused to point back to camp. The campfires of the Huastecs flickered in the gathering darkness, casting a surreal blanket over the landscape, like fireflies in an autumn mist. Nothing stirred, as if for a moment the world and everything in it was frozen in time.

"Feel it?" Tonah whispered. "Feel the silence in the crack between the worlds; that moment when time stands still?"

Tonah's words didn't make sense to Caleb, but he felt the strangeness of the moment and a melancholy enveloped him. He felt the weight of eternity and the futility of man's struggle on the earth. In a cosmic sense, a person lived for only an instant and then died. Did his deeds on this earth matter? Caleb shivered involuntarily and reached out to grasp Shanni's hand. He felt her life energy reach out to his, their auras merging. Lightheadedness over came him and the landscape shimmered.

Tonah perceived the change in Caleb and added quietly, "We will sit here. Continue to stare lightly at the campfires. As darkness falls, they will aid you in entering the spirit world. Let yourself go and follow the flow into your dream."

As in a dream, Caleb sank onto the soft sand and sat cross-legged, dimly aware of Tonah's and Shanni's presence nearby. A knot formed in his stomach as he began to relive his nightmare. He didn't want to do this, but he felt outside himself, inexplicably drawn forward with a morbid fascination, as if watching the agony of a stranger. He began to speak in a monotone, attempting to verbalize the disjointed images that flashed before his inner eye. *Dark clouds hung overhead as he raced his pony across the grassy knoll. Night was falling and he must reach the river before it was too dark to cross. He looked down at his bare feet, clinging to the side of the galloping pony and recognized himself as the boy who had learned to ride bareback, wild and free, through the rolling meadows of his father's ranch. But somehow it all was threatened; he felt it in every cell of his body and the urgency of it was driving him wild with panic.*

The rain whipped his face, blinding him as the pony slowed, fighting to keep its footing on the slippery grass. Somehow through the rain and his tears he saw the river, dark and somber, as if frozen into an icy painting fading into the darkness.

The pony pulled up at the river's edge as a flash of lightning outlined a rider on the other side, shrouded in a shawl and hunched miserably in the pouring rain. Somehow he knew it was his mother, waiting for him, to guide him back home.

He spurred the pony into the roiling water and kicked clear, holding to the pony's mane as he splashed frantically alongside the plunging animal. Lightning flashed as he fought to keep the outline in sight, but the figure was fading, swallowed up in the storm.

He was halfway across now and a surge of hope caused him to kick faster. He would make it across in time, despite the whipping waves that threatened to pull him and the pony under. He felt the pony's feet hit bottom, and the stout animal lurched, finding its feet and climbing strongly for shore. He released his hold and crawled out onto the muddy bank, fighting for breath. He looked up as the lightning flashed and he saw the dim figure slowly receding in the distance.

"No!" He screamed. "I'm here! Don't leave me!"

But his words were whipped away by the wind as the figure faded from view, leaving him alone. He sank to his knees in abject horror. His mother was gone, suddenly and completely. For the first time in his life he knew abandonment. He felt totally and completely alone, and somehow in his child's mind he knew. She would never return.

Caleb stirred weakly as the fires of the camp flickered back into view. He brushed a hand across his brow. It came away wet with perspiration and he wiped it absently on his thigh. Nausea rose in him as he climbed weakly to his feet and swayed in the darkness.

Shanni was beside him, weeping silently and grasping his hand tightly. He felt Tonah's strong hand on his shoulder, guiding him back toward camp. He shivered uncontrollably, his stomach knotted with pain. What was happening to him? The nightmare was enveloping him, leaping from his dream into his world, and he was sinking into madness! How could he make it end? How could he regain the steely control that had carried him coldly through life since his mother's death?

The sun was high when Caleb emerged from his lodge and blinked in the sun. The usual sounds of camp reached his ears and he heard the daily cadence of the trainees in the background on the practice field. He felt curiously refreshed, as if a burden had been lifted from him, and he was ravenous!

He strode across camp toward Tonah's lodge, intent on finding breakfast. Tonah sat nearby in the shade of a blanket supported by four slender poles. Shanni was absent, likely with the other trainees on the practice field. Tonah nodded his greeting, and did not seem surprised to see him.

The aroma of roast venison reached his nostrils, distracting him from Tonah's greeting and he hastened to the fire to remove one of the wooden spits strung with chunks of meat. Impatiently, he started to pull the meat away with his fingers, but jerked back as the heat singed his fingers. Presently he managed to get the meat onto a plate, and secured a cup of coffee. He walked over and sat down by Tonah as he ate with relish.

Tonah smiled, but waited patiently until Caleb had eaten his fill. "I suspect you feel much better today," he opened.

"Like my old self, and starved as you could see. But I never want to go through last night's experience again! It's no wonder a man forgets his nightmares as quickly as he can! What was that all about, anyway?"

"It's complicated, and yet it is simple. As a small child, you had no way to comprehend or to accept your mother's sudden death. You sublimated the loss and carried the hurt all these years. You never knew how to release it. It is enough for now that the burden has been lifted from you and you've started the process of healing. I recommend you go about your regular activities, train with the warriors, and ground yourself in the physical world. We'll see if you sleep normally and rest well."

"But when I think about it..."

"Try not to think about it," Tonah interrupted. "You've carried that burden around a long time. For now it is best to live normally and regain your equilibrium. We'll revisit your dream at the appropriate time."

"Fine by me. I'd as soon never remember it again. Why revisit it at all?"

"There may be a warning in it. Sometimes our inner self utilizes our dreams to tell us things that our conscious mind ignores."

"I've never felt so out of character, and so out of control. I am not comfortable in the world of dreams and omens. Give me a horse and gun and let me scout for the enemy! No more of that!"

"Many things are out of our control when we are children, and only children can experience the true terror of abandonment, even though it is unintentional and unavoidable. As an adult we do a good job of sublimating those memories, for they are just too painful. You've reached deeply into that well and now it best that you close it back up for awhile."

"Where's Shanni?"

"She was worried and wanted to stay here to see about you. I told her you would awaken refreshed, and insisted that she keep her daily schedule of training. Her being here would focus you on last night's experience and that is not what is needed."

Chapter 13

TOSHNI PLACED THE offering in front of the stone idol and bowed reverently. He backed away and turned to face the supplicants before him. More and more of the Huastecs had been coming to make offerings as the hardships of the journey increased. Toshni found his influence growing as the people sought answers to compelling questions. Were they doing the right thing to continue the journey into the unknown? Had they somehow offended their gods, and brought this trouble down upon themselves? Was there still a way, if they could find it, to repair the damage and restore their former life of relative safety?

Toshni was a simple man who did not seek power for himself. Yet his power was growing, along with that of his sons, who were increasingly involved in leading the rituals of worship. But with the increased power came responsibility for people's lives as they looked to him for answers. He had been placated in the confrontation with Matal, but not convinced. As the hardships of the journey increased, his misgivings grew. As they journeyed farther into the unknown, their peril grew. It was only a matter of time until some new calamity would fall on them. Then the people would see that he was right, and follow him back to the land they knew. Yes, another confrontation was coming soon, and he must prepare.

THE CARAVAN HAD STOPPED for the night. Campfires appeared as the Huastecs settled down for the evening meal. Shanni finished her meal and walked to the edge of camp, preoccupied. Stars lit the night sky, brilliant in the clear desert air. The quiet peacefulness was at odds with her sense of foreboding for they were not safe here. Food and water were scarce, and there was always the haunting fear that conditions would worsen as they continued south into the unknown. She was aware that Toshni's followers were growing as people's fears drove them to seek solace in the rituals of the past.

She heard low voices and paused. There was little privacy in the camp and she did not wish to intrude as people stole precious moments to themselves. She saw movement and made out Ambria's slight form as she approached out of the darkness.

"Good evening, Shanni," Ambria greeted, surprise in her eyes. Her face was flushed as she took a deep breath to calm herself. "I did not expect to find you here."

"I left camp to clear my mind. It is peaceful out here."

"For you, maybe. Matal and I can only find a few moments alone, and each time is torture. I want him so I can hardly resist his advances. Do you ever feel that way with Caleb?"

"Yes, when Caleb and I are alone together I am swept up in him. All I feel is desire."

"Then why do we deny ourselves? It is our nature to want the man we love. I thought you and Caleb would have married by now."

"We decided to wait until the Huastecs were settled so we could return to his ranch in Colorado."

Ambria shook her head. "Who knows how long this journey will last? We're only now realizing how big the outside world is. This journey could take years."

"That's what I was thinking as I walked out here tonight. I was wondering if Caleb and I made the right decision to wait. It seems that life goes on wherever we are; maybe we should pursue our happiness wherever we are. We might never see Colorado again."

"I think we hold on to the past because we understood life there. Here everything changes; there is never a day when we can feel safe and in control of our lives. My father says this journey was a mistake, and will be disastrous if we continue. He wants us to go back home. More and more of the Huastecs are coming to agree with him."

"What does Matal think?"

"Matal said that we would not have begun the journey if we could have survived in Mesa Verde."

"Then how can your father advocate going back?"

"He believes that we offended the gods. If we can appease them, then they will protect us and restore our life of peace in Mesa Verde. He is about at the point to refusing to go further. Another misfortune and he and his followers will pull out of the caravan."

"And you will have to choose between your duty to your family and staying with Matal."

"I've thought of that. It may sound selfish, but I must look to my happiness. I will stay with Matal."

"Then you should marry, and soon."

"Matal and I reached the same conclusion, tonight. What about you and Caleb?"

"So much has happened to us lately that we've been distracted from sharing our feelings. Caleb is a strong man, used to being in control. His involvement in sorcery is confusing him, making him question his sanity. I fear it is coming between us. Now Tonah insists that Caleb must go on his spirit quest before another attack is launched against him."

"Won't that be dangerous?"

"Yes."

"Then you face the same dilemma as Matal and I. Do you postpone your life together, or do you marry now and face the future together?"

"You are right. Putting off the decision is in itself a choice, and I think a poor one."

"Maybe we could have a double wedding," Ambria brightened. "Let me know what you decide. I must go now."

Ambria glided away toward the camp, leaving Shanni alone under the stars. Ambria is only a few years younger than me, Shanni thought. Why do I feel so much older?

She reached out with her prescience, seeking clues to the future, but she could not pierce the clouds of potentiality. She sensed both danger and opportunity; a future that they could and must determine by their actions. Realization formed in her mind like the clear pool of a mountain lake: She and Caleb must decide. They must take control of their lives and shape events. They could not wait for the fates to decide for them.

CALEB WAS RIDING in advance of the caravan as the Huastecs stopped for the noonday meal. He rode over to the shade of a rocky outcropping and dismounted. Following long habit, he removed his rifle from the saddle scabbard and sighted it, his muscles moving fluidly as he practiced stepping, turning and aiming, although he did not fire. They could not spare the ammunition, and could not risk the noise. Satisfied, he replaced the rifle and reached for his revolver. In one fluid motion, he drew the gun and pointed, the smooth walnut handle familiar in his hand.

Walpi rode up and halted, watching. Caleb turned, smiling, and replaced the revolver with a deft motion.

"One cannot practice too much," Walpi opened.

Caleb nodded agreement. "It helps clear my mind. I understand physical action."

"As do I. Success in this world depends on it."

"Then you do not believe in sorcery?"

"Oh, I believe. I grew up with shamans. But my predilection is for physical action. I think they saw it early and gave up on me. I've never regretted it."

"I think my predilection is for the physical also. I want no part of sorcery."

"I'm afraid I cannot help you with that. And you don't need my help mastering weapons. You do well enough on your own."

Caleb nodded, acknowledging the compliment. He'd had to learn knives and guns to survive when he went out into the world alone. His world had demanded it. Now he'd seen a different world, a world equally dangerous and frightening. Would he be forced to learn sorcery to survive in it?

He shook off the thought, annoyed. He didn't need the distraction, the feeling of uncertainty. He looked back at Walpi. "Any idea what we face further south?"

"More of the same. Hot, dry desert with little water. I have the scouts out, searching for the best route. We have enough food for the present, but the people are getting tired of dried meat and beans."

"Any chance to hunt fresh game?"

"We're traveling down a long desert plain, with mountains to the east and west. As the plain narrows, we may be able to hunt in the mountains, but it will increase the danger of attack.."

"How so?"

"Where there is game, there will be people, and they will not welcome strangers."

Caleb nodded agreement. This was a harsh land, with few resources. Natives would see their encroachment as a threat. "We'll need to approach them," he answered. "Get permission to hunt the food we need."

"If we can," Walpi agreed. "But it may not matter."

Caleb raised his eyebrows in silent question.

"This caravan cannot go unnoticed, and we have much of value to bandits. It is a matter of time until we are attacked. I'm surprised we've gotten this far without trouble."

"Constant heat, lack of food and water, dissension within the ranks, and bandits looking for a quick score. Any other worries to keep me from being joyful?" Caleb returned with a wry smile.

"And then there is the spirit world. Who knows when or how they will come at us."

Caleb felt the old misgivings return. For a moment there he had forgotten and his mood had improved.

"I could have done without that reminder," he said, swinging smoothly into the saddle and reining his horse around. Walpi spurred up beside him as they galloped back to the caravan. They left the horses at the edge of camp and separated to find their respective camps.

Shanni stood up from the campfire to greet Caleb as he walked up to join her and Tonah. He nodded his greeting and ladled food into his plate. He settled down to eat in the shade of an awning strung beside Tonah's cart. The sun beat down relentlessly; there was no getting away from the heat.

"Anything new today? I've been out front scouting. Land looks all the same, hot and dry."

"Matal was by, checking on us. He looked tired. Said more and more people are siding with Toshni. If we don't break out of this desert soon, there'll be another confrontation. I think he's disgusted, ready to let them go."

Caleb nodded, remaining silent. He wasn't surprised. Matal would only go so far in enforcing his leadership, and then let them go with good riddance. He knew if the bands split, each group for itself, they'd be picked off one by one. But people didn't think with their emotions; they just acted, for better or worse. And things were getting worse.

"Well, I guess we'll cross that bridge when we come to it. We've got enough problems to fill the day."

"Each day we make progress," Tonah agreed. "We must endure. Our only hope is to find sanctuary to the south. There is nothing for us here, or back where we came from. The people will come to see this."

"In time, I hope," Caleb nodded. "Now they are only aware of the discomfort and uncertainty."

"Which we all share, in one form or another," Tonah replied. "Enough for today that we travel and make progress in peace."

"I agree," Caleb responded, rising. "Sometimes it is best to stay focused on progress and not buy trouble."

Shanni rose, and took Caleb's arm. "Let's walk until time for the caravan to start. We've hardly seen each other."

She steered toward the edge of camp, and they walked in silence, enjoying the break from the chores of the day. One forgot the simple pleasures in life, Shanni thought, remembering the quiet walks with Caleb at Mesa Verde. It seemed a long time ago, in another life.

"I talked with Ambria last night," she began. "She's in love with Matal, and afraid that her father and the dissidents will force her to choose between him and her family."

"If Toshni pulls out, every family will have to choose. It'll be disaster for those who go, and for those who stay."

"And where will that leave us?"

Caleb stopped, puzzled. "Why, we'll stay of course. There's no question of going back."

"If we go forward, we may never be able to return to your ranch in Colorado. We may struggle for years to find a homeland to the south."

Caleb paused, thinking. "I guess I'd never faced that possibility. I always figured you and I would return as soon as we got the Huastecs settled in their new home. That's what kept me going; knowing we'd return someday and settle down on my ranch."

"Ambria and Matal want to get married soon; they feel it is a mistake to postpone their life together with the future so uncertain."

"They're showing wisdom beyond their years. They shouldn't postpone life, betting on the future." Sudden realization hit him. "And," he added, "Neither should we!"

"Then you feel we should marry now also?"

"The sooner the better. It's been hell having you so close, and yet we couldn't be together, sharing our life as man and wife. It is unnatural and adds to the uncertainty of the journey. At least married, we have each other."

"It is a big decision, and who is to know which is best. I believe we should follow our hearts."

Caleb took a deep breath, organizing his thoughts. "I've always felt it was the right thing to do. We've waited too long already. Let's get married, and let's do it now!"

Chapter 14

THE DAY HAD been hot and long, but Shanni was swept up in the excitement of her wedding preparations. The doeskin gown she had so carefully stored for the journey came out, as her attendants carefully brushed out the creases. As she went to put it on, she was suddenly apprehensive, for she had gained muscle and weight in the heavy workouts with the warriors. What if she could no longer wear it? She let out a silent sigh of relief when it slipped on, fitted like a glove to outline her lithe form, tall and radiant. Her black hair cascaded down her back, shining in the light of the candles of the lodge. There would be no water lily to adorn it this time, she thought wistfully, thinking back to the night they had almost wed. Kaibito's attack had ruined their plans, and had almost cost Caleb his life. She chided herself for postponing their wedding this long. What was she thinking? But now it would all be made right; at last she would be the wife of the man she loved.

It was unfortunate that Ambria and Matal had delayed their wedding until they could convince Toshni to cooperate. It was a difficult time for the family and Ambria had elected to wait a few days, wanting no dissension to mar her happiness. But she had insisted that Shanni continue with her plans. After all, a marriage was a unique event between two people, and every couple must find its own way.

Shanni emerged from the tent followed by her attendants. She stood tall, her graceful body outlined by the white doeskin gown she had so carefully stored for this moment. The celebration was more subdued than the one at the Navaho camp, for the Huastecs were traveling in a strange and hostile land. Resources were scarce, but the feast pots were boiling and the women had managed to make fresh corn breads from the store of grain to accompany the stews.

The music began, with wooden flutes leading the melody accompanied by chimes and animal-skin drums. Brightly colored costumes had been donned by the young men and women and they danced in great circles, caught up in the music, the tinkle of their jewelry blending with the rhythm of the music.

Caleb stood by Tonah, watching with a lump in his throat as Shanni advanced across the camp. He had never seen her more beautiful, and realized again how deeply he loved her. He realized that with her, however life unfolded, he would be complete.

Stars were appearing overhead in the gathering dusk, with the light of a half-moon casting shadows across the desert. It seemed that time stood still, as the dancers stopped and stood, watching Shanni make her way to the altar to join Tonah and Caleb. Her dark eyes met his, and she smiled. In that smile was the timeless love of a woman for a man, for the soul mate each longed for, the soul mate that made life complete.

When she reached Caleb, she took his arm and they turned to face Tonah. Tonah, clad in the multicolored robe of the shaman, nodded silently and the attendant draped a long red sash across Caleb's shoulders, with one end continuing across Shanni's shoulders. Then they turned to hold hands, facing one another.

The music stopped and a hush settled over the assembly. Shanni's voice was clear and strong on the night air as she completed the ancient words of the Huastec marriage vows:

"In the presence of my people and my gods, I, Shanni, daughter of Kochina and Raphael, granddaughter of Tonah, in the fullness and celebration of my womanhood, declare my love and devotion for you, Caleb Stone. From this time forth, for as long as I am upon the earth, this I promise you:

"To be your mate, and to fulfill you in all things as a man,

"To adhere to you above all others, and to support you in all things right in the sight of the gods,

"To bear your children, and to bring them up strong in the beauty and love of the world,

"To provide for your needs that you may walk strong upon the earth,

"And to join you always in the celebration of life.

"From this day forward we are one, inseparable. I take you for my husband, forever."

Shanni's eyes were dark pools of sincerity, melting Caleb, drawing him to her.

Caleb spoke the Huastec wedding vows he had learned from Tonah.

"In the presence of our people and my God, I, Caleb Stone, son of Jonathan and Elizabeth, in the fullness and celebration of my manhood, declare my love and devotion for you, Shanni. From this day forth, for as long as I am upon the earth, this I promise you:

"To be your mate, and to fulfill you in all things as a woman,

"To adhere to you above all others, and to support you in all things right in the sight of God,

"To love and protect our children, and to join you in bringing them up strong in the beauty and love of the world,

"To protect you and provide for your needs that you may walk strong upon the earth,

"And to join you always in the celebration of life.

"From this day forward we are one, inseparable. I take you for my wife."

He kissed her then, slowly, gently as the attendants tied the ends of the sash together. Caleb felt the frustration and yearning subsiding within him, replaced by a quiet peace. This was their moment, and even the world stopped as they committed their lives to each other. It was a solemn promise, and he knew they would keep it until death.

The dance of celebration began. Young couples formed concentric circles, moving in opposite directions, in step with the music, forming a great kaleidoscope of color and movement. Shanni and Caleb were drawn to the center of the circle where Shanni placed her hands behind his neck as he placed his around her waist and they danced in celebration of their love. Caleb remembered with bittersweet emotion when they had danced thus, long ago on the plaza at Mesa Verde. Life had seemed simpler then, like a dream that vanished in the mist of the dawn.

The hours flew, and then they were hustled off in the midst of the throng to his tent near the edge of the camp. Sentries were posted at a distance as the celebrants began retiring to their beds. Tomorrow the journey would resume, and reality would again impinge on their lives. But at least for tonight, their world had been filled with love.

Their tent was spacious, and the attendants had arranged it comfortably for their use. A small fire by the door cast warmth into the interior until Caleb gently closed the flap and turned to face Shanni in the dim light of the candles.

They stood, suddenly shy, holding hands and embracing gently. After a long moment, Shanni stood back from him, looking into his eyes as she dropped the robe and loosened her hair to fall in a spray over her shoulders.

"Love me, Caleb," she whispered. "Fulfill me as a woman. I have wanted you for so long!"

Caleb drew her to him and felt her fingers loosening the buttons of his shirt.

Far into the night, Shanni awakened in Caleb's arms, savoring the closeness of him as he slept. His strong arm nestled her head, and his chest rose gently as he breathed. If she could just preserve this moment, her happiness would be complete. But unwanted, her prescience cast images before her eyes in the darkness. Tomorrow they must again arise to reality, and their constant peril. Soon Caleb must risk his life on the spirit quest, and she knew the danger was real, more terrible than perhaps even he suspected. And she could not help him.

She snuggled closer. In order to have their happiness together, she had brought him into the world of the Huastecs, and in that world she could lose him forever. Shanni blinked back silent tears as she hugged him to her. To have such happiness torn from her would be more terrible than never to have experienced it at all.

Chapter 15

THEY HAD FINISHED the morning meal when Caleb excused himself and strode across camp toward the area where the horses were temporarily corralled. Shanni sipped her coffee and gazed dreamily at the far horizon, somehow beautiful today as she sighed. Was this a dream? Would she awaken to find that their marriage was yet to be fulfilled? But no, it was true and she knew a peace and happiness of which she'd only dreamed.

Caleb returned with his two horses saddled, and threw supplies behind the saddles. "Come," he said. "We have a long ride for today."

"What on earth?" Shanni breathed her surprise. "Aren't we going with the caravan?"

"We'll ride back across the border, into the Arizona Territory. There's a justice of the peace there in Douglas, across from Aqua Prieta. We're married, as far as I'm concerned, but by making it legal in the United States, you'll have my ranch if anything happens to me."

"Don't tempt fate, talking like that!" Shanni replied. "Why would I want the ranch anyway, if anything happened to you?"

"Go along with me on this. I learned from my father the importance of getting the paperwork done legally. Getting a marriage certificate will also document your U.S. citizenship, and give you the protection of its laws. That will be important to you, and to our children.".

"It seems so cold, somehow, so businesslike. We're just married. Can't we have a few days to ourselves, without worrying about the world and its challenges?"

"I wanted that, too. But each day we travel further into Mexico. Soon we'll be too far to return. We must go now."

"All right, I'll get dressed for the ride." Shanni arose and went into her tent. Caleb led the horses to the side of camp and greeted Tonah, who stood quietly waiting for the caravan to start.

"There is risk in riding alone. I could request that Matal send some of the men as an escort," Tonah opened.

"No. I thought of that. We can travel faster alone, and an armed force crossing the border into Douglas would attract too much attention, perhaps result in our being detained by the authorities. I've ridden those trails alone in the past. We'll make out fine."

"Why the sense of urgency? Surely you could get a priest to carry out the ceremony when we approach a town further south."

"Shanni and I are man and wife, based on our vows before God. But my country will not recognize our marriage without the proper ceremony documented in writing. If I do not return from my spirit quest, then I want her to inherit my ranch in Colorado. If all else fails, she'll have a home to return to."

"Are you that concerned about your spirit quest?"

"Shouldn't I be? You yourself told me I'll face death, with the outcome uncertain. I will be risking death just by going out into this desert alone."

"You are right," Tonah agreed. "The future grows more uncertain, for you and for all of us." He turned as Shanni walked across camp to join them. "Have a safe journey," Tonah added, as they swung into their saddles and Caleb led out north.

The ride to Douglas was hot, dusty and uneventful. The town was little more than a village, with a few false-front stores lining the street. Caleb found the justice of the peace, who performed the civil ceremony and accepted his fee. At Caleb's request, he completed two marriage certificates in longhand, listing both Caleb's and Shanni's birthplace as Colorado, and affixed his signature and seal. His wife and a neighbor signed as witnesses. Caleb carefully folded one of the certificates and placed it in his saddlebag. The other he placed in an envelope and posted it to John Stowe, his attorney in Durango, with a note requesting that he file it at the courthouse of jurisdiction over Mancos. He'd done all he could to protect Shanni's rights, and those of their children, to inherit his land. Maybe it wasn't romantic, but what better way to show his love and commitment to Shanni?

Shanni had no way of understanding the system of laws outside Mesa Verde, for it was a strange world from which she'd been sheltered. But she was learning fast, and she perceived that Caleb was responsibly doing the right things to protect her as his wife. There was much to learn in order to survive in the world outside Mesa Verde.

She could feel that he was less tense on the ride back, as if a weight had been lifted from his shoulders. Why was he so apprehensive and edgy? But he was leading out front, silent, pushing to regain the caravan before dark. She surveyed their surroundings, seeing only faceless desert and low hills. Nothing stirred as they steadily covered the miles back to safety. Caleb pulled the horses to a walk as they came in sight of the caravan, moving slowly down the long valley far to the south, and then he reined the horses to a halt in the shadow of a rocky outcropping...

"I feel your relief," Shanni said, "Although I do not fully understand it. I just want us to be together and enjoy our happiness."

Caleb turned to her and smiled. "Me, too. At least for a while, I want to lay down our burdens and just be together."

"And then?"

"The world will draw us back, and again we'll be fighting to survive."

A fleeting shadow caught Caleb's attention and he turned as his horse shied, bumping into Shanni's mount. She saw the dim outline of a puma slithering across a rock outcropping to disappear in the shadows..

Caleb had drawn his revolver instinctively as his eyes searched the rocks. He motioned and reined back. "What's a puma doing out in this heat? It must be rabid!" he exclaimed.

"What is rabid?" Shanni asked.

"Sick. A sickness that makes it mad, out of its mind and dangerous."

Shanni felt an involuntary shiver run up her spine. Her vision blurred and the landscape vibrated, turning negative with light and dark colors reversed. She felt the eyes of the puma, fire-red, watching, and she *knew*. Caleb was right, the puma was mad, but not from a sickness, for it was no longer a puma; it had become the evil sorcerer that possessed it.

Caleb's first shot struck the puma as it gathered its muscles to spring. The puma recoiled, twisting to the side, aborting its attack. It attempted to regain its balance and tottered as Caleb's second bullet smashed into its skull. Shanni saw the silvery brightness of the sorcerer's awareness release the puma and streak southward to disappear into the darkness.

"What is it?" Caleb asked, replacing his revolver. "You look like you've seen a ghost."

"Not a ghost," she answered. "Worse than a ghost. Didn't you see it?"

"See what? I saw a puma and I killed it."

"There was a sorcerer controlling it. The sorcerer was behind the attack."

"That again," Caleb muttered, shaking his head. "Much more of this sorcery business and I'll be mad, rabid as that puma. I saw a wild animal poised to attack, and I used my gun to kill it. That's the reality of it, and without a gun, it could have killed me. That's the real world in which the Huastecs must survive."

Shanni sat still, tears welling in her eyes. Caleb caught himself and reached out to her. "I'm sorry, Shanni," he said. "I didn't mean it that way. I believe you saw what you saw. But you see what I believe; I believe in what works, and we live in a world where weapons are necessary to survive."

"It isn't that," she answered softly. "It wasn't your words."

"What then?"

"I realize now that we cannot postpone the inevitable for our happiness. If you do not learn to defend yourself in the spirit world, soon, you will be destroyed."

"And if I do."

"You may be destroyed anyway."

Anger flared in Caleb's eyes. "All right. I'll go on the damn spirit quest if I must, but I *will* take my guns."

Tonah was concerned when they related the confrontation with the puma, and sent for Aurel.

"There is no time to waste," he opened when Aurel arrived. "Please go to the cart and unpack my drum and spirit sticks. We must begin the preparations tonight."

"What do we do?" Caleb asked, finishing his dinner.

"Tonight we prepare you, and tomorrow at dawn you go forth."

"Can't I go with him? Surely my spirit powers could help."

"No. Each person must find his own path. Soon power will call you to your own spirit quest, and even I cannot help. Caleb must walk out alone, with only a canteen of water and a knife. And he must stay until it is time to return."

"How will I know?"

"When you are no longer the man you are now. When you are changed."

"Changed how?" Caleb's frustration was growing. "Why should I change? Why should I want to?"

"I know you think I'm talking in riddles, and that's the problem. Many things of the world cannot be explained in words, they can only be experienced. That is the spirit quest."

"So I'm risking my life without knowing why or how. Can you see why this seems insane to me?"

"Yes," Tonah agreed.

Caleb waited for Tonah to finish. The silence stretched out. "Well?"

"That is all I can say. You must trust yourself to survive the experience, and to learn what you must know to continue."

"All right. If I must, I must. But I'm not walking out into that desert. I'm riding, and I'm taking my guns."

"They will be of no use to you," Tonah returned. "They could be the distraction that weakens you, causing your death. Your only weapons will be your intent, and your detachment. They will focus your strength and assure your survival."

"I'm not going out there without my horse and my weapons," Caleb repeated.

Tonah thought a moment, and he knew Caleb. Once Caleb's mind was made up, he would not change. How could he make Caleb see that the weapons were a crutch that could harm him instead of help him?. And then he realized he could not. Caleb's way to power would be a different and more dangerous way. But it was his destiny and Tonah could not change it. He realized that he must step back out of Caleb's way.

"So be it. It is your choice." Tonah replied.

Caleb glanced at Shanni, who remained silent. Even Tonah seemed uncertain. He suddenly realized all this was uncharted territory, even for Tonah. He would be on his own. He fought down the dread building in his stomach.

A candle cast dim light inside the tent as Caleb entered and removed his shirt. At Tonah's bidding, he kneeled, sitting on his feet and gazing forward. Aurel began a low, rhythmic drumming as Tonah removed containers of colored sand from his box of supplies. Silently, Tonah motioned for Caleb to watch the sand painting that he began to construct on the dirt floor. Tonah's hands moved with the skill of long practice as he sprinkled the different colored sand, blending the colors into a geometric design that seemed to glow in the dim light.

Caleb shifted uncomfortably, his feet getting numb from the unaccustomed position. He could feel the slow beat of his heart pulsing through his veins, and felt it settle into rhythm with the beat of the drum. His eyes blurred, and he blinked rapidly, trying to regain control. He stared at the sand painting and it seemed to undulate, like a wave of water across the surface of water. The colors became luminescent, glowing and running together like quicksilver. But the colors did not merge, instead, they swam, wriggling like snakes to form ever-changing designs. Again he shifted uncomfortably, the pain of his feet becoming a distraction.

Tonah noted his discomfort and spoke softly. "Move to a sitting position, cross-legged and ease the discomfort. There is much yet to do."

Caleb shifted to the new position and felt the circulation returning to his legs. This is better, he thought, and then the flowing colors drew his attention back into the sand painting. Caleb was dimly aware of the steady drumming. It had become part of the background, only dimly perceptible just below his level of awareness. Somehow his entire body of itself seemed to pulse in rhythm to the drum. He felt himself swaying slightly, like a man in a boat as the waves lap by.

Tonah completed the painting and set the containers aside. He reached into his leather amulet and carefully lifted out a pinch of yellow powder and placed it in the palm of his right hand. He dipped the tip of the index finger of his left hand into a tin of water, and began rubbing the powder into a paste. He took a twig and heated one end in the flame of a candle until it flared into flame. He shook the flame out, leaving the burning ember, and reached across and grasped Caleb's forearm and pulled it forward. He touched the glowing ember to Caleb's arm in two swift dots, as Caleb jerked back in surprise and pain. What the hell?

Tonah began daubing bits of the yellow paste from his palm into the red welts of the burns. Caleb started to protest, and he flushed. Perspiration sprang out on his lip and forehead, and his stomach lurched. He felt dizzy and burning hot. The tent was suddenly stifling, like a steam bath. He had to get out and get some air.

Caleb started to get up and fell on his side. He'd lost his balance. Which way was up? Waves of nausea swept over him, and he heaved.

He blacked out, and then felt the dirt floor on the side of his face as he regained consciousness. His left eye slowly opened and he focused on a lump of colored sand at the corner of the painting. The sand began to enlarge, growing like a volcano out of the floor, covering his consciousness to become a mountain blocking out his surroundings.

He moved feebly, trying to get his hands underneath to push himself up. His vision swam and he felt like he was drowning in a tub of steaming water. He felt perspiration running down his nose and dripping onto the dirt floor. Panic engulfed him. Tonah and Aurel had disappeared. He was alone! And he was dying! He had to do something.

When consciousness returned, he was lying on his back. His eyes focused on stars overhead, and he turned onto his side. Somehow he had gotten outside the tent. He was cold, shivering in the night air. He gasped, trying to catch his breath. What was happening? He needed to get up and get help! He started to rise, but blacked out from the exertion. At last his body stabilized and he slept.

Cold water on his brow awakened him. A piercing ache pounded inside his head with each beat of his pulse. He opened his eyes and tried to focus. He was still outside. Someone had placed a blanket over him and he recognized Aurel placing a compress on his head. Caleb felt miserable and sick. He was so weak he could hardly move. Then he remembered the paste and a surge of anger added to his misery. What had Tonah done to him? He tried to speak, but his tongue was swollen, like cotton in his mouth.

Aurel lifted his head and held a canteen to his lips. Caleb drank gratefully, and felt his stomach lurch. He propped himself into a sitting position, and Tonah's form swam into view.

"What the hell did you do to me?" Caleb demanded. He felt betrayed. Tonah had poisoned him.

"There is a frog far to the south. It perspires a type of poison to discourage its enemies from eating it. When dried, the perspiration can be used to make the paste I introduced into your system last night. It prepares you physically and mentally for the rigors ahead, increasing your stamina and resistance to infection. Without it you would have no chance to survive."

Caleb was panting for breath as he struggled to regain his strength. "You could've told me what you were doing! I've shot men for less."

Tonah stretched out his arm and Caleb recognized the two small red scars on his forearm. "It is part of the spirit quest. It is necessary. If I had told you, you would not have understood, and you would not have agreed to it. I did what I had to do."

Caleb didn't know what to say. He felt miserable, and his head pounded. Now his spirit quest was delayed. He could not go out like this.

"Now we will carry you out into the desert and leave you to begin your quest."

Caleb couldn't believe what he heard. Like this? He was helpless!

As if reading his mind, Tonah continued. "I will give you something to make you feel better when we get there."

Tonah and Aurel lifted Caleb to his feet, and helped him on with his shirt. He had slept all night in his jeans and boots.

"Not without my guns and horse," Caleb gasped. "I'm not going without them."

"I haven't forgotten," Tonah pointed. Aurel grasped the reins of his horse, saddled with his gun belt hanging over the saddle horn. Caleb's head swam and he blinked to clear his vision. Yes, the rifle was in the scabbard.

Aurel helped him to climb up into the saddle where he clung to the saddle horn. Tonah led out, walking and Aurel followed leading the horse. Caleb looked around and blinked. The entire camp was gone. Had the caravan left already? He stared, trying to clear his vision. Where was the tent? Then he realized what he thought was the tent had been a fold of canvas that Aurel now carried. He had not awakened in camp. He had been moved. Where was he, and where were they going? He'd only started and already he was lost.

Chapter 16

AUREL STOPPED AND looked back at Tonah. The walk had been long, and the stops for rest were becoming more frequent. Tonah's strength was failing, Aurel noted with dismay. The man who was more like a father than a mentor to him was growing feeble. What would he do without Tonah? The thought filled him with anxiety. He realized how both he and the Huastecs depended upon Tonah's strength and wisdom in these times of trouble.

"Are you all right?" he asked.

"I am not ill, but the years weigh heavily upon me. Even the smallest exertion leaves me without strength for days."

"What can I do to help?"

"No one can help when the strength of the human body fails. I have been fortunate to learn the skills to prolong my time upon the earth."

"You have always seemed so strong, as if time could not touch you."

"The spiritual strength does not diminish. It is fixed at birth. The spiritual part of us remains a part of the universal consciousness, but our mental and physical bodies are part of the earth and must eventually fail."

"Why is that so?"

"Because of the enormous energy compression necessary to make the physical world, and our bodies so that we may reside in it. Even with the energy stored within us at birth, we must eat and sleep our entire life in an attempt to replace the energy we use. It is an awesome process."

"If we replace the energy, why do we become old and die?"

"Because ultimately the energy decay overcomes the focused energy. Energy in its pure form is unordered and chaotic. Energy must be harnessed and put in order to create what we know as the physical universe, but even it eventually decays. Our bodies are made from the energy bundles of dying stars."

"Can I learn the skills to prolong my life as you have?"

"It requires more than a set of skills. First, one has to have a purpose that attaches him to the earth. When one's life purpose is known to him, there is a compelling attachment to life in order to complete the work. When the desire is strong, the body responds and utilizes energy to keep going. Without my attachment, my body would have died over a hundred years ago."

Aurel was speechless, his mind in turmoil at the implications of Tonah's statement. "Why, that would mean..." he stammered. "You must be over a hundred years old!"

"Nearer two hundred," Tonah nodded, leaning on his walking staff. "Normally I would have advanced to the next level of existence long ago, but my attachment to the earth was very strong. My life's work was to prevent the extinction of the Huastecs. The potential to accomplish my mission did not come into existence until recently. I had almost lost hope."

"But we're lost in a strange and hostile land, and our danger increases by the day."

"Yes, but the process has been set in motion. Despite our trials, we are moving in a new direction, one which offers hope to the Huastecs. And Power is providing us with the skills we need to accomplish our purpose."

"I don't understand. Who is developing these skills?"

"You, Shanni, and Caleb are at a critical juncture. That is why his spirit quest could not wait, despite the need for him here. Others are developing and will surface when their time is right. It is all based on potentiality, and nothing can hurry the process."

"But I haven't been allowed to start on my spirit quest," Aurel protested.

"You have already started, and so has Shanni," Tonah's voice was soft as he gazed into the distance at the haze of smoke beginning to rise behind a range of low hills.

"I don't understand," Aurel repeated.

"You will," Tonah said quietly. "Soon you will."

Aurel and Tonah rounded the stone outcropping leading to the Huastec camp and stopped horrified. Smoke rose from overturned carts blazing in the afternoon sun. Most of the horses and carts were missing, Aurel noted at a glance. He recognized Toshni and a few of the old men, giving directions and aiding women who were administering to the wounded.

Aurel ran ahead, and Toshni turned at his approach. "What happened?"

"We were attacked by a large force of bandits, nearly half a hundred. They planned the ambush well, timing it when we stopped and dismounted for lunch. They must have been watching us for days."

Aurel's eyes scanned the broad valley. Bodies of riders and horses still littered the landscape. Only a few hours had passed since the attack.

Remembering Tonah, Aurel hurried back to help him catch up to the survivors.

"Were many killed?" Tonah asked.

"Two of our people, that we've found. We've concentrated on helping the wounded. Matal and a small force were out scouting. They heard the attack but it was over too quick for them to get back in time to fight. They've gone in pursuit."

"Why. They're needed here."

"Because the bandits took Shanni, Ambria and the other young women, along with most of the horses and carts."

Motioning to Aurel to follow, Tonah followed Toshni among the wounded. Canvas, blankets and other materials at hand had been stretched over poles to make crude shelters from the sun. The wounded had been tended and made as comfortable as possible. They would be moved to more permanent shelter among the rocks in the coolness of the evening.

Tonah stopped suddenly, recognizing a still form.

"Yes, it is Walpi." Toshni confirmed. "He was guarding the rear of the caravan when the main force attacked from the front, drawing many of our riders forwards to meet the threat. Walpi and two of our young men were split off by a second force. They fought well, killing most of the attackers in that group, but our warriors were killed, and Walpi was badly wounded. He is not expected to live.

Tonah leaned over the still form and reached out to feel the pulse in Walpi's neck. He held his hand two inches over Walpi's chest while he listened to the labored breathing.

"He is dying," Tonah confirmed, turning to Aurel. "Prepare a shelter and get my supplies. There is no time to lose."

Aurel rushed away to do Tonah's bidding while Tonah sat down heavily. He gazed out over the still landscape. Matal was following his heart and not his head in pursuing the larger force. He risked his own life and that of his men. But he could not doubt Matal's courage, and his desire to rescue Ambria and the others. But he would return, if he returned, without success. Tonah drew a deep breath and took stock. Caleb was lost to them during the spirit quest, and Shanni was a captive. With their strength divided, they were vulnerable to attack by the sorcerers. He must remain vigilant, but his strength was waning. And there was Walpi. Without the channeling of fresh energy into his life force he would surely die. Tonah shook his head in weariness. He had intended to remain alert to help Caleb when the confrontation in the spirit world took place, as it must. But now Tonah had no choice but to place his focus on protecting the Huastecs, and Walpi. With regret, Tonah realized that Caleb was on his own.

The men had carefully moved Walpi to the shelter erected at the edge of camp, and Aurel laid out Tonah's supplies. Tonah sat wearily, watching the flames of the small fire, gathering his strength. "You must be my hands for the healing," Tonah said in the quietness after the others departed. "I do not have the strength."

Fear flashed in Aurel's eyes as he turned to Tonah, but he covered it and said quietly, "I will do as you will."

"Good," Tonah nodded his approval. "Please get the sand and begin the sand painting. As before, I will help you with the fine points."

Aurel gathered the containers of sand and began to create the images, remembering to channel the lines of natural energy that coursed through the earth. Aurel had studied hard and learned well, Tonah noted, and now it counted. A false move and all their efforts to save Walpi would be for naught. Perspiration formed on Aurel's forehead as he worked, oblivious to the passage of time. There was no one there for the drum, so Tonah tapped a stick rhythmically on a leather canteen. It was essential to the healing that Walpi's heartbeat and life rhythm be synchronized with the repetitive tapping, for that would help channel the earth energy. Darkness had fallen and the firelight cast flickering shadows over the three men battling with death.

Near midnight, the painting was completed. This was as far as Aurel had come in his apprenticeship. Tonah perceived Aurel's anxiety as he moved into uncharted territory. Aurel looked up expectantly, waiting for Tonah to take over, but Tonah waved a weary hand. "Hold your hands palm down over the earth on each side of

Walpi's chest. Close your eyes and feel the energy potential. It will begin as a tingle, and then pulse through your hands. Then you must use your *intent*, to will it to rise. You will feel it start to flow upward, and then you must channel it with your hands, bending it to course through Walpi's body. You will be frightened by the power of the surge, but you must not react, and you must not draw back. If you fail, Walpi will die."

"You must do this," Aurel insisted. "I will do it when I have the training. We cannot risk a man's life while I learn."

"I would if I could, but I cannot. My strength is gone. It is up to you."

Fear rose in Aurel as he looked down at Walpi's still body. If Walpi died, he would be responsible for Walpi's death, even though he was unprepared. And his people would remember and never have confidence in his healing. Without their belief, he could not succeed as a shaman. There was too much at stake, all his years of development would be wasted.. It was not fair to ask him to do this.

"I cannot do it," Aurel said with finality, turning to Tonah. But Tonah did not hear, for fatigue had claimed him. He lay quietly on his side, unconscious.

Panic seized Aurel and he froze, unable to move. He did not know what to do, and he knew that he must act. His breath rasped in his throat and his body shivered. He wanted to run, to get away. Realization struck him like a thunderbolt; he had been born for this moment. This was the turning point, where he would go forth successful, fulfilled, with potential, or he would fail and with it his life would be a hollow shell, no matter how long he lived. He had not asked for the responsibility of life over death. He did not want it, but it was here. He must choose, and live with the awesome responsibility of that choice for the remainder of his life.

Aurel took a deep breath, and his hands shook as he placed them palm down beside Walpi's still body. He steadied himself, concentrating, trying to remember Tonah's words. He would feel a tingle, the energy would start with a tingle and then it would surge. He waited, feeling desperately in the still air, waiting for a sign. Nothing happened, and he fought down the fear that surged in him. He would not run. No matter what happened, he would not run from this. Deep in his mind he remembered Tonah's coaching from the past. *"You must will it, and then step back and allow it to happen. Your intent must be focused but not attached. Think of it like a pebble thrown into a quiet lake. You must act to set the process in motion, but you must let it go to get the result. It is a weird feeling, to act and not to act at the same time. But you must learn to do it, and to know how it feels when it is happening."*

Time stood still as Aurel hovered over Walpi, concentrating, feeling for the nuance of energy that would signal the start of the energy force. The sound of Walpi's breathing slowly dipped below his consciousness, and the flickering firelight dimmed into darkness. He was alone in the universe, with his hands. He was only aware of his hands, reaching out, seeking, seeking.

Perspiration covered his brow, and his legs trembled from the tension. It was not working. Walpi's life was slipping away and he could not help it. Panic rose in him and his concentration broke. He looked around wildly. He must awaken Tonah. Tonah must help him!

He poured water onto a cloth and bathed Tonah's brow. The cool water caused Tonah to stir weakly and drink from the canteen. "What has happened?" he asked weakly.

"Walpi is dying and I cannot summon the energy. Without your help he will die!"

Tonah sighed and then took a deep breath. "Here, mix this with water and drink it," he said, removing a powder from his amulet and handing it to Aurel.

"What is it?" Aurel asked.

"It will help you to see what must be done. Now hurry, there is little time."

Aurel dropped the powder into the cup of water and watched it dissolve. He raised it to his lips and drank it down, trying to ignore the bitter taste that pierced his palate and caused his stomach to lurch. He felt a rush, and his face flushed. His extremities began to tingle and he became light-headed. He sank to a sitting position beside Tonah. His vision shimmered, and he became aware of bright colors or coronas around the objects in the tent. As he glanced at Tonah, he saw multi-layered bands of color emanating from Tonah's still form.

"What you see is the life force," Tonah answered his unasked question. "Now look at Walpi."

Aurel turned to Walpi's still form and was startled with the sudden realization that there was no corona around Walpi. As his eyes adjusted, he realized he was seeing through Walpi's body to the faint glow that pulsed around Walpi's heart and extended up into his brain.

It was like a banked fire, Aurel thought. Only the embers remained, slowly dying.

"Nothing you have done has worked," Tonah said quietly. "What you see is the last of his life force ebbing. Without new energy, Walpi is doomed."

"But you must tell me what to do!" Aurel cried out. "I've done everything I know. You must help me!"

"I cannot. I can no longer generate the necessary energy."

"Then show me the way."

"The way lies within you, and only you can choose. At this point, so much energy must be transferred to revive Walpi that you yourself may die!"

Aurel caught his breath. He had forgotten that he might be risking his own life to save Walpi's. When Tonah had saved Caleb's life, he'd told Aurel that one often faced death to generate the energy necessary to save another's life, but he had thought it was a figure of speech, a way of verbalizing the serious intent needed to summon the life energy. But now he realized that Tonah had literally risked his own life to save Caleb's, and Tonah had many more years of experience than Aurel. The risk was real and Aurel had no time in which to gain the necessary experience.

He suddenly felt trapped. He felt closed in by the tent and the stifling air was suffocating him. He crawled outside into the night air gasping for deep breaths. He looked up at the quiet stars, still and timeless in the desert sky. Not me, his mind screamed. This is not my time and Walpi's life should not be my responsibility. I cannot do this!

And then Tonah's thoughts pierced his perception like a lance: *Every man faces his moment of truth. If he fails, he spends the remainder of his life a mental cripple, seeking power and fame to convince himself that he is something that he is not, a man of character, and dying a thousand deaths in the doing. Go now and find the answer within yourself, and then return and save Walpi.*

Not knowing how to proceed, Aurel climbed to his feet and stumbled out of the camp into the night. Shadows loomed and the ghostlike boulders shimmered with strange hues that seemed to reach out to him. His head swam, and his vision dimmed, and then he saw it. A round shadow that lay on the gravelly floor of the dry wash caught his attention, drawing him in. Involuntarily his feet moved toward it in a halting walk. He bent over to stare into the blackness and found himself tumbling down a long tunnel in pitch darkness.

His senses overloaded and he blacked out for a moment. When he awakened, he was at the edge of a small village set along a stream, framed by snow-tipped mountains on the horizon. The landscape colors were unusually brilliant, giving the village a surreal quality. It must be the effects of the potion that Tonah had me drink, Aurel thought.

He saw a figure approaching, walking gracefully, and made out the face of a young woman beneath the shawl that covered her hair. She looked familiar and Aurel had the feeling that he knew her. "Welcome to Ibora," she greeted, reaching out with a mug of cool water for him to drink.

Aurel drank, realizing he was very thirsty. "I do not know Ibora," he answered. "Where is it located?"

"How can I answer?" she replied. "South of the mountains and west of the moon?" She is right, he thought. Without a common reference point, a landmark that both understood, Ibora could be a few miles away, or a continent away, from the Huastecs' camp.

"Maybe it doesn't matter," he agreed, climbing to his feet. Without answering, she turned with him and they began walking toward the village.

"My name is Ionia," she said, "And you come to us seeking knowledge. My father will serve as your guide."

A feeling of uneasiness began deep in Aurel's stomach and he drew a deep breath. How did they know why he was here, and where was "here"? Was this real or was he hallucinating from Tonah's potion? Did it matter? Nothing he had been able to do had helped Walpi. Unless he could find the way to save Walpi, there was no future for him back with the Huastecs.

As they neared the village, a tall man rose from beside a lodge and stood quietly watching their approach "This is my father, Wonan," she introduced, as Wonan stepped forward smiling to shake Aurel's hand.

"Come," he said. "First we will eat and then we will talk."

Wonan led into the lodge and they sat down to food and drink. A low fire burned in the center, casting flickering shadows along the wall as they ate quietly, talking little. Aurel ate hungrily, fighting the fatigue that had overcome him, making every movement an effort. Time seemed to slow, and his eyelids drooped as he attempted to finish his meal. He became aware that both Ionia and Wonan had stopped eating and were staring at him intently. As he returned their gaze, Wonan's piercing eyes seemed to grow into large pools of darkness, drawing him in. Aurel gave in to his fatigue and his despair and sank into unconsciousness.

He awakened refreshed and looked around the lodge. He was alone, and he could see the sunlight streaming into the entrance. He was still clothed, so apparently they had placed a blanket over him where he slept. He got to his feet and walked outside, feeling refreshed from the sleep.

"I see you are feeling much better," Wonan waved him over to the campfire. The smell of food cooking over the open fire greeted him and he felt a surge of hunger.

"Seems all I've done is eat," Aurel apologized, helping himself to the food.

"One of life's priorities," Wonan answered with a smile. "One must eat when one is hungry, and sleep when one is tired. Only then can a man have the strength for other things. Sometime we forget that to our detriment."

"I am grateful for your hospitality, but I feel a sense of urgency. I must find the way to save the life of a friend and warrior back in my village."

"We will start at once and help all we can, but only you can determine the time it takes."

Aurel didn't like the implication. Again all the responsibility was being placed on his shoulders as Tonah had done with his admonition.

"The sooner the better then," Aurel answered, not knowing what else to say.

Aurel followed as Wonan led away in a walk from the village. There was no sign of Ionia or the other villagers as they looked back at the quiet lodges scattered along the meandering river. The place had a surreal, otherworldly quality that made Aurel uneasy.

They walked for hours, along dim paths among the low foliage that dotted the foothills of the mountains. Finally Aurel broke the silence. "Where are we going?"

"To find your answers." Wonan answered with surprise. "I thought that was what you wanted."

"It is, but where are we going exactly, to find them?".

"I thought you knew. We will search until you find what you are seeking. Only you can know that. I have no way of knowing what the answers you seek will look like."

Aurel paused and stared at Wonan, not believing his ears. He thought that Wonan was to be his guide and take him to the solution to capturing the energy to save Walpi's life. Wonan was only walking him around in the wilderness, and Aurel was in no mood for having his time wasted. "Let's go back," Aurel said sharply, trying to hide his anger.

"As you wish," Wonan agreed turning to lead back down the slope to the village.

Ionia stood up to greet them as they returned. She smiled brightly and took Aurel's arm. "Come," she said brightly, "I must show you around the village." Wonan nodded his agreement and waved his leave to Aurel as he entered his lodge. Not knowing what to say, Aurel let himself be led away by Ionia. His mood softened as he became aware of Ionia's lithe form beside him as they walked.

She had a natural grace and a girl-like quality to her personality. She was totally at ease, with quick smiles that lit up her face. Aurel felt he had somehow known her all his life.

"You don't remember us, do you?" She asked quietly as they crossed the village and walked along the stream.

"I'm afraid I don't know what you mean."

"Don't I seem familiar to you?"

"Yes, I've had the feeling that I already knew you. You seem familiar somehow, but that couldn't possibly be. I'd remember you if we'd ever met."

"In this lifetime, perhaps, but humans are shielded from the memories of past lives."

Aurel stopped and looked at her fully. "I don't understand."

"In another life we were lovers. You were killed before we could realize the dream of a life together. Now the universe has given us another chance."

So that was it! Somehow he'd stumbled into another world of possibility, as real as his own. Somehow he'd influenced a potential future into reality that permitted him to fulfill his destiny. But what about Walpi?

"Don't you see," Ionia interrupted quietly, as if reading his thoughts. "This is your real world. You are waking from a bad dream, a dream in which you were unfairly given the responsibility for Walpi's life. What happens when your dream becomes a nightmare?"

"I wake up," Aurel answered.

"And that's exactly what you've done here. Soon you'll remember our relationship, the people of the village, everything. You've been through a bad shock, it will take time for you to get well. Then we can live in peace and in love for the remainder of our lives."

Aurel let out a long breath. So he was not responsible for Walpi, and his life with the Huastecs had been a dream! But why couldn't he remember? Was it the potion, or had he been in a coma? And what had he come here to find? Already his motivation was dimming. What did it matter, anyway, if it was all a dream?

The days passed into weeks as Aurel found his old love awakening for Ionia. While he could not remember their past life, this one was good enough and he let himself surrender to happiness. He enjoyed the pleasant days with Wonan, hunting for food among the deer in the forest, or fishing in the river. Entertainment of music and dancing filled the evenings, and Aurel felt his old strength and confidence returning. His body had matured and become strong with the physical training and already he was becoming a favorite in the games with the village men. Soon his natural gifts would make him a leader of the people. He and Ionia began making plans to be married.

One morning he walked alone along the river. He had slept well and was feeling particularly good as he appreciated the beauty around him. It was a good life and he was lucky to have found it. And Ionia made it perfect. With her, his life would be full and complete.

He stopped to gaze across the river, and an eddy in the current near his feet caught his eye. He looked down at the fish that swam by, leading his eye to the quiet water nearby. He stared at his face reflected by the still water, and he saw a stranger. Shocked, he recoiled and caught his breath. His brain became a beehive of confusion as he staggered, gasping for air. The landscape reeled and he dropped to his knees to steady himself. He looked up at the mountains and he knew, without knowing how he knew. All the answers he sought were within himself. His body, like all human bodies, was a reflection of the universe. He had sought answers outside, and had created only illusions. The only reality was within oneself. As realization grew, he felt a great sadness and tears welled in his eyes. He saw Ionia approaching. She saw his face and stopped, her hand going to her mouth as she gasped.

"I must go now," Aurel said simply. "I must save Walpi."

"No! You cannot! That's not real! You're throwing our lives away!"

"I must save Walpi," he repeated, almost to himself.

"You cannot. You will die if you try."

For a moment, Aurel reached out and grasped the unfolding of the universe. All were one, connected. His life would only matter if it were lived in harmony with that unfolding. He could not know the plan, only his part in it. His life could only be fulfilled, could count for something, if he made the right choice and did the right thing.

He fought the longing and sadness welling up in him. He had only to reach out to her and his nightmare would pass, as it had before. But it would not be the right thing. Sadly he waved to Ionia and felt the darkness of the tunnel returning.

He felt the cold wind of the night desert, and opened his eyes to stare up at the quiet stars. How long had he been gone? Nearly a month, for he had spent weeks with Ionia and the villagers. He had been gone much too long to save Walpi.

He climbed to his feet and walked unsteadily back to the camp of the Huastecs. He approached Walpi's lodge and found Tonah and Walpi as he had left them, as if suspended in a time warp. As his mind cleared, he realized he'd only been gone a short while in the physical world. His eyes adjusted, and he saw that Walpi's life force had lessened. Now the glow was faint, pulsing softly with the beat of his heart. How had he held on? His wounds were grave and he had lost much blood. Only his heart, beating on, had forced his body to hold onto life.

Aurel sat down beside Walpi and centered himself. If he must die so that Walpi could live, so be it. A strange calmness came over him, a feeling of acceptance. Now he could look inside himself and find the answer to saving Walpi's life. He went into a deep trance as his perception flashed across the universe, seeking. Like a billion stars, the neurons of his brain fired brightly, making new connections and sorting data known and unknown, reaching down into knowledge accumulated through millions of lifetimes. Aurel became one with the universe, and felt its benevolence, its love for its creatures. And he began to awaken to this life on this plane, and without knowing how he knew, he knew what to do.

Aurel arose to stand over Walpi. Gently he placed his hand over Walpi's heart and reached up with his other hand, reaching for the energy that would save Walpi's life. As he waited searching, he sent the energy of his body coursing along his arm, through his hand, into Walpi's body. He felt the energy drain, and steadied himself, breathing deeply. This was as Tonah had warned. He could transfer his own energy, but only if he became a conduit for the universal energy could they both live.

He felt a tingling, a niggling in his palms, as a soft blue glow began to grow above his outstretched hand. His emotion started to surge, and he caught it. He became detached. He no longer felt the elation of success nor the fear of failure. He felt nothing at all, yet he was alive, for he felt the total focus of his being on the tingling in his hands. The tingling, the search for the universal energy, had become the focus of his being. It was all he cared about.

The tingling intensified, building up heat within his hands. He resisted the temptation to draw away. He must receive the energy and channel it. Still the heat built, and instinctively he turned his palms to the side, feeling the energy surging downward like a column of water roaring from his outstretched hand down through his body and through his palm into Walpi. Walpi's body jerked spasmodically as the energy surged through him. Aurel began to move his palms, shaping and channeling the flow as the energy became a blue-white vapor pulsing between the cosmos and the earth. He brought his palms inward so that he was channeling the energy directly into Walpi, enveloping his body with multi-colored streams of light writhing and sparkling as the energy reformed itself into a blue column extending skyward.

Aurel felt the glow and heat creeping slowly up his arms. His arms and hands were becoming the energy; they were being consumed by the flames. He began to ease his palms apart, and watched the energy slowing, widening, to cover Walpi's entire body in a fog of blue energy. The odor of ozone filled the air, and then the energy began to fade.

Awareness of his surroundings returned, and keen pain pierced Aurel as his cramped back cried out for relief. He straightened slowly, gasping for breath, and wiped the perspiration from his face. He staggered to the edge of the shelter and gazed at the quiet stars overhead. The world looked different, and it felt different. For Aurel, the world would never be the same.

Chapter 17

CALEB'S EYES WERE bloodshot from lack of sleep. However, the tonic Tonah gave him relieved the nausea. In fact, his system was alternating between fatigue and feelings of euphoria as the drug took effect. Tonah had explained how the treatment last night was required to purge his immunological system by draining his adrenals, which forced his body to achieve a new and higher level of resistence to internal and external attack. He felt too tired to reply, but still he resented Tonah taking the actions without warning or explanation.

Tonah and Aurel watched in silence as he drank the potion, and then Tonah nodded. "Do not attempt to follow us," he said, as he and Aurel turned to walk away along the narrow ravine.

Caleb blinked and surveyed his surroundings. He was in a dry wash enclosed by broken rock walls. It was no different from the landscape he and the Huastecs had traveled through for days. But as his vision cleared, he noted a peculiarity. Each object he looked at gave off a glow, like an aura, of colored light. And the colors changed as he swung his gaze from light to shadow. Somehow his color perception had shifted, for he was seeing brighter and deeper reds given off by boulders that had absorbed the heat of the sun, and cooler, yellow and blue pastels emitted from rocks that lay in the shadows. He turned to his horse, standing nearby, and was astonished at the surreal image of the animal's core of red that faded into yellows and greens near the surface of its skin, and faded into a blue aura that radiated out from its coat.

Everywhere he looked, he could see the pulsating color as if the object were a living, moving being. As the landscape wavered, he felt nausea rising, as if he were on the heaving deck of a sailing ship as it bore through a rising sea.

He turned and led the horse into the shade of the wall and sat down to settle his stomach. What was he supposed to do now? Maybe he should walk, seek out water and a place to camp for the night. Slowly he got to his feet and mounted, nudging the horse forward up the sandy wash.

Hours passed, marked by the arc of the sun passing its zenith and setting toward the west. The horse was tired, hanging its head as it walked. Caleb sat loosely in the saddle, surveying the surroundings. They had moved for hours, but had made no progress that he could see.

The long shadows of approaching nightfall provided relief from the blazing sun as Caleb pulled the horse to a stop in the shelter of a rock formation. He dismounted stiffly and drank from his canteen. He poured water into his hand and held it to the horse's mouth, watching it nuzzle the precious drops. It wasn't enough. The whole canteen would not be enough for the size of the animal. He loosened the girth and pulled the saddle and blanket from the horse's back. He removed the bridle and scratched the horse's ears.

"If I could give you more, I would," he finally said. "Maybe we'll find water in the morning."

He threw his blanket down on the sand and fell into an exhausted sleep.

A half-moon had risen when he awakened suddenly and sat up. The horse had gone, apparently to return to the caravan. It was just as well, Caleb thought, for he could not look after the animal where he was going.

In the dim light of the moon, the strange auras returned, outlining the boulders and outcrops in his path. He was becoming accustomed to the colors, but wondered when they would recede and his vision would return to normal. His senses seemed unusually alert, amplifying every sound, smell, and visual clue. He was hypersensitive to this strange world, and edgy.

Then he heard the sound, a click of metal on stone and he froze, watching. The aura writhed on the boulders that filled his vision. He waited, hardly breathing, and then his eyes made out the man standing next to the boulder, and saw his hands move. With the automatic reaction of long practice, Caleb brought his rifle up and fired.. The man stood unmoving. Panic surged in Caleb; had he missed that close? He fired repeatedly until the figure wavered and fell into the shadows. Crouching low and scanning the rock for others, Caleb crept toward the spot where the man had fallen. He reached the area and stopped, sweeping the area with his eyes. There was no one there! He wiped his tired eyes and blinked. Had the shadows played tricks on him? Was he seeing ghosts?

He pushed on, making a winding path among the boulders that had fallen in confusion from the rocky crags above. He gazed up at the moon, providing the dim light in which he traveled. He might have been on the moon, he thought, for all the desolate landscape that stretched out in front of him. He turned up the canteen and drank the last of the water.

He spun at a noise behind him and saw the dark outlines of three men standing in the wash, their sombreros glinting strangely in the moonlight. He saw the silent flashes of their handguns as he swung his rifle and aimed shots in their direction. His rifle clicked on an empty chamber and he dropped it, reaching for his revolver. Realization struck and he stopped. Their shots had made no sound. He had seen the flashes, but there had been no bullets. If they had been real, he would have felt them, or heard them ricocheting off the rocks.

And then he heard a sound that caused the hair to stand up on his neck. The men were laughing, a low guttural chuckle that welled to the abandoned hilarity of men sharing a good joke.

Caleb stood, his pulse pounding in his ears as the outlines faded into the darkness. He had to get a grip on himself, he thought. He'd emptied his rifle at shadows. Now he had only his handgun for defense when the enemies were real.

Near dawn fatigue overcame him and he sat down in a cavelike depression that had eroded out of the side of the stone wall. He had no food and no need for a fire, but he was thirsty. He must find water and soon. But for the moment, his strength was gone. His eyelids drooped and he was soon asleep.

The sun was up when he awakened, sharply separating the shadow of the cave from the floor of the desert in front. He was aware of his thirst, and swollen tongue, before he opened his eyes. Dimly the landscape swam into view, and again the auras danced in varied colors across his vision.

Something moved, catching the corner of his vision, and he looked down at the rattlesnake coiled a few feet back from his stretched-out feet. Instinctively he drew them in, bending his knees up under his chin. The eyes stared in an evil glare as the reptile's tongue flicked out, sensing the air.

Food! Caleb thought, reaching for his knife.

"That's gratitude for you!" he 'heard'. *"I could've bitten you and left you to die, and now you want to make breakfast of me!"*

Caleb wiped his hand across his eyes, clearing his vision. He must be hallucinating.

"Don't try it!" the 'voice' continued. *"I am the only chance you have of getting out of this alive."*

What do you mean? Caleb thought.

"Without water and food, your body will die out here; and without a guide, you will lose your sanity as the apparitions continue to be sent against you. Already you have succumbed to the attacks of the spirit beings."

I'm having trouble determining what is real, Caleb thought.

"The problem for you is that both worlds are real. Your life is threatened in both and you must defend yourself in both."

This cannot be happening! Caleb thought, drawing his revolver out of the holster and taking aim.

"Suit yourself." The rattlesnake's aura began to change color, the bright patterns merging into a uniform color that faded from green to yellow to red as the snake's body wavered.

With fierce intent, Caleb deliberately squeezed the trigger and felt the gun roar in his hand. The bullet slapped the earth, smashing sand and gravel up in a cloud of dust. As the dust cleared, Caleb realized that once again he'd fired at an apparition.

AGORA, THE SENTINEL watched the priests gather in the darkness of the pyramid. Torches cast flickering shadows over their faces as they gazed into the crystal supported on the stone altar. Choctyl the priest scanned the landscape through the eyes of the condor that soared on long wings, riding the air currents that rose from the floor of the desert. They had watched as Alphonso and his men raided the Huastec camp, and dispersed the group. Now was the time. With their targets separated, each could be finished off individually. Agora turned to the Guardian who had agreed to return for a brief period. The Guardian was pure light, too bright to look upon. Composed of pure energy held together by forces unknown on earth, it draped itself in a fabric of other-world origin to keep from blinding Agora and the other sentinels. Its time here would be brief, for it had worlds to see to, and resented the enormous energy drain required to return to earth. Because of their gravity, the planets were avoided by higher life forms to avoid the gravity and energy drains that limited life span and mobility.

"What is your wish?" Agora prompted the Guardian.

"Each of you will select a target, and direct the attack in the physical world," 'It' said. "Agora and I will direct the attacks in the spirit world. Go now and begin. I cannot stay long."

The priests bowed and filed out of the chamber.

"And us?" Agora prompted.

"Why do you think, with our powers, we do not interfere in the matters of men?'

A good question, Agora thought. Why hadn't he thought of it?

"Because they are not worth the expenditure of energy." The Guardian answered its own question. "Minor life forms on an insignificant planet simply cannot create enough mischief to warrant our interference. Now those life forms that can control galaxies must be watched closely and sometimes defused. The power of humans is confined to the earth, so what does it matter?"

"Then why did you return?" Agora caught himself. He did not mean to sound impudent.

The Guardian let it pass. He expected little of sentinels, only once removed in progression from humans, the lowest of all forms of sentient life. "All life forms are part of the Universal Consciousness, and cannot be separated from it. It permeates all life throughout the universe. But humans, to begin their cycle of development, are purposely prohibited from prior knowledge of the universal consciousness when they are born. All they know is what they learn in life on earth, which keeps them from causing trouble in the matrices controlling the evolving universe, or 'the future', in earth terms. But occasionally some develop the ability to see beyond the veil, into the other worlds that exist alongside theirs. They begin to interfere with the causality of the matrices, and because of their free will, they are very difficult to rein in. We've learned it is best to terminate the lives of those with paranormal potential before they can learn to use it. That's why I took the time and energy to return."

Agora was thinking quickly. He hid his shock that the Guardian would deign to make any explanation of his actions or motives. And such a long explanation was out of character. Usually a Guardian communicated in monosyllables, if at all. Why would the Guardian care what he thought or knew, as a mere sentinel? Unless...unless the Guardian itself had something to hide. That was it. Something the

Guardians had done in their past lives on earth was threatened. But what? And how could anyone on earth threaten a Guardian?

"A generous explanation," Agora answered, quickly remembering to cloak his thoughts. "Thank you for sharing your wisdom with me."

"We see you becoming a very effective Guardian when you move to the next level," the Guardian returned. "I am merely helping you along."

And further obligating me, Agora thought. What could I find out that they do not want me to know? But Agora knew he'd taken enough risk for one day. He nodded sagely and remained silent.

SHANNI WAS ONLY dimly aware of her surroundings as the cart bounced over the uneven trail. She and the other women were packed into the cart, and she leaned semiconscious on the woman beside her. Her head throbbed from the blow of the rifle butt that had rendered her helpless and oblivious. Memory returned, and she recalled the chaos of the attack. Using Walpi's training, she had grabbed her rifle and killed two of the attackers. But there had been too many riding through the camp on horses, and now they were prisoners. There was little talk as the women endured the hardship of travel on top of the trauma of capture.

Shanni glanced up at the sun and took her bearings. The band was traveling westward at a fast pace. The leader, called Alphonso by his men, seemed intent on reaching his destination. They ate a cold supper, and then, using the horses of the Huastecs to supplement his own, Alphonso changed the teams and resumed travel. Shanni tried to doze to ease the pounding in her head. Near midnight they entered rolling hills with scrub plants, and climbed higher into mountains supporting scrub forests. The cool air refreshed her and she sat up to take note of their surroundings. There was no trail, but evidently their captors knew where they were going, and picked their way through narrow valleys to minimize climbing by the tired horses.

Near dawn they entered a dirt trail and turned to follow as it wound ever higher into the mountains. As the sun rose, they approached a rude mountain town, its single street lined with a few wooden dwellings. Alphonso and the advance riders pulled to a halt and the carts stopped. The tired horses stood, heads down, their breath visible clouds in the brisk air.

Alphonso left the building accompanied by a man whose bearing and dress told Shanni he was of some importance, a manager or leader of the town, perhaps. The men approached the cart and looked inside.

"A good haul, Jefe," Alphonso said proudly. "Just like I promised."

"They look worn out. Are any ill?" The man's cold black eyes swept the group. His hair was full and carefully combed, and his drooping moustache carefully trimmed. Alphonso's deference reaffirmed Shanni's initial conclusion that he was the real leader of the operation. But what was it? Why had they been brought here?

"Some were injured when they resisted our attack on the camp. The women fought as fiercely as the men, a surprise that cost us the lives of good men," Alphonso answered.

"What's done is done. See that their wounds are treated, and that they are fed. We want them in good shape for Vera Cruz. I'll send Hoven around to check their virginity, and we'll sort them then."

"As you say, Jefe," Alphonso grinned, licking his lips. "If any are found unsuitable for shipment, I would welcome the opportunity to take them off your hands. My men and I can make good use of them."

"We'll see," Juan Zegarra answered, noncommital. "Even a used woman commands a good price in Vera Cruz."

Alphonso kept a straight face and held his tongue. Juan was already negotiating. If Alphonso was to have one of the women, he'd have to pay the price. And who knew what she might bring in Vera Cruz? With Juan, there was always the issue of money.

Alphonso waved the carts to move forward, revealing the group of men strung out on foot, herded by mounted horsemen. The men were strung together with rope, and much the worst for the forced march. Dried blood caked the heads and faces of many, from battle or more likely from brutal treatment from the riders, Juan thought. Well, no matter now.

"Clean them up and take them to the mine," Juan ordered.

"Right away," Alphonso answered. He must get to Hoven, he thought. A quick bribe and he could pick the woman he wanted for himself.

The women had been given food and allowed to bath. Now they waited in a large room, talking quietly among themselves. Shanni did not know where Vera Cruz was, but she'd gathered from the conversation that they were to be forced into bondage, and she suspected the worst. She'd faced that fate with Kaibito, and she had learned. The training with Walpi and the hardships of the journey had changed her. As a leader of the Huastecs, she was responsible for the lives of the other women, and she was determined this time to seize control of events. No longer would she wait to act. But how? What should she do? She would need a plan, and soon, for they had little time.

A woman entered the room accompanied by two female attendants. She was old, with a fierce demeanor, but well-dressed. Evidently she commanded some respect in this closed mountain community.

"I am here to examine you," she said coldly, without greeting. "You will do as I say and you will not resist. If you resist, you will be punished."

She pointed to the nearest woman and the attendants seized her by the arms. The woman unlocked a door into the next room and they disappeared, closing the door behind them. Shanni heard the sounds of a struggle, and a scream cut off suddenly.

Anger flashed in Shanni and she reacted, throwing open the door and dashing into the next room. The woman looked up, startled, as Shanni's eyes took in the scene of the Huastec held down on the table. Shanni seized the nearest attendant and swung her violently against the nearest wall. The attendant sank unconscious to the floor. The old woman stepped back, startled, and then hurled herself at Shanni as the other attendant fled screaming from the room. The woman was strong, and struck with an unexpected savagery, thrusting Shanni backward. She stumbled against the wall, her breath knocked out of her, as the woman's hands grasped for her throat. Fingernails slashed her flesh as stars swam in front of her eyes, and she reacted, slamming the woman around, face to the wall, and delivering a swift punch to the kidney. The woman shrieked and turned, beast-like. Her face had changed into a hideous flush, her mouth pulled back into a grimace of strong, animal-like teeth. Her eyes flashed insanely as she held out a hand, emanating a physical force that lashed out at Shanni, throwing her backward.

The door burst open to admit Alphonso and several of his men, guns drawn. Alphonso fired a shot into the ceiling, the noise bursting like a cannon in the closed room. Momentarily stunned, Shanni stopped and turned.

"Seize them!" The woman shrieked. "Tie them from the rafters. I'll teach them to resist."

One of the men ran outside and returned with ropes. Shanni and her compatriot's hands were tied and they were stretched up, feet off the floor, to hang by their wrists. Shanni bit her lip at the pain but made no sound. But the woman knew, and smiled evilly.

"Got your attention now, have we? If you don't like my examination, maybe you'll like that of the men better!" She nodded and Alphonso grinned, moving closer. He reached up and caressed Shanni's arms, drawing his hands carelessly down her body. She convulsed involuntarily, repulsed at his touch. Alphonso laughed and stepped back. "If she fails the examination, she'll learn to welcome my touch, but this is not the time or place!"

He stood watching as the woman turned and entered the room with the remaining Huastecs. "You must be very stupid," he said, "To cross a powerful brujeria like Hoven."

He shook his head and walked outside, slamming the door behind him. Shanni's companion, Mala, gasped at the pain as the rope ground into her wrists, cutting off circulation. Shanni knew she must act now, while they could seize the initiative. She fought back anger and composed herself, breathing deeply.

She concentrated on the rope binding her wrists, and sent her awareness upward, along the length stretched tight with the weight of her body. She sharpened focus, directing her intent at the rough strands, burning into the fibers like a lens. The rope began to stretch as the fibers softened, and smoke curled up as they began to burn. Suddenly the rope snapped and Shanni fell to her feet. She dashed to Mala and lifted her up, slackening the rope and untying her wrists. Shanni dropped her to her feet and signaled silence as they crouched and approached the door to the other room.

Chapter 18

CALEB STRUGGLED ALONG the rocky draw and found shelter from the blazing sun under an overhang. Thirst gnawed at him as he drew his shaking hand across his brow. The unremitting heat and lack of food were taking their toll as he teetered on the edge of consciousness. Was this Tonah's plan, or had the spirit quest gone dangerously wrong? He licked his lips and looked around. Nothing stirred. He was in real trouble, for if he passed out now he would die. Yet he lacked the strength to continue. His thoughts rambled, uncontrolled as he rested, trying to regain his strength. His tired eyes scanned the landscape, and again the colored auras glimmered off rocks and boulders. Would they never end? He felt trapped in a nightmare world, neither sleeping nor awake, and was about to perish.

After all I've been through, it's come to this, he thought. All because against my better judgment I let myself be talked into this damned spirit quest. My father warned me against demons and sorcery, and I knew better. Bitter self-recrimination filled him and he hung his head.

Fatigue overcame him and he napped briefly. When he awakened, dusk had fallen, the long shadows cooling the heat of the sun. He struggled to his feet and wandered slowly up the gravelly wash. Nothing changed, the rocks, the gravel, the sand scattered out in all directions to the horizon of low hills. Direction meant nothing. What did it matter where he walked?

In the shadows he saw a small outcropping of creosote bushes, dry and dormant from lack of water. Deep inside the earth their roots lay waiting for the rain that would revive them. The tragedy of the plants struck Caleb and he stopped, stunned. The plants could not move, and could not choose their course of action. They could only stand, endure, and wait. If the rain did not come, they would die. Yet they, like all life, dreaded death and fought to live. How privileged was man, who had all the choices and the means to fulfill them! Sadness overcame Caleb and he began to weep silently. The auras of the plants broke down through his tears like a prism and he saw a rainbow of colors spread like a morning mist over the clearing.

A last vestige of sanity warned him that he was hallucinating, that he had lost control, but he was too tired to care. A great fatigue enveloped him and he saw the futility of fighting it. Like the creosote bushes, fate had fought him to a draw. He could not go on, he could only stand and wait.

"*So the great warrior of the Anglos has come to this,*" a voice 'spoke' in his mind. He blinked and looked up. Where was the voice coming from? "*Did you think the spirit quest would be so easy? Only when you come face to face with your death do you understand life. You cannot have one without the other.*"

"Who is speaking?" Caleb demanded, looking around.

"*I felt your pain and I responded to it. I am the being in front of you.*"

"You are a plant, and plants cannot talk."

"*True, but we can communicate. All living beings can communicate, on some level.*"

I'm going insane, Caleb thought, panic flashing as he turned to flee.

"*Where will you go?*" The voice read his thoughts. "*You have been running from life all your days and it hasn't worked. Now you must stand and face yourself.*"

I've got to get out of this place, Caleb thought feverishly, gasping for breath. I'm in a nightmare and I must wake up! He began scrambling among the broken rocks and boulders. The shadows moved, causing him to lose his direction. Still he struggled, for he must get away. Minutes passed and he slowed, catching his breath. He looked up and realized that he was back at the same place, looking at the same creosote plant. He had wandered full circle.

"*It has nothing to do with bravery or fear,*" the plant continued as if there had been no interruption. "*At some point, you are run to ground and your death stands in front of you. Only then do you realize how precious your life is to you, and how sadly you've misused it. The greatest sadness of life is the realization of what you've lost. If you can face death down, and postpone it, you will return to your life with a new power and sense of purpose. You will understand the importance of choosing, and taking full responsibility for your choices. Until then, like all humans, you walk through life in a daze, uncomprehending.*"

Caleb sank down on the cool sand. The plant was right. He'd thought he had all the answers, but he'd been too busy with the details of life to really stop and think. And now, at the abyss, he realized that all that didn't matter.

He saw a glimmer in the shadows, a darker shadow creeping slowly forward. His eyes were playing tricks again. He blinked, and wiped away the perspiration on his brow. On top of a boulder, he saw the outline of the panther with burning eyes emerging out of the whirling mist of the aura. Caleb started to react, and caught himself. He'd been fooled enough by the apparitions. This too would pass. He smiled, he wouldn't be fooled this time.

The outline of the panther solidified, its black body hugged the boulder as it gathered its feet to lunge at Caleb. Damn, it looked real, he thought, apprehension rising. He could almost feel its breath. Suddenly the panther lunged, and the world stopped!

Caleb's body froze and he could only perceive as the rugged desert scene became a tableau of light and shadow that began to pulsate. His stomach lurched as a feeling of nausea swept over him. Then he saw "through" the gravelly wash, the boulders, and the body of the panther, suspended in mid-air. Tenuous strands of light emerged, connecting everything to everything with pulsating light. Beads of pure energy danced back and forth along the strands, weaving themselves into bundles that aggregated, making the "things", the rocks, boulders and other manifestations of ordinary reality.

Behind the strands was the Void, a darkness so deep that he was drawn involuntarily into it. He fought down panic, helplessly, as the strands of light dissolved and the blackness enveloped him.

And then he felt the Presence. Tiny points of light emerged, moving, coalescing. As they gathered, they began to swirl slowly, creating spiral aggregations out of the darkness. Caleb felt emotion from the Void, a benevolence and sense of caring as the Presence saturated his being. The Void was not empty; it contained a Universal Consciousness that created all life out of nothingness and then loved and nurtured its creations. Caleb sensed the potentiality in the Void, the potentiality that caused entities of energy to appear from nothingness to spin and dance, and then disappear again into the Void, as fireflies twinkled on a summer evening. Some of the entities did not disappear. Instead, they combined, becoming particles and then aggregations of particles that grew at incredible speed into increasingly diverse and complex structures, flashing, colliding, in a fireworks display of cosmic proportions. The particles began to boil in kaleidoscopic colors, like rainbows within rainbows, twisting and turning upon themselves until the Void was filled with a writhing cauldron of emerging existence.

Caleb recalled his father's words, reading from the Bible: "In the beginning was the Word..." and Caleb understood how reality came from potentiality, a potentiality held in place by the conscious will of the Presence.

The cauldron of energy grew and the aggregate began to separate into swirling spirals of heat and light. As the aggregates grew, Caleb realized the points of light were stars, created from the unimaginable energy from the Void. And through it all ran the strands of energy, of light, like dewdrops on a spider's web.

Caleb's perception shifted and he saw his body as a collection of entities of energy immersed in the Void and pulsating with it. Every part of the universe, every "thing" in it, was interconnected. Man "swam" in the ocean of energy like a fish swam in water. His body and that of every living creature organized the energy that created and maintained it, and focused it in a way that perceived the universe, each in its own way according to its nature. In time, each creature, like the bundles of energy of which it was made, returned to the Universal Consciousness that had created the potentiality and dreamed it into existence out of the Void.

The swirling, boiling, multicolored vision began to fade and the barren desert landscape began to take form like a cracked and faded painting. Caleb felt silent tears running down his cheeks at the awesomeness of the revelation that he would never die. Like a caterpillar that morphed into a butterfly, he and all life changed into a different kind of being, and then more and more beings, as they moved into dimension after dimension, unending. Caleb understood how Beings composed of light and energy, when they visited earth, would blind mortals and overwhelm them with trembling and terror.

The desert scene was reasserting itself and the leaping panther re-emerged into view. Ordinary time had been suspended and Caleb realized that he had somehow been in control of it. For an instant he could "jog" the ordinary passage of time with his *will*, and in that instant he could expand subjective time and project his awareness to explore the mysteries of other worlds for hours, days, and years and still return within the "second" of ordinary time.

The universe was an awesome Consciousness, pulsating with life! Words could not describe it!

With his *intent*, Caleb "released the world" and the panther completed its lunge, teeth bared, as deep in Caleb's brain, a survival mechanism triggered. Honed over millennia of human evolution, it lay hidden and dormant in the neocortex, the reptilian brain that had protected man long before he was a sentient being. Faster than human thought, the mechanism reacted reflexively and Caleb's hand flashed to his revolver.

The panther screamed in pain as his shot caught it in mid-air, twisting the sleek body half around. Its momentum carried it onto him, clawing and biting as it vented its rage.

His revolver knocked clear, Caleb desperately clawed at the knife at his belt and struck again and again, sinking the long blade deep into the thrashing black body.

It was over in seconds that seemed like hours. Hot blood ran down Caleb's head and neck, but he was too tired to tell if it was his own. He gazed at the still form of the panther, and heard it draw a deep, rasping breath. Still alive! Panic seized him as he looked around for his knife.

And then he saw it. The panther's body became opaque and he saw its life force pulsating like a glowing blue-white egg of pure energy. He reached out and his hand touched the energy, his fingers pushing through the surface without resistance. The energy crackled and streamed up his arm, and he felt the jolt as the power entered his body. And then the egg expanded, becoming a column of light that extended out of sight into the sky. It glistened as energy pulsed downward, through his body into the ground. Instinctively, he pulled his hands back to shield his eyes, and the energy quieted, fading to a faint glow that soon dissipated into the shadows. The sickening odor of scorched hair assailed his nostrils and he sat, gasping for breath.

A flickering caught his eye, and he turned to see the creosote bush enveloped by yellow-blue flames. The flames burned brightly but the bush was not consumed. After a moment it dissipated, leaving the plant unharmed. He wiped his eyes, unbelieving, and then he understood. What appeared to be fire was the life-giving energy that permeated all living beings..

Caleb again felt his awareness shift. His mind centered and he entered into a state of immense clarity. He looked into the face of the emerging universe and felt its overwhelming sense of caring. The heart of the universe was emotion; its very existence depended upon the desire of all life forms to be alive and to experience life. The universe experienced life through its beings, and the beings themselves drew their life-force from the energy of the universe through a mutually-reinforcing symbiosis. Caleb's soul soared as he was liberated from the cares of the world. He understood that life on the earth was only a phase, important at the time, but now he realized that it was only a temporary attachment. He was no longer tethered by his desires to the wants and needs of life on earth. He could accept with equanimity the time when his life on the earth would end and he would move on.

He looked down at his body, crumpled near the body of the panther. He saw the blood pumping steadily from his wounds and realized he was dying. Did it matter? He saw now that he would move on to a better place, a place of new experiences and new possibilities, unfettered by the bounds of the earth and its gravity. But was he being selfish? Had he fulfilled his purpose upon the earth? Was his love for Shanni so shallow that he could abandon it, and her? No, his work had just begun. He could now see the challenges he faced to defend himself and Shanni in both worlds, and there was no turning back. Even if they ran, the spirit beings would find them. His only course of action was to live and to go forward.

With his new understanding, he knew that he must return. He had much work to do.

THE DISTANT BOOM of the revolver broke Goyathlay's reverie as he sat meditating on the promontory. He opened his eyes to the sky, every sense alert, as he reached out with his perception, sampling the cool wind that blew in from the west.

He arose silently and climbed down to the desert floor. He swung into an easy gait that covered the distance, going toward the faint echoes of the sound.

An hour later he entered the clearing outlined in the moonlight. He saw the man lying silently, and the dead body of the black panther. He grunted, and reached for his amulet, the small leather bag tied around his neck. He carefully selected a powder and sprinkled it over the panther's body. The dust became iridescent, swirling like a dust devil into the air. An outline took form and Goyathlay recognized the Sentinel, hovering over the clearing, and felt its evil intent. Goyathlay removed a tiny mirror and reflected the light from the moon onto the outline, which coalesced into a bright ball of pure energy and flashed away to disappear in an instant over the horizon.

Goyathlay's face remained impassive as he turned his attention to the silent form on the floor of the clearing. The man was near death, bleeding from his wounds. He was an Anglo and of no interest to Goyathlay. He dismissed him from his mind and turned to the panther. The pelt of the panther would bring him great medicine.

He skinned the panther with practiced ease, folded the pelt and turned to go. The moonlight fell full across the still form of the man, and his outstretched arm. Goyathlay saw the two angry red scars and he stopped. He recognized the marks of a powerful sorcerer. The man was no longer an ordinary Anglo; he was a man of knowledge, and Goyathlay knew that he could not leave the man behind.

He laid the pelt aside and moved into the shadows, gathering clay dust and dried leaves of the creosote. He spit to make a paste, and began to plug the bleeding wounds. He cut strips of cloth from the man's shirt to bind up the injuries for travel.

He drank water from his gourd and sat down to gather his strength. Centering his mind, he entered the trance that would enable him to walk all night with the body of the man across his shoulders.

The morning sun was well up into the sky when Goyathlay climbed the narrow foot trail and rounded the bend into the mountain park of the Huichols. The Huichols were a tribe with powerful shamans, beyond even his own ability to heal. They had remained hidden even from the Spanish invaders in the wild fastnesses of the Sierra Madres. Few knew of their existence, but Goyathlay had used the Sierra Madres, which the Apaches called their "Mother" mountains, for the shelter they provided in times of trouble.

The lookouts had alerted the village, and young men came out to meet him and relieve him of his heavy burden. As they took the man into a nearby shelter, Chinto, the village leader and head shaman walked out to meet Goyathlay.

Goyathlay stood, trance like, with his eyes closed. He took deep breaths and slowly opened his eyes. As he returned to the world of ordinary reality, he became aware of the fatigue of his long journey, and gratefully followed Chinto into his lodge where food and water waited.

There was no need for talk, as Chinto waited patiently for Goyathlay to eat and drink. When Goyathlay had eaten, he sat back tiredly and nodded his thanks.

"Chinto's hospitality is great, and I am grateful."

"It is little enough for an old friend. You came far?"

"I left before the moon was at its height in the night sky."

Chinto thought a moment, calculating rapidly. In the trance-walk, Goyathlay had covered more than sixty kilometers. It was an admirable physical feat. Goyathlay would not have undertaken it unless it was of grave importance.

"Then you need rest. We can talk later. Do not concern yourself; we will care for the Anglo. He is of some importance to you?"

"I do not know him. I heard the sounds of his battle with a black panther. When I arrived he was unconscious and bleeding to death. I was about to leave him to his fate when I saw the spirit quest scars on his arm."

"Ah, then he is apprenticed to a shaman." Chinto spoke with certainty.

"I believe the shaman is from a strange tribe that travels south, through the badlands. He found me, through the spirit world, and made me aware of his presence. He sought nothing. I sensed goodwill, and believe he only wanted to avoid intruding into my boundaries in this land."

"A good sign," Chinto agreed. "But what of the Anglo?"

"It appears the shaman has sent him on a spirit quest."

"But that's never been done with an Anglo. What could the shaman be thinking?"

"It is an act of great courage, or great desperation. Only the shaman can reveal his intent, if he chooses to do so. We will have to seek him out."

"In the meantime, enough talk. Rest yourself while we attempt to save the life of the Anglo, and then we will see."

CONSCIOUSNESS RETURNED TO Caleb through a dim mist, a shield of spidery strands that swam across his vision. He felt light, suspended in space, as he sought to sit up. He found that he could not move, his arms and legs were encased in a downy cloud that cradled him, but nevertheless held him prisoner.

He looked through the glimmering gossamer strands and saw a blue light emanating from a crystal, supported in the center of a stone altar. He was in a cave, with light streaming in from an opening in the roof. As his eyes cleared, he saw the shadowy outline of robed men standing in a circle around the crystal. Along the wall were tall stone statues, of gods or men, he could not tell. He felt a sense of dread, of foreboding, in this place. It was a place of Death. And then realization hit like a bolt; he was in the cocoon that had imprisoned Shanni in the pyramid of the Sentinels, and this time he was alone. There was no one to rescue him and guide him home.

Anger flared in Caleb, and he renewed his efforts to burst forth from his bounds.

"Excellent," he heard the voice from the chamber as the blue light intensified, glowing brighter as in driven by a bellows. Faint memory stirred in Caleb and he recalled Tonah's admonition. He must detach from all emotion. Somehow the Sentinels used the strength of a human's emotion against him.

He lay back tiredly, and memory returned of the peace he had found in the desert. After understanding the design of the universe, this dimension of life was of little importance. They could only kill his body, and terminate his existence upon the earth. What did it matter when he would go on to realms of greater power and discovery? He closed his eyes, breathed deeply, and prepared to rest.

CHINTO ENTERED THE lodge where his apprentices had completed the preparations. He looked at the Anglo, lying still as death in a coma. He adjusted his vision from long habit and looked into the life energy, hovering precariously around the heart and brain. The man was near death. Chinto sharpened his perception and looked closer. A second aura surrounded the first around the brain, dimly as if trying to cloak itself.

Chinto involuntarily drew in a deep breath as he straightened, backing away. Beings from the spirit world had seized control of the Anglo, and terrible things happened to the shaman who crossed them. He would have to proceed carefully to keep Caleb alive until he could confer with Goyathlay.

Chapter 19

SHANNI BURST THROUGH the door into the room containing the Huastec women. Hoven was bent over examining a woman and turned at the noise. Their eyes locked, and rage engulfed Hoven as she flung herself forward, clawing for Shanni's eyes. Shanni was rocked backwards at the fury of Hoven's attack. And then Shanni's fury matched Hoven's as they battered and clawed around the room, the Huastecs scampering to get out of the way.

But Shanni was a woman now, strong and tempered by Walpi's training of the warriors. Her training took over and she countered Hoven's attack, and launched heavy blows that slammed Hoven into the wall unconscious.

"Quickly," Shanni shouted. "To the horses."

She opened the door to the street and looked out. The horses remained tied where their captors had left them to herd the Huastec men on foot to the mine. "Grab a horse and ride out, now!" she added, racing to the hitching rail.

"What about our men?" Mala shouted as she mounted and spun the horse around.

"No time now. Maybe later. Now ride!" Shanni leaned over and pulled the rifle from the saddle scabbard as a man came running out at the commotion. Without thought, she leveled the rifle and fired, knocking the man off his feet. She turned and galloped after the women riding desperately down the narrow mountain road.

They rounded the curve out of sight of the town, and the women slowed, letting Shanni ride to the front. She began looking for a way off the road for she knew the men at the mine would soon be in pursuit.

She saw a narrow canyon lined with pines leading away to the west and spurred toward it, the Huastec women following. Soon the rough terrain forced them to pull to a walk, letting the horses pick their way as they wound along a small stream. The canyon narrowed, forcing them into single file as they climbed higher, the tall pines giving way to scrub brush along the sheer cliffs. Shanni's apprehension grew as the canyon narrowed. A box canyon would be a trap.

They paused in an open area to look back down the long canyon they had climbed. As she'd expected, she saw a band of mounted men climbing toward them. Shanni looked around at the narrow canyon. This was a good place to make a stand.

"Dismount," she ordered. "Tie the horses further up the canyon, and bring your rifles. They'll be here before dark. We'll stop them before they can sneak up on us in the dark."

Mala and the others rushed to comply. Within minutes, they were stretched out on the ground, rifles ready. Now, Shanni thought grimly, we'll find out if all of Walpi's training was worthwhile.

Juan Zegarra was waiting when Alphonso Alvarez dragged back into the village after dark. Alvarez had a crude bandage around his left arm, and several of the men rode bent over the saddle. But what infuriated Zegarra most were the bodies slung over the saddles. Fully half a dozen of Alvarez's men had been killed!

"Madre Dios!" he swore, as he strode out into the street to grab the bridle of Alvarez's horse. "Did your men shoot each other in the dark?"

"Hell, no!" Alvarez was in no mood for Zegarra's second-guessing. He was wounded, and he was mad. To hell with Zegarra! "Help me get my men inside and seen to. Then we'll talk."

The wounded were taken into the room vacated by the women only hours before. Zegarra sent for food and soon the men were settled as well as possible. They were a sorry sight, Zegarra thought. Not much use for defense even, let alone finding the women.

After Alvarez had eaten, Zegarra summoned him into his office. "Well, what happened out there?"

"We ran into an ambush. The women rode up a canyon and then cut down on us with rifles. Every shot hit a man! It was all over in seconds."

"You let a bunch of women ambush you?"

"Well, we thought they was panicked and just trying to get away. We never expected them to turn on us and fight."

"So you just rode in and let them shoot you to pieces!"

"I've never seen nothing like it. They shot better than most men. They've had some training with weapons, and by somebody who knows what he's doing. The fight was over in thirty seconds."

"And you just turned tail and ran?"

Anger flared in Alvarez's eyes. "We turned and got out of rifle range. I left men to keep them bottled up while I got the wounded back. I am not in any mood for second-guessing by you or anyone else!"

Zegarra took a deep breath and let Alvarez's insolence pass. He'd better get in control of events or they would fall down around Alvarez's head and take him along.

"We'll need to round them up first thing tomorrow, and get them on the way to Vera Cruz. I need my men back to work the slaves in the mine. We don't need to waste time on this flare-up."

Alvarez was sullen. "Reckon you plan to just ride up there and bring them back?"

"No. I plan for you to do so. That's what I'm paying you for."

"You done with me? Reckon I could use some rest, with the big day tomorrow."

"I'm done. But I want this fixed tomorrow."

Alvarez turned and walked out the door. Zegarra picked up a cigar from the humidor on his desk and put it in his mouth, lost in thought. What if Alvarez wasn't up to the task? If the women were fighters, they could waste time and tie up manpower rounding them up. And time and manpower were two things he didn't have. Damn! Why was he cursed with such poor tools as Alvarez and his men? Twelve trained soldiers would be worth more than all of Alvarez's men, and a hell of a lot less trouble. Maybe he could get DeVila to send some help. No, Zegarra thought, DeVila would smell a rat and want to know too much. No, he'd have to complete the dance with Alvarez, such as he was. But they had to capture those women tomorrow, or kill them before they escaped.

Shanni and the others had shared what food they found in the saddlebags, and drunk their fill from the stream. At least they had water for themselves and the horses, and the horses could graze. Only a few men had been left behind to cut off their escape, and she doubted they'd try to attack. After seeing what had happened in the ambush, they'd be satisfied to sit tight until reinforcements returned in the morning. Which meant she and the others must act tonight.

"We're lost if we wait until morning. They'll return with reinforcements and we'll be trapped. We must break out tonight. Here's what we've got to do."

Mala and the others gathered around as they discussed next steps. It was a desperate plan, but it was a plan, and the alternative was slavery for them in Vera Cruz, and for their men in the mines. It was life, or death.

Zegarra was awakened by gunfire far down the mountain. "Damn Alvarez's men," he grumbled. "All they've got to do is sit tight and wait for us in the morning. They don't have to amuse themselves keeping the women awake." Then he came fully awake, thinking. Alvarez's men were uncouth and undisciplined, the kind of men who'd want to amuse themselves with the women. They'd be stupid enough to try to take the camp, and the women wouldn't be much good for sale in Vera Cruz, even if they were alive.

He got up and paced the floor, and then looked out the window at the stars. No use in riding down there at night. What was done was done, and they'd clean up the mess in the morning.

Shanni led as they slipped through the tall pines to the camp, outlined in the trees by the dull coals of a dying fire. Clearly they had not expected attack. Three men were sleeping, while one man sat up, dozing, with a rifle in his hand. They had a choice; they could kill the men where they slept or attempt to take them prisoner. They didn't need prisoners, but desperate as they were, she knew that she and the others couldn't just kill them. Waving the others into position, she called out, "Don't move, we've got you surrounded."

The guard on sentry snapped awake, as the sleeping men's eyes opened. Without warning, a rifle opened up to their right, in the trees. A sentry they'd missed!

The woman next to Shanni screamed in pain and fell, to lie still. Further away in the darkness, she heard shouts and the sound of returning gunfire. At the same time, the sentry spun his rifle around and began firing. Using the sentry's fire as a cover, the men on the ground threw their bedrolls aside and scrambled into the shadows. It was kill or be killed now, and the training took over. Swiftly and savagely, they fired until the enemies were silenced, and then rose to advance carefully and check the bodies.

Two of the women had been killed in the initial surprise from the sentry, and several had been grazed by bullets. But they could ride, and there was no time to waste. The gunfire would have alerted the village. They took guns, ammunition and supplies, and the two bodies of the women back to their camp. The shock of the firefight was wearing off, and several were weeping as they placed the two bodies near the sheer wall of the canyon and covered them with stones. There was no time for mourning, or for a decent burial.

Shanni trembled uncontrollably. She had not asked for this responsibility. What strange twist of fate had made her the leader? Now she was responsible for the lives of the others, and for rescuing the Huastec men enslaved in the mine. Maybe she should just ride out with the surviving women, and try to save them, leaving the men to their doom. Everyone stood to die if they stayed and fought. Her powers in the spirit world would not help her here; these men understood only guns and knives, and would stand or fall by the bullet

She took a deep breath and knew what she had to do. She could not shirk her duty. They had to seize the initiative, hit hard and hit quickly before the enemy could marshal his forces against them. This was what they had trained for, and what they had to do to survive. Alvarez's men would show no mercy if they recaptured Shanni and the other Huastec women, so they must be ruthless in their counterattack. They must be totally committed to win at any cost. Anything less meant death.

She gave the signal and they mounted, riding out single file down the canyon in the darkness.

Even with the horses taken from the camp, they were still short. If they rescued the men from the mines, many would have to ride double. They could not outrun their pursuers, but maybe they could get well away from the village before dawn. And then they would have to run and hide. Eventually they would have to fight, likely without help from Matal and his hunting party. Who knew what was left of the Huastec caravan? Shanni looked up to take her direction from the stars as she led the silent group down the narrow mountain trail. Tonah and the Huastecs seemed so far away, and she felt so alone.

Shaking off her uncertainly, Shanni thought quickly. At first light they could expect pursuers from the mining village. If she and the others had any hope of rescuing the remaining hostages, the men who had already taken to the mine, it would have to be now. Yet she knew the gunfire would've alerted Alvarez and his men. On the other hand, the last thing they would expect would be an attack! They would expect the women to run for their lives. She and the other women must seize the moment. Quickly she gathered them around and outlined her plan.

Shanni left a sentry with the horses as she and the other women fanned out on foot, circling the mining village. They were unfamiliar with the terrain, which slowed their progress in the light of a waning moon. Shanni's heart throbbed strongly in her ears with the tension. Never had she expected their lives to depend on guns in the ordinary world, where her paranormal skills were of little use. Caleb had been right. One had to exist first in the physical world, and it could be irrationally ugly.

Fortunately there were few buildings, and they quickly located and eliminated the one with Zegarra's office. The men would be housed in a barracks close to the entrance to the mine. As they climbed along the side of the dirt trail, the outline of a low building appeared backed up to the edge of the mountain. Miners' gloves, pickaxes, and other gear was strewn near the entrance to the building. This must be where the men were housed, Shanni thought. And they wouldn't have much time to recover if she picked the wrong building. Motioning to the others, they circled toward the front, their eyes making out more detail as they approached.

And then she made out the sentry, sitting quietly under a low porch, near the entrance to the building. She could not tell if he was awake, but had to assume that he was watching. There was no choice, he would have to be taken out silently. She whispered to Mala to circle around back with two other women, to search for additional sentries. Shanni had learned a hard lesson at the enemy camp; she did not intend to be surprised again. Mala nodded and led away silently in the dark.

Shanni and the remaining women crept closer. Shanni whispered to them to take defensive positions to cover her as she moved forward. She took a deep breath and felt herself trembling. Walpi's training had been thorough, including how to kill an enemy silently with a knife. But that had been training, an abstract exercise. This was for real, and the sentry, however unworthy, was still a person. What was she becoming? A killer no better than those she killed? Where was the dividing line? What made one action right and another wrong?

Shanni stopped and took a deep breath. This was not the time. She must focus or risk her life and that of the others. The choice was simple and as old as mankind. When the circumstance demanded it, one must be willing to kill in order to survive, or one perished at the hands of those more ruthless. It was a hard choice, but as long as there were predators, it was a necessary choice.

Shanni crept forward, removing the knife she'd found in the saddlebags. Her thumb unconsciously felt the wicked sharpness of the blade. Had it taken life before? She reached the end of the building and glanced around the corner. The man sat silently, in profile, head up. So he was awake! How could she approach him without being seen? She glanced again, and saw his head nod, then sink to his chest. He was dozing. That would have to be enough. Hugging the shadows, she began inching along the face of the building under the eave.

She was close enough to hear the man's even breathing. His head came up and she froze, not ten feet away. Would he sense her presence? His head started to nod, and Shanni sprang.

Her left hand flashed around the man's head, to close over his mouth as her right hand flashed down and back in a savage arch. She felt the hot splash of blood as the knife bit deep, severing the man's throat back to the bones of his neck. His body reacted violently, leaping from the chair and tearing away from her grasp. She heard the raw rasp of air gushing from his lungs, a scream silenced by the severed vocal cords. He smashed against the wooden wall as Shanni leapt back, trying to avoid the thrashing of his body. He fell forward, his limbs trembling, stirring the dust. Shanni watched the scene detached. It was as if she were watching from the sidelines as another person performed the deed. She had not known that it took so long for a man to die.

She tried the door and was surprised to find it unlocked. She drew a deep breath and entered. A lone lamp provided scant light at the end of the long room, outlining the bunks and the sleeping men. She saw the Huastec men, and her eyes searched the room for others. They were alone. Evidently Alvarez and his remaining men slept elsewhere. Quickly she crept down the line, awakening the men. They were groggy and slow from the work in the mine, and Shanni quickly grasped why the door had not been locked. After the hours in the mine, the men were too tired to run far, and the sentry had only to raise the alarm.

Soon the men were up and moving, following Shanni outside and down the ravine to the Huastec women, rifles ready to defend their retreat.

"We must have additional horses," Shanni whispered to the gathered group. "Zara, you lead the men back to Hester and the horses, while Mala and I get horses from the corral."

"Should we push our luck?" Mala questioned. "It'll be daylight soon"

"And certain pursuit. On foot, we'll be ridden down like dogs."

"Then at least let us help," Orna said. "You mustn't risk your lives alone."

"Work in the mine has weakened you and the other men, and there's a hard ride ahead. We'll need your remaining strength for a running fight."

Orna nodded his understanding and motioned the men to follow him. Shanni, Mala and six of the women warriors turned to creep silently toward the horses.

Alvarez got up groggily and padded to the door of his quarters. When in the village, he used a room in the communal dining building adjacent to the miners' barracks. He stepped outside and stretched, preparing to relieve himself. His tired eyes wandered to the barracks, the porch covered in shadow. The sentry would be there, he thought, watching. Grunting, Alvarez walked along the building and around the corner for privacy. His eyes adjusted to the night as he looked unconcerned along the timbered ravine.

He blinked. Had he seen shadows moving in the darkness? And then he recalled that he had not seen the sentry, but only thought he was hidden by the shadows. Alvarez buttoned his pants and returned along the wall, turned the corner and walked toward the porch of the barracks. As he approached the shadowed porch, his eyes adjusted and he looked into the staring eyes of the sentry's body, lying flat in the dust, a dying grimace on the face circled by a pool of blood.

Alvarez's skin crawled with revulsion as he turned wildly and ran along the porch. He tore the door open and grabbed the gun belt beside his bed. He turned and rushed back outside to fire into the air, the blast of the gunshot ripping the silence to reverberate down the canyon.

Shanni and Mala had reached the corral and saddled two horses. Other horses stood, bridled, ground-hitched, waiting to be saddled when the gunshot broke the stillness.

"Quickly," Shanni shouted to Mala. "Open the corral and push the horses out ahead. And then ride for your life!"

Shanni swung into the saddle and lifted her rifle. Leaning forward, she urged the horse into a run after Mala's fleeing horse. There was no need for caution now.

The sound of gunfire roared to her left as she leaned forward across the shoulders of her running horse. She heard the sharp crack of bullets overhead, and then they were free of the village, charging headlong down the narrow trail. They turned off and backtracked up to where Hester held the other horses, and found Tucan and the men waiting. They caught the horse's bridles and swung up bareback, some riding double until everyone was mounted. They would need more horses to get back to the caravan, but for now they could put distance between them and the village, until they found a place to hide.

Shanni could hear the tumult in the village as Alvarez shouted commands to his men. They'd soon have the horses from the cart to catch up the other horses. And then they would come after Shanni and the Huastecs. And this time they would want more than prisoners, they would want blood.

Chapter 20

GOYATHLAY HAD RESTED well and awakened hungry. He exited the lodge and walked across the narrow camp to join Chinto, who sat calmly by the cook fire. A woman ladled food into a bowl and handed it to Goyathlay, nodded, and turned away. Chinto sat quietly while Goyathlay ate. Goyathlay needed to replenish his reserves of strength after the long trek, and then there would be time for talk.

Goyathlay finished his meal and took a long drink from the ladle in the water jar. Satisfied, he settled back comfortably and nodded to Chinto.

"The man sleeps," Chinto opened. "His wounds were not fatal, and his body has stabilized from the loss of blood. But his mind is in another place, captured by evil spirits."

"Why do they care about an Anglo?"

"They fear what he will become."

"Then they will not release him?"

"Our normal methods of exorcizing the evil spirits are not effective. A barrier has been set up. Even I cannot penetrate it."

Goyathlay was silent, thinking. He knew Chinto's ability as a powerful shaman. "That requires much strength. I am surprised that the spirit ones have it."

"I sense the power of a Guardian behind them."

Goyathlay frowned. "A Guardian has vast powers and responsibilities in the other worlds. Why would a Guardian concern itself with an Anglo?"

"We have not found the answer. But only something of grave importance could summon a Guardian's perception back to this world."

"And if the Anglo's spirit remains there, he will die."

"Yes. More accurately, their intent is to kill him."

"And we cannot help."

"It is too late to ride on his perception and get through the barrier. Now it is all up to the Anglo."

"But he cannot know what to do. Only one trained in the way of the sorcerer could know what to attempt in order to escape. Even then it would require much power against a Guardian."

"True," Chinto agreed. "The fate of the Anglo is in his own hands. We cannot help; we can only wait."

Caleb drifted in and out of consciousness. Through dim perception, something deep inside him told him he must act to save himself, but when his energy began to rise, fatigue overwhelmed him and he sank back, giving in to the torpor that soaked through his being. Where was Tonah? Why hadn't he come to rescue Caleb? Anger started to well up in him. Tonah had sent him on a spirit quest and now abandoned him. Did shamanism overshadow friendship? Had Tonah's years of sorcery deluded him into betrayal of a friend's life for some impersonal training ritual? And what of Shanni? Would not her love cause her to reach out to him?

He felt confused; he was not thinking straight. He reached down inside himself with an effort. He was indulging, allowing himself to feel victimized. He must put all that aside, detach himself, and fight to live.

His memory went back to when he and Tonah had rescued Shanni from the spirit beings. He recalled with a start how Tonah had warned him about feeling emotion. The spirit beings used a person's most powerful emotions, fear and anger, against him. He tried to detach from his feelings as the beings stirred outside the cocoon. The light intensified, and he felt the cocoon shrink, slowly suffocating him. He gasped, and fought down the panic that welled up in him.

The image of his father swam into view. Behind him stood the barn and the mountains of Hesperus Peak outlined in the dim light of the stars. A chill wind soughed down from the heights as Caleb stood looking up at his father, trembling.

His father was beside himself, frantic, as he looked from his son, only four years old, to the dead body of the panther lying nearby.

"Son, what in God's name did you do?"

Caleb felt hot tears run down his cheeks, the aftermath of terror and bewilderment.

"I don't know, Father. I don't know!"

His father held the lantern higher, the unused shotgun in his right hand. "I've told you never to come out at night. That panther could've killed you!" John Elias Stone shook with a mixture of anger and fright. His only son could have been killed by the marauding cat that had been terrorizing his livestock.

"I'm sorry, Father. I heard a noise and I was worried about the colt."

A flurry in the shadows and his mother ran into view, clutching a long shawl about her shoulders. She rushed to Caleb and knelt, holding him close. He buried his face in her bosom, warm and safe. She kissed his hair as she hugged him, rocking gently.

"Mary, I don't know what's happened! The panther attacked him and it is dead. Not a mark on either of them. This cannot be happening. It is impossible," John Elias said, shaking his head.

Mary looked up. "Our boy is safe. That's all that matters."

"But Mary, it's impossible." John repeated unbelieving. "It's witchcraft!"

"It's the Lord protecting our son, praise be! We'll not second-guess our Lord."

John Elias shook his head wondering. "We'll not speak of this," he said. "Not ever."

He put his arm around Mary and Caleb and helped them back into the house. Mary took Caleb up to his bed in the loft, with John Elias close behind. She tucked him into bed and pulled the comforter up snug.

"Did I do wrong, Momma?" Caleb asked.

"No. What you did was right. The Lord gives every creature the right to life, and the ability to defend it. Isn't that so, John?" She turned a sharp glance in John Elias's direction.

"It's so, Son." he said. "You did right, and I'm glad you're safe! Praise the Lord!"

Mary stood up, gazing down at Caleb. She stroked his head. "Go to sleep now and have pleasant dreams."

She turned to John, standing awkwardly. "And I love you, John Elias," she said softly. "You can accept what you cannot understand." Quietly she led him down the stairs from the loft.

The pressure increased and Caleb felt the life force being squeezed out of him. Deep down in the core of his being something awakened to life, slowly like a leviathan shaking off slumber. He was no longer Caleb Stone; he was Life itself, raising itself out of the muck of the primordial sea, clawing its way to higher ground, heaving, gasping with an emotionless determination, a single aim of focused intent, *the will to live!* He heard the voice of his mother calling across eternity, *Trust Yourself.* And Caleb opened his eyes.

COLD FEAR FILLED the pit of Shanni's stomach as she took stock. They'd captured too few horses, and most of the Huastecs were riding double. They'd easily be ridden down if they ran far.. They had no food, and little water, and the sun was rising in the east.

She gathered the small band together in the dim light. The women were haggard from lack of sleep and the exertion of the rescue; the men were all in from the unaccustomed labor in the mines. Without rest, they could not manage the long journey back to the caravan.

Shanni turned to Mala, "First we find water. Then we find a place to hold up. They'll follow at first light, and they'll have supplies for the chase. We'll have to hit them before they expect it."

Oron, leader of the men prisoners spoke up. "I agree. Without supplies and horses, we'll be finished in the desert."

"Quickly, then. We know the way to the stream where we retreated, and it is near the road. Go there and fill every canteen and container we can find, then we'll set up an ambush along the road."

Zegarra was beside himself with fury. Alvarez and his men had made one blunder after another. And now he took over. "I want every man that's left on a horse with a gun at first light," he screamed at the men assembled in front of his office in the moonlight. "I want food and water for six days. We'll catch every one or your men will die trying. This is your last chance to redeem yourselves."

He turned and entered his office to retrieve his rifle and ammunition, in addition to the six-gun strapped to his waist. He placed bandoleers across each shoulder. When he emerged into plaza he looked as fierce as he felt. Even Alvarez was subdued. He'd never seen Zegarra so enraged. It wouldn't do to cross him now.

Without a word, Zegarra strode to his horse and mounted, turning to swing his gaze across the mounted band. Less than half the men they had when they brought the prisoners in, and all because of Alvarez's stupidity. They couldn't afford more losses. They had to hit the prisoners before they could get organized. He climbed on his horse and led out at a gallop in the dim light.

Zegarra had trackers out as the sun began to light the eastern sky. They saw where the escaping prisoners had left the road and pulled up. Zegarra spurred forward. So they thought they could hide in his backyard. This would be easier than he'd thought. "After them!" he urged. "Don't give them time to dig in."

As they entered the ravine, the brush and trees forced them into a single file, with the trackers out front. Zegarra ordered more men forward, fanning out to flush their quarry before they could escape. Alvarez charged up beside Zegarra, his concern overcoming his caution. "We'd better ease up and watch out," he blurted out. "The women can shoot as well as men. I'm telling you, they're all dangerous as hell!"

"Maybe that's why they've cut through you like a knife through butter!" Zegarra retorted. "You're buffaloed by them."

"I'm bluffed by nobody. I'm facing facts, and we can't afford to lose more men."

Zegarra drew up at the genuine concern in Alvarez's voice. Maybe he had a point. And then he heard the first fusillade of shots, and the screams of mortally-wounded men. The melee was close ahead, but unseen in the dim light of the forest. The gunfire continued, so at least some of the forward riders had survived the ambush. "Swing around!" he shouted to Alvarez and the men. "Flank them and finish them!"

Alvarez and the men went crashing out of sight in the tall brush, as Zegarra and two men eased forward cautiously. The firing had stopped, and his men would hear if the prisoners attempted to escape. It had cost a few men, but it would be over quickly.

He entered the scene of battle and saw the scattered bodies of his men. The gun belts and ammunition had been stripped from their bodies, and the horses were gone without a trace. Alvarez and the flankers eased in quietly from the other direction. "Did you see them?"

"Not a trace," Alvarez replied. "They disappeared like ghosts."

"They must've led the horses on foot to avoid detection. They can't get far that way. Push after them!"

The trackers were on foot, attempting to sort out the hoof prints in the matted forest floor. Zegarra realized that having Alvarez and his men ride around had mixed their horses' hoof prints with that of the escaping prisoners. These must be trained fighters, and he was learning the need to respect them.

The trackers circled wide and soon picked up the trail of the escaping prisoners. They had scattered to make less noise, but all were heading back toward the road. With additional supplies and horses, they must intend to run for it. "Get some men back on the road quickly," he shouted to Alvarez. "We'll push from behind to assure they don't double back!"

Without a word, Alvarez waved to several of the men to follow him and spurred for the road.

Shanni stopped, gasping for breath as she led the horse toward the road. The wound to her arm was not serious, but she had to stop the bleeding. She hastily tied a bandanna around her arm and continued forward. She must reach the road with the others. They had enough horses now, and the supplies would have to do. Their orders were to gain the road and ride for their lives.

She heard the noise of riders ahead, and stopped, attempting to gauge the source of the commotion. There was an exchange of gunfire, and then the sound of retreating hooves. Some of the Huastecs had gotten away, at least for now.

She eased through the brush, leading the horse. She could make out the dirt road ahead, through the trees. Every nerve tense, she strained to hear in the sudden silence.

"Don't move, or I'll shoot you down like the bitch you are!" Alvarez's voice broke the stillness, and Shanni's heart lurched. She turned to see Alvarez's face grinning behind the raised rifle pointing at her. Two of his men hastened forward and bound her hands behind her back. She winced at the pain, but did not cry out. They raised her into the saddle and led the horse back to Alvarez, who took the reins. "Keep looking," he ordered the riders. "There may be more stragglers.

The sun had risen, lighting the ravine and the enclosing forested hills. As Shanni swung her gaze across the valley from the road, she realized that anyone remaining would be easily seen. She could only hope that the remaining Huastecs had ridden out in time. She heard the yells of riders, and the thrashing of horses through the brush, as Alvarez turned the horses and led her back along the roadway to the village. As she looked back down the mountain, she could see riders entering the roadway with more captives. It had been a desperate plan, and some had gotten away, at least for the present.

They entered the village and Alvarez led her to a storeroom. He pulled her down from the horse and dragged her inside, tossing her on the dirt floor. Dim light came in through cracks in the crude boards, and a narrow window high in the wall. She heard the chain being secured to the door, locking her inside, and then she was alone.

Alvarez strode across the dirt road to the porch leading to Zegarra's office and paused to watch the returning riders with their prisoners. Zegarra's horse was already tied at the rail, so Alvarez knew he had returned early. Emboldened by their success, Alvarez entered the office and faced Zegarra, sitting behind his desk. Zegarra looked haggard. The easy life had spoiled him, Alvarez thought. He's not used to losing his sleep.

"I captured their leader, the witch that caused all the trouble," Alvarez opened. "Hoven says she's no virgin, so she's no use to you. I'm taking her for myself."

Anger flared in Zegarra's eyes. He didn't care about the woman, but he detested Alvarez's insolence. Alvarez was the kind of man to overstep his bounds; sooner or later he'd have to kill him. But not now. Now he had to keep ahead of events, and of Alvarez. He needed just a little more time.

"How much are you willing to pay for her?" Zegarra shrugged carelessly. "That was the deal, remember? You want her, you buy her. I've got to salvage something from all you've cost me."

Alvarez flushed at the insult. "See here, you can't lay their escape on me. My men done their part."

Zegarra waved a dismissive hand. "Water under the dam, let's don't waste our time on it." He waited, staring at Alvarez.

"She's useless to you now. Why should I pay for her?"

Zegarra's eyes bored into Alvarez's. "It's the principal of the thing. You pay me and she's yours."

Alvarez flushed with anger. Zegarra was holding him to the last ounce of flesh, and he hated him for it. He'd kill Zegarra someday, and serve him right.

"All right, the hell with it. Five pesos, just for your damn principle!"

"Done," Zegarra replied, standing up. Alvarez retrieved the money and laid it on the desk.

"What about the ones that escaped?" Zegarra asked, changing the subject.

"I've got Jose with six riders after them. They won't last a day."

"Their orders?"

"Capture them or kill them. We can't afford for any to get away."

Zegarra nodded thoughtfully. "All right then. Get the prisoners into the mine, and let them sleep there after work. Maybe they'll be more pliable when we let them out to return to the barracks."

Alvarez nodded agreement and turned to exit the room. Zegarra heard Alvarez's boots pound along the wooden porch as he strode toward the mine. Things were coming to a head, he thought, and timing was everything. There were not enough men to work the mine, and DeVila would hold him accountable when the next shipment was short. His plans had been carefully put in place, and it was time to ride.

Shanni heard the chain rattle on the door and saw Alvarez enter. Her hands were behind her back, and the wound throbbed. She tried to sit up but could not. Alvarez stood over her in the dim light. "You belong to me now," he gloated. "I paid Zegarra five pesos for you, and I aim to get my money's worth. She-devil or not, I'll tame you!"

He turned to walk to the door. "I'll see you tonight, and if you try any of your tricks I'll skin you alive!"

Zegarra packed quietly while he waited for darkness. While Alvarez was occupied with the woman, he'd get the pack horses and load the silver he'd been hiding away. It would be enough for a new start in Vera Cruz, far over the mountains from Mexico City. DeVila would be furious at his disappearance, of course, and suspect him, but there was no accounting for the silver output from the mine. He could not be accused of stealing, and with the chaos in the central government, he'd soon be forgotten. He'd take on a new identity in Vera Cruz and pursue business worthy of a gentleman.

Night had fallen when he secured the pack horses and loaded the saddlebags packed with silver ingots. He led away into the night, along a trail that wound over the mountains to the east.

Alvarez entered the storeroom with two of his men. One held a plate of food and a canteen. Alvarez drew his revolver and pointed it at Shanni. "Untie her and watch her while she eats," he ordered. "And stand clear, she's a tricky one."

The man set the food down and untied Shanni's hands. Her arms were cramped and she struggled to a sitting position. Her wound throbbed painfully, but the bleeding had stopped. She picked up the plate of food, and began eating. She would need her strength for whatever came.

Chapter 21

CALEB FILLED WITH a terrible resolve as he slowly sat up. He was totally detached from all emotion, and his body felt like iron. The mist entrapping him began to give way. He stood up and saw the shadowy beings dimly as the head priest channeled the blue beam of energy that surrounded him. In the background, he saw the bright luminous being, partly covered, adding its energy to the field that drove him slowly backward. He did not fight the force, instead he accepted its power, allowing it to course through his body. Surprisingly it felt cool, like a cool stream that meshed with the energy field his body had absorbed from the panther. He felt himself expanding, growing in size to tower over his tormentors.

Choctyl reeled backwards, cursing. "More power! More power! We cannot let him escape!"

The Guardian smiled and "reached" upwards, pulling a beam of pure energy from the farthest reaches of the universe. He pointed his other hand at the crystal and the beam intensified, driving Caleb backwards, pinning him to the damp wall. Caleb gasped at the surge of power that threatened to overwhelm him and then reached deep down within himself and knew from the core of his being that he would not yield. They might be able to kill him but he would not yield. Perspiration ran down his chin as he reached out, his hands deflecting the energy toward the opposite wall. Instantly steam boiled, radiating the heat and the power across the dark room.

Caleb gazed across the room at the Guardian and realization struck that it would not let up. It had tapped the unlimited power of the universe and it could continue forever. Doubt began to creep into Caleb's resolve, and as he faltered, he realized his mistake, for his body began to weaken.

Caleb pulled himself together with an effort. He was in the valley of the shadow of death, and he had no fear, for the Guardian was evil, and he feared no evil. The being could kill him but it could not conquer him. His spirit would live on, and in the higher dimensions he would find the Guardian and expunge it from the universe. The battle was not over, it was only beginning, and he was dying.

And then he sensed a brightness at his left shoulder. A luminous egg formed in the dark air, and radiated appendages of pure light, white and intense. Involuntarily his eyes closed, as if he were looking into the sun itself. A voice spoke to him, "*Have no fear, your time has not yet come.*"

Caleb felt the appendages encircle him, like arms hugging his body, shielding him from the energy beam. The energy beam flashed into a rainbow of colors, swirling and breaking upon each other like the waves of the ocean. Caleb's mind was drawn into a vision of the evolving universe. He saw creation itself and felt the positive emotion that brought the world and every living thing into being. It was like he was a dream, a dream-being of the Creator. A great peace swept over him as he realized that there was a plan for life directed by caring beings from the higher dimensions.

An explosion rocked the cave and Caleb momentarily lost consciousness. When he came to, he crawled out of a hole in the rocks and found that he was again alone in the desert. He moved to the shade of a boulder and sat, catching his breath. Caleb looked at the rocks, the desert, and the world around him and he knew. His world was forever changed. He now saw the world of ordinary reality as a dream world, a marvelous world of opportunities. For the spirits that came into this world, the choices were limitless, with both pleasure and pain resulting from those choices. Could this not be heaven? For this life was where spirit became flesh and every person's dream was possible.

Why had he been saved from death? What had singled him out?

"*You have but to ask, and it will be revealed to you.*"

Caleb turned his head, startled. Who or what had spoken? There was no one in sight. Was he hallucinating again?

"*You have been given great power, and are forever changed. Use it wisely, for the purpose it is intended. You are now part of the positive evolution of the universe.*"

"Why me?"

"*A pact was made with one of your ancestors hundreds of human generations ago, and sealed in her genetic code. It was passed down through your mother. She was never alone, and neither are you.*"

"How come I never knew?"

"Because you grew up focused on the ways of the physical world. You denied your gift and pushed it down into your subconscious, where it lay dormant. When you accept it as real, it will become available to you at will."

"So you've been there all along?"

"Yes. The term used on the earth is 'guardian angel'"

"But how do you have the time, I mean, do you wait around to step in when I'm in trouble?"

"You think in human terms. I am not a unique creature, like a man. I coalesce when you create the need for me. In the past, that has only occurred in life-or-death situations. Now you have moved to a new level, where what was hidden in your subconscious is now part of your conscious. Now you can summon and direct 'my' power at will. I am a part of the ocean of consciousness that permeates creation, both the physical and the underlying 'dreaming' that brings it into being. At the appropriate time, you will become a part of that consciousness and you too will direct energy into creation."

"At death?"

"Aging and termination of the body results from entropy. The energy utilized to create and maintain a human body must eventually return to the universe from which it came. For a time the person is permitted through a physical body to live and harness powers in the physical plane. That too must pass, in order for the universe to continually evolve. It is all part of the plan."

"Where do I go from here?"

"There are beings who misuse the energy. They are the ones who attacked you. You must neutralize them, some in the physical world, and others in the spirit world. Now that you have crossed the threshold of knowledge, you can apply your powers in either."

"Is it wrong to kill them?"

"Some beings have used their gifts for evil, and we can only act on the physical world by using beings in the physical world. Through you, and others who have become enlightened, we can terminate the evil being perpetuated contrary to the plan of creation. But you must approach it as a duty, with detachment. You must not allow human passion, particularly malice, to overcome you in completing your work. Destructive human emotions such as greed, envy and hate, have corrupted the plan of creation and brought pain and suffering into the world."

Caleb shook his head, dazed. "Where are you? Who am I talking to?"

"Those are human terms. Does it matter? I can manifest in any manner appropriate to get a human's attention. Look to your left."

Caleb turned his head, and saw a man standing a few paces away, his back turned.. He was of average height, dressed in tan work pants and shirt. Dust from the desert covered him, as if he had come a long way. Caleb again saw the multicolored aura that had encased objects since he'd undergone the preparation by Tonah. Tonah saw the beings, and had set the stage for Caleb to do so. His resentment at Tonah faded. Tonah had done what he had to do, and now Caleb had received the same charge.

The figure shimmered in the light of the sun, and morphed into a tall, thin form that was strangely familiar. The man turned and Caleb was looking into the face of his father. The hair raised on the back of Caleb's neck as he fought down rising panic. Involuntarily, he reached out a hand, shielding his eyes from view.

"*The answer was there all along,*" his father said. '*We just did not recognize it. It is in many places in many traditions. In our tradition, it is found in the Bible's book of Matthew, 7:7. 'Ask and it will be given to you; seek and you will find; knock and the door will be opened to you'. I accepted on faith but did not understand. If humans understood and acted on their understanding, there would be no evil left in the world.*"

Caleb moved his hand and started to speak, but already the figure was fading, leaving only the quietness of the desert. Caleb stood up and turned his gaze to the hole in the rocks that was the doorway into the Underworld, and the beings who had tried to kill him. He took a deep breath and started toward the darkness.

TONAH AWAKENED FROM a deep sleep and collected his awareness before opening his eyes. He heard Walpi's even breaths, and felt the strength in them. Tonah opened his eyes and sat up slowly. Aurel lay on the dirt floor where he had fallen. Concerned, Tonah adjusted his eyes and looked into Aurel's body for the aura of life. Aurel had entered a coma, with his life force drawn up into a core of energy that surrounded his heart and extended to his brain. Aurel had utilized all the strength in his young body, taking it to the brink of death. He had risked his life to save Walpi's.

Next he scanned Walpi's body and found the core of life energy had expanded, sending streamers along the circulatory system into his arms and legs. The energy pod was growing and Tonah knew that Walpi would live, but he would never recover his strength as a warrior.

Tonah climbed to his feet and sought out the remaining Huastecs in camp. He requested that two young Huastecs dip bowls of stew and carry them, along with water from a canteen, as he led back to the two silent figures. Tonah ate from one of the bowls as he watched the two awaken Walpi and gently spoon stew into his mouth. Tonah finished eating and filled his cup from the canteen. He drank slowly, and then took a long breath. He set one of his helpers to beating the spirit drum, sending its low thrumming through the tent, while the second returned to the campfire to secure hot water.

Tonah knelt beside the still body of Aurel, and gently rolled him onto his side. He secured a blanket and covered Aurel's body, still as death. Aurel's breathing was shallow, barely audible, his spirit trapped in the netherworld, and Tonah knew he must bring his spirit back.

CALEB CLIMBED DOWN the long tunnel to the chamber that had held the priests and the Guardian. The Guardian had disappeared, but the priests remained. His eyes locked on their leader, the one who had directed the Guardian's strength against him. The other priests stepped back into the shadows, leaving him alone with the leader who they had called Choctyl. Choctyl's black eyes burned with a feverish intensity as he faced Caleb across the dimly lit room, and then with a sudden movement he jerked the robe in front of his face and launched himself into the air, up the narrow passageway leading to the outside world of men.

Without thought, Caleb leaped to follow and found himself flying, weightless up the narrow tunnel! What manner of madness was this? When the doubt flickered in his mind, he felt himself falter, starting to fall, and caught himself. Now was not the time. He would not question his new-found powers.

As Choctyl reached the surface, he morphed into a spotted predator, a jaguar, and bounded across the broken boulders of the landscape. Caleb felt the earth underneath his feet and glanced down at the black paws of the lithe and powerful black panther that followed Choctyl's flight. Caleb realized that he had absorbed the life force of the predator that had tried to kill him and now he was utilizing that force to stop Choctyl.

Caleb bounded effortlessly over the broken ground, the body honed for sureness and speed over countless years of evolution, as he gained on the twisting body darting in front of him. Choctyl glanced back to see Caleb gaining and turned, dashing into shadows behind a low ridge. Caleb closed the gap and leapt into the shadows, his panther eyes instantly adjusting to the change in visibility.

Choctyl had run to ground, and attacked viciously, biting and clawing at Caleb's face. His body responded, slapping out mightily with both paws, driving Choctyl backwards against the wall of stone.

Caleb closed the distance, his powerful jaws seeking the throat instinctively, sinking feline teeth deep into the soft flesh. Choctyl roared with fear and rage, scrambling to get to his feet, but Caleb had a death grip, choking the life out of the thrashing body.

With a last scream, Choctyl released his perception and attempted to withdraw his life force from the jaguar, back to his sanctuary. But it was too late. Caleb's newfound strength flowed interchangeably between the worlds of men and of sorcery. Choctyl realized his mistake too late, and he died with the jaguar in the physical world.

Caleb released the still body and leapt nimbly to the top of a boulder. As he stood, looking down at the scene of combat, he felt his body changing. He was releasing from the body of the panther and he remembered that his human body lay somewhere to the north, injured in the physical world. He had forgotten to establish a marker, a beacon to guide his return. After all he had gone through, was this to be his mortal mistake? Was he to wander aimlessly, unable to return to the physical world? Tonah, he thought desperately; he must try to reach Tonah. Tonah could guide him back.

IT WAS NEAR midnight when Tonah completed his work and sat back, tired and covered with perspiration. Fortunately Aurel's youth gave him a reserve of energy that Tonah could draw on to supplement the reduced energy he was able to transfer. His days of healing were over. It was good that he was transferring his knowledge to Caleb, Aurel and Shanni.

He sat back, closed his eyes and centered himself. Across his vision floated the face of Shanni and he felt her agitation. But she was not yet perceiving in the spirit world, so whatever she faced was within the physical world, and that was where she must learn to survive. He spread out his perception like a blanket, a mist that thinned and wafted across the desert into the spirit world that had no boundaries and was not measurable.

He sensed a presence and opened himself to it. A familiar face appeared, the face of the shaman he had seen on the mesa; the man known as Goyathlay.

"*You seek me?*" Tonah projected.

"Yes. The Anglo with you has been injured. His body is here, with powerful shamans, but his spirit is trapped in the netherworld and we cannot revive him."

"Is he dying?"

"His body is strong. He will recover if his spirit body returns."

"Did he leave a guide or a marker?"

"None. We have no way to find him."

"Then I will go. I will leave a marker so you can find me when he returns."

"It will be as you say. We will keep a vigil."

Tonah adjusted his perception and retraced his steps to the desert where he and Aurel had left Caleb to begin his spirit quest. He picked up the trail and began to follow Caleb's tracks as he rode and later walked leading the horse. His trail in the physical world was easy to follow, but when he entered the spirit world, Tonah knew it would take all his skill to attempt to follow.

Chapter 22

MATAL HELD UP HIS hand, halting his warriors as riders appeared, rushing down the mountain road in the distance. Quickly he led the group off the trail out of sight, and peered out along the road in the early morning light. Two riders left behind by the bandits had ambushed his men, killing two and pinning the remainder down all night. There had been no time to catch up, and they were too few to stand and fight. He'd hoped to reach the place where the Huastecs were prisoners and to develop a plan for rescue. The alternative, a poor one, was to return to the caravan, assemble reinforcements, and start over.

As he watched, he noted another band of riders emerge in pursuit of the first group, and his tired mind clicked. Some of the Huastecs must have escaped.

"Those must be our people!" he shouted, spurring back upon the trail toward the oncoming riders. "They'll need help!" The remaining three riders followed Matal, but the tired horses could do little more than trot.

Mala recognized the riders and spurred forward. "It's Matal!" she shouted, turning in her saddle as the horses raced around a long curve., The riders met with shouts of greeting, and Matal quickly led them off the road to take up defensive positions.

The bandits had not seen Matal's riders, and emerged around the curve at a gallop. The Huastecs' first volley knocked three riders from the saddle before the return fire forced Matal and the others to withdraw to better cover. The bandits turned and spurred back out of range.

Matal and the others prepared for an attack, but the riders dismounted, apparently to carry on a heated conversation. Mala saw several waving their hands in emphatic discussion, and a couple of men walked away in disgust.

"What's going on?" Matal whispered.

"Don't know," Mala answered. She had seen that the horses of Matal and his men were spent. Like it or not, they had to stand and fight, which would play into the hands of Alvarez and Zegarra back at the village. This was not a good place to make their stand, and they couldn't hold out long with their limited supply of ammunition.

Then they saw some of the men mount their horses and ride back up the trail, to turn off and begin circling around the Huastecs' position.

"Trying to flank us!" Matal breathed.

The remaining bandits conversed and then the group broke up, returning to their horses. Soon they rode back to leave the road and disappear into the brush.

"Spread out, form a perimeter!" Matal ordered. "Look for them to come in from any direction!"

The Huastecs took their positions and waited, sweating in the morning sun as the minutes ticked by.

After more than an hour, Matal looked questioningly at Mala. "Do you suppose they went back for reinforcements?"

"They would've returned by now. It's not that far. Besides, they would've left pickets to watch us, keep us pinned down."

"Strange," Matal shook his head.

"Fan out, but be careful. See if any of the bandits are left."

The Huastecs began walking through the brush. There was no sign of the enemy. The group reassembled at the horses. "What do you think?" Matal asked.

"I guess he didn't pay them enough," Mala responded. "They had horses, guns and supplies, more than most villages provide. I guess they decided it was better to take what they had and leave than to risk a bullet."

"Are there many left up there? We'll need to rescue Shanni and the others and then head back."

"Only a few riders. We've had several firefights, putting many out of action. And now it looks like the rest may be deserting. We'll have Alvarez, their leader, and the mine guards to face for sure. There's no place for them to run to. And there's Zegarra, the mine superintendent. We could overrun them, but they'll have our people as hostages."

"Then we'd better make a plan, and try to implement it tonight." Matal turned to the others. "Spread out, make cold camp and eat. Try to get some sleep. We'll move tonight."

THE FOOD WAS tasteless, but Shanni ate. She would need her strength, and didn't know when she might eat again. "I could use some water to wash it down," she said quietly.

"Give her water," Alvarez ordered, holding the muzzle of the revolver steady. If she moved, he'd kill her, despite the five pesos. But she seemed subdued. Maybe he'd taken the fight out of her. But it didn't matter, he'd make sure she was beyond resisting before he took his pleasure with her. He'd beat the fire out of her.

One of his men retrieved a canteen and walked toward Shanni.

"Hold it!" Alvarez shouted. "Didn't you learn anything? Don't get in reach of her or she'll tear your head off!"

The man backed up uncertainly, still holding the canteen.

"Lay it on the floor and kick it over to her."

The man did as directed, sliding the canteen within reach. Shanni reached out slowly to drag the canteen closer, and lifted it to her lips. She drank and then finished the food.

Alvarez relaxed a little, but still held the revolver leveled.

"I need to go to the toilet," Shanni said, looking up at Alvarez.

Alvarez grinned. "Help yourself. Walk outside and go. I'll be right behind you, with this gun leveled."

"A woman needs her privacy."

"Forget it. You can go out, or go in your pants. Makes no difference to me."

Shanni sighed. "Do these men have to go, too?"

Alvarez thought a moment. No need to share her with them, He'd earned his own private show. After all, he'd paid five pesos. "You men wait inside. We'll be right back."

Shanni stood up, and walked around Alvarez, careful to stay clear of the revolver. She walked through the door and stepped out into the sunlight, her eyes half-blinded after the dim interior of the storeroom. The ground had been leveled for the storeroom, and fell off after a few feet into the brush of a ravine. There was no place to run, or to hide.

"That's far enough," Alvarez ordered.

Shanni stopped, and turned to face him. Slowly she slid her rider's pants down, and squatted to urinate. Alvarez flushed, grinning, and let the muzzle of the revolver drop carelessly. Shanni finished, and focused her intent. She *willed* the revolver to stay down as she stood up and pulled her pants up carelessly. And then she launched into a forward roll that closed the distance toward Alvarez.

Alvarez jerked his arm to bring the muzzle up, but somehow it locked, the revolver stuck. He glanced down in surprise as Shanni rolled up, flashing her right hand out with stiff fingers to strike knifelike at his throat, crushing his larynx..

Alvarez dropped the revolver, his hands flying to his throat, his face turning purple as he strangled, trying to scream. He fell to the ground with a loud thump.

Shanni swept up the revolver and pinned herself against the wall as the first man emerged, gun in hand. She shot him at point-blank range, and raced down the back of the building and around the corner. Quietly she turned to the narrow window and peeked in a corner. The second man stood well back from the door, silhouetted in the light. She shot him in the back, the force of the bullet carrying him through the doorway out onto Alvarez's body.

Shanni raced for Zegarra's office. He'd have to be neutralized before the sentries could get up from the mine and investigate. She rounded the building and came up to the window. The office was empty, and Zegarra was gone!

She turned, and started around the corner. A revolver roared, and she saw Hoven standing in a doorway across the street. She whirled into a kneeling position and fired twice. She saw the bullets smash into the door frame, but Hoven's body was already opaque, dissolving into the mist. No time for her now, Shanni thought, racing to the corner of the storeroom which was closest to the entrance to the mine. She waited until the first sentry emerged from the mine, gun in hand.

"It's over," she shouted. "There's nothing left to fight for. Alvarez is dead, and Zegarra is gone. You can walk, or you can die. Your choice."

The other two sentries had arrived at the entrance and heard Shanni's words. They looked at each other in disbelief.

The first man holstered his revolver and lifted his hands. "Reckon I'll walk," he called out. "Nothing holding me here."

"All or none," Shanni shouted. "I'm in no mood for tricks."

"Put your guns up," the man ordered the others. The Huastecs began arriving at the entrance.

"Leave the rifles and revolvers on the ground," Shanni ordered, "And walk clear. Moton, you and the others pick up the guns. If they try anything, kill them."

"We won't try anything," the guard assured her. "We're not bucking a stacked deck."

"Don't look back," Shanni ordered.

The three men hurried down the road. They'd be back for supplies after she and the men were gone, but what would it matter?

Swiftly they ransacked the buildings for supplies. The horses were gone, so they'd have to walk. It couldn't be helped. At least they were free, and they had food and water. And, if need be, they had guns and could use them.

She led out at a walk down the narrow mountain trail. She rounded a corner in the narrow trail and there in the shadows stood the silhouette of a woman. Shanni blinked as the outline split into three, spreading out to block her path. As her vision cleared, she recognized the figure as Hoven, standing with a rifle held ready across her chest. But Hoven was a brujeria, a sorceress, why would she confront Shanni in the world of ordinary reality?

Then the realization struck Shanni; Hoven had sensed Shanni's mental powers but could not gauge their strength. So she gambled that Shanni's fighting ability would be no match for hers and she could end the threat by killing Shanni now.

Hoven's eyes burned with hatred as Shanni glanced from one figure to another. Only one figure could be real, and she must choose the right one quickly. If she fired at a phantom, the real Hoven would kill her with the real rifle.

Shanni licked her lips, revolver in hand at her side. Hoven smiled and shifted the rifle as Shanni fought down panic. What to do? How could she choose? And then she remembered Tonah's admonition long ago to listen for the heartbeat. That separated the ghosts of childhood from the beings of ordinary reality, and only the 'real' beings were to be feared in the physical world. Shanni pushed out her perception in a flash, fine-tuning her hearing across the distance separating her from the three 'Hovens'.

And she heard the heartbeat from the Hoven to the right. Hoven perceived the probe and knew. She shrieked and snapped the rifle forward, firing. Shanni had already reacted without thinking, dropping to one knee as she raised the revolver and returned fire. Hoven's bullet went high as Shanni's bullet hit hard, knocking Hoven off her feet. Hoven scrambled in the dust of the road, twisted to her feet like a cat and leaped forward, levering shot after shot from the rifle.

Bullets splattered the gravel as Shanni rolled to her right, using Walpi's training to outrun Hoven's aim, seeking cover from the low depression along the side of the trail.

Hoven's rifle clicked on an empty chamber as she stood grimacing, radiating pure hatred like a fog across the space separating her from Shanni. The spreading red splotch on her tunic showed that Shanni's bullet had found its mark. Hoven's sorcery was keeping her alive as she cast the rifle aside and sped forward, drawing her revolver.

Rage engulfed Shanni and she stood up, firing deliberately at Hoven's knee. The knee was flung backward by the force of the bullet, smashing Hoven forward into the gravel. As Hoven raised her revolver, Shanni fired, and a dark hole appeared in Hoven's forehead. Her head snapped back violently, and then recoiled to the side, the hatred fading like dying embers in the dark eyes frozen in death.

A shimmering appeared around Hoven's body as Shanni blinked. The shimmer intensified into a blue haze that hid the body momentarily, and then a violent flash blinded Shanni. A foul aroma of putrefaction reached Shanni's nostrils and she turned away, repulsed.

Without thinking, Shanni turned around and walked past the corner to where the Huastecs stood, waiting.

Mala, on watch at the foot of the mountains as the sun sank in the afternoon sky, saw movement up the dim trail. She wiped sweaty eyes and peered into the glare. Presently she made out a group walking at a brisk pace. Who would be walking out here? And then she recognized Shanni!

"Hey, wake up everyone!" Mala shouted. "Our people are free!" And she ran out to greet them.

Chapter 23

TONAH CENTERED HIMSELF and reached out, spreading his awareness like a mist across eternity. He became a receptor, sensing the faintest emanations and fine-tuning to the awareness that was the being known as Caleb Stone. And Tonah recalled the time when they had sat quietly by the Chaco River, discussing the rescue of Shanni. They had shared the peaceful sound of the water, and grounded themselves in the stones. That was a key point in the matrix, a node where their life lines had crossed. It was the place to start the search for Caleb, but would Caleb remember?

CALEB FOUGHT DOWN the feeling of panic. Never had he felt so lost and so alone, falling through the black void of eternity. Now he understood why Tonah had insisted on a guidepost, a sign as a guide back to the world of ordinary reality. He remembered the smooth pebble from the Chaco River that had grounded him in his prior spirit journey, but he had no pebble now...or did he? The memory flowed back like a vivid dream, and he recalled sitting with Tonah by the quiet waters of the river.

Time had stood still as they sat, not doing but perceiving. For the first time, Caleb had experienced the peace of becoming centered, a condition in which all his intellectual and emotional faculties were in perfect harmony with total acceptance in an uncertain world. With an intuitive leap, Caleb realized that moment that he and Tonah had shared would always exist, frozen in time like ink under glass, locked forever in the tapestry of eternity.

He wished he could be there again, sharing that moment, anchored in the reality of that time and place. The sense of falling slowed and Caleb's volition began to assert control, driving him like a shooting star across the void. There was a moment of uncertainty, a shimmering as he opened his eyes to the emerging world of ordinary reality. Tonah sat nearby, eyes closed, motionless as a statue. Caleb heard the quiet ripple of water over stones.

Tonah opened his eyes and smiled. "You remembered."

"I didn't know what to do. I'm not sure how I got here."

"Does it matter?"

"I guess not. Is this real, or am I dreaming that we're here?"

"What is 'real'? There are only experiences and interpretations. A sorcerer accepts what is, and works within that reality to achieve his purpose. He does not attach or cling to explanations."

"This seems real enough," Caleb responded. "I even smell the desert sage."

Tonah smiled again. "Check your pulse."

"What?"

"Can you feel your heart beating?"

Caleb paused, and then he reached his right hand toward his left wrist. "I can't detect my heartbeat." he answered, puzzled.

"That's how you know. Soon it will be automatic for you to know without having to check."

"So we're not really here." Caleb shook his head slowly.

"Not correct. We are really here, but in the world of nonordinary reality. Both worlds, and many others, are real but different. They operate with different laws of nature."

"But my body is not here."

"Your spirit body is here, but your physical body remains in ordinary reality. That is why you must see to its care when you leave it to enter the spirit world, and take pains to assure that you can find your way back to it."

"Then I must return to the site of the panther's attack. I was wounded, maybe seriously. My body is there."

"No. Your body has been moved by the sorcerer Goyathlay to a village deep in the mountains. There he and the healer Chinto prevented you from bleeding to death. They await your return to your body."

"But how do I find my way back?"

"That is why they contacted me. I must lead you back."

"And if you had not found me?"

"Your body would slowly die."

"What do I do now?"

"Now it is time to go."

Caleb felt a tremor and the landscape fractured, like a mirror cracking, and his vision dimmed. He felt a sense of loss, of sadness as he left the place of peace to return to the world of men. He followed Tonah, racing like a beam of light into the void. And then he was falling, falling, falling through eternity.

In the village of the Huichol, the body of Caleb Stone sighed and took a deep breath. His eyes opened and he blinked, gazing at the attendant in the dim light of the lodge as his consciousness climbed up from the deep pit of oblivion and assembled itself, interpreting reality. "Water," he gasped. "Please give me water."

The attendant held water to Caleb's lips. Caleb drank and then laid back, closing his eyes. The attendant rushed out to summon Chinto.

Chapter 24

A CLAMOR AT THE edge of camp alerted Toshni to the arrival of Shanni, Matal, and the surviving Huastecs. He arose from the kneeling position in front of the altar and backed away, bowing to the stone god. He exited the shelter, shading his eyes from the glare of the sun, as he gazed at the approaching group.

The riders were apparitions of gray dust, their tired eyes hollow from exhaustion and lack of food. Toshni's experienced eyes swept the band. Many were missing and he knew that meant they would not return. He shook his head sadly. The Huastecs had paid dearly for abandoning their gods.

Men from the camp met the riders and led their tired horses away. Matal and the others walked to the cookfire and sat down quietly while food was served. Toshni walked over and nodded his greeting. There was time enough for talk after they had eaten.

Matal broke the silence when he finished his food. "How many people did we lose?'

"More than twenty died in the attack, and nearly a dozen since then of their wounds, mostly trained fighters."

"We lost nearly a dozen escaping from Alvarez and the mines."

Toshni thought quickly. That was nearly half of the warriors trained by Walpi and his men. The remainder of the Huastecs were older men and women, and young children. Deaths from age and accidents had further reduced their number until now, nearly half the Huastecs who started the journey had perished. And the journey had scarcely begun.

"Too many," he observed finally.

"Yes, too many," Matal agreed.

"Rest now," Toshni admonished. "We will decide what to do tomorrow."

Matal nodded agreement and got up. The others had already sought their beds, exhausted from the long ride. Without a word he went to his tent and stretched out to fall asleep.

Ambria watched sadly from her father's tent. Tomorrow Toshni would lead his followers north and she would have to decide whether to abandon her family, or to leave Matal behind. Duty or love; she must choose.

Shanni stopped inside her tent to clean up before bedtime. Exhaustion had claimed her and she fought to keep her eyes open. Still she felt a deep pang of disappointment, for neither Caleb nor Tonah had greeted her. Had Caleb not returned from his vision quest? And where was Tonah? Was he helping Caleb? Concern filled her with dread, but there was nothing she could do now. She must rest and regain her strength before she could be effective. If only she were not too late! Tears welled up in her eyes. Death had stalked the Huastecs, and many had died. What if Caleb did not survive? Her feverish mind welcomed the warm oblivion that sleep brought.

She awakened the next morning, still tired but alert. The sleep had refreshed her mind, while her fatigued body would require days to recover. She dressed quickly and stepped outside to see Tonah seated with Aurel at breakfast. As she approached, Aurel ladled food onto a plate and handed it to her. Shanni smiled her thanks and sat down.

"Good morning, Grandfather," she greeted. She tried to hide her concern as she saw Tonah up close. Dark circles clouded his eyes and his face had aged visibly since she'd last seen him. He looks like he is dying, she thought with a chill. Would this nightmare they were living never end?

"Good morning." A trace of Tonah's warm smile returned. "Much has happened."

"Caleb?" Shanni's intensity showed. "Has Caleb returned? Is he all right?"

"He has not returned, but he has completed the spirit quest and is recovering. He will return soon."

"Recovering? He's been hurt?"

"He will recover fully. His quest was successful. He faced death and conquered it. He is forever changed."

Shanni caught her breath. What did that mean? Would he be a stranger to her now? Some sorcerers were seduced by the power in the spirit world and detached from human cares and desires. Could Caleb have changed into a different person, a stranger to her? Would he still love her?

"How about you?" Tonah asked softly. "Have you returned the same person?"

Shanni flushed, remembering. She had fought with guns and knives. How many had she killed? She had felt detached, with no regrets, no concern about taking a life, and no shame. She had killed without remorse in order to survive. In the past she had shuddered at what she had perceived as Caleb's ruthlessness. Only now did she understand his world and what he had to do to survive in it.

"No," Shanni answered. "I am not the same."

Uval, one of Toshni's sons, approached the group. "Father is calling a council for the camp. We will meet in front of the tent of the temple. When all are assembled, we will decide our future course of action."

As Uval walked away to alert others, Shanni turned to Tonah and Aurel. "So soon? We've only just arrived, and Matal rode day and night to find us and lead us home. He is too tired to confront Toshni now. Does Toshni think only of himself?"

"Remember the prophesy of the sentinel in your dream catcher," Tonah replied. "It said that all of the Huastecs would perish if we did not take a different course. That course may not be one that we would wish. We must hear what Toshni proposes and then decide."

Shanni was appalled at the condition of the camp as they walked through on their way to the meeting. Food was scarce and no horses had been left to hunt for more. Without horses, the few remaining carts were useless, providing only firewood for the fires. And they needed to find water, soon. Time was running out for the Huastecs.

As they approached the crowd, Shanni saw the looks of fear and despair in the faces of the people. All had been touched by the deaths of the warriors, and some families had no one left to bear their burdens on the journey. The Huastecs had experienced death, suddenly and brutally, and now they sought answers, and some reason for hope.

Toshni stood in front of the tent sheltering the stone god. Smoke rose from the offering on the stone altar as two of his sons tended the fire. Toshni's white hair crowned his creased face as he spoke.

"Friends, I am sorry to disturb your rest. We have suffered a terrible blow and need time to recover. But time is what we do not have. We are running out of food and water, and we lost most of our horses. How long can we survive on foot in the desert? It is clear that we must decide now what to do. Every hour we delay increases our peril. The choice is clear: do we continue into the unknown, or do we turn back?"

"This is not an indictment of Matal's leadership. He has done well and I commend him. But he cannot bring forth water from the rocks, nor food down from the heavens."

"At least we know what is behind us. We can survive the journey back to the Navaho. If we must, we will assimilate into their nation and survive on the reservation. It may be a poor choice, but it gives us life."

"My family and I as well as other families who agree with us are leaving today. We urge all of you to join us."

Matal had listened quietly. He was tired, and sick at heart. Did it matter anymore whether he held the Huastecs together? Circumstances showed neither he, nor anyone else, held the key to their survival. Maybe they should all give up and turn back. He stepped forward, and when he spoke his voice was strong.

"I have fought to hold us together for the safety in numbers. We were few enough at best to face the hazards of the journey. But we had hope that together we could finish the journey and re-establish our people, so that the Huastecs could survive and prosper as a nation in a new land. The Huastecs will not survive as a people if we return. I must go forward, where there is still hope."

"What about Tonah?" A woman spoke from the crowd. "What does Tonah say?"

Tonah stepped to the front and turned to face the assemblage. "When I sent my spirit body into Shanni's dream catcher, I was told that all would perish if we did not change course. The sentinel could not advise us of what course to take for the future is not fixed. We chose from the limited choices that we had. Maybe now, after our suffering, the choices are different. Maybe survival does demand that we perish as a nation in order to survive as individuals. Each of you must now decide for yourself what is the best course."

"What is your choice?"

"My time is short, but I will go on. I believe our future lies to the south and that we must find the Center and reconnect with our ancestors."

Toshni spoke up, quieting the murmur in the crowd. "Each of you must decide, and tell us your choice by the evening meal. We'll divide the supplies and be ready to leave before daybreak."

The next morning, Shanni stood next to Ambria, who wept silently with her arm around Matal's waist, as they watched Ambria's father, mother and brothers lead the entourage out of camp. The stone god had been placed in a wooden palanquin borne by four men, and the few horses laden with supplies. All of the families with old people and young children had elected to return with Toshni. Only two dozen of the trained warriors had elected to continue, with half a dozen horses. Their first priority was to find water, and then food and additional horses. The die was cast, Shanni knew. They would never see their families and friends again. Now each group must find its own destiny, and somehow she must find Caleb.

Chapter 25

CALEB AROSE WITH the dawn, dressed and stepped out of the shelter into the sunlight. He saw Chinto seated nearby. Goyathlay was not in evidence. He walked over to join Chinto.

"I see your energy has returned," Chinto greeted.

"I cannot believe I am healing so fast."

"It is due to the potion your shaman gave you. It stimulates your life energy. For a time, your body can absorb an enormous amount of punishment and snap back."

"Then why wouldn't we utilize it all the time?"

"Because there is a price to pay, a tradeoff. The body ages much faster, like the brief life of a bird, whose metabolism is very fast."

"It appears I will have some scars; the panther was real."

"Yes. It existed in the world of ordinary reality, and could have killed you. But your scar ridges will eventually flatten, leaving only the color, the paleness against your skin."

"The marks of my spirit quest," Caleb added.

"Precisely."

"I am grateful for all your help, but much time has passed since I was with the Huastecs. They are in a dangerous land and I need to be with them."

"Much has happened," Chinto agreed.

"You know?"

"Only in a general way. I feel the disturbances in the matrix of events, and sense much struggle by the people. But I do not sense total disaster."

"Then I should plan to return right away."

"Not quite yet. Our paths may not cross again, and Power has brought you to me for the final step in your teaching. You must be introduced to the world of plants, the other sentient beings on this planet."

"I know plants, but I didn't know they were sentient. Only humans can think and talk."

"Only humans can think and talk in human terms. We are extremely arrogant to think that our reality is the only reality. Every living being has a reality depending upon its perception of the world."

"Help me to understand why I need to know about plants."

"Because plants are essential to our existence. They keep our bodies alive. Without them, we could not exist on this earth. Think about it. What if you had no plants to eat, and no oxygen to breathe? Plants feed our bodies, and convert the air into oxygen that we breathe. But there is much more. As a shaman, you will utilize the power of plants in healing. Much you will teach yourself, but you need an introduction, a place of understanding from which to start. That is my task while you are here."

"When do we begin?"

"Now." Chinto stood up and picked up a canteen and a leather carry bag. He set out from camp, with Caleb following. Chinto's camp was hidden high in the hills of the Sierra Madre where the rainfall and cooler climate supported alpine grasses and evergreens, a stark contrast to the dry, lifeless desert at the base of the mountains.

They climbed in silence for hours, winding upward along the slope of a mountain until they gained the ridge and sat down on flat stones to survey the valley from which they had come. Caleb's gaze fell away across the evergreen slopes, down to the narrow stream that split the valley, and the lodges of the Huichol scattered along its banks. In the distance, the blue haze hung on the slopes of the ridges that marched in steps to the horizon. Caleb felt a sense of timelessness, of eternity. It was as if time stood still in this wilderness.

"Time is an invention of man," Chinto said, reading Caleb's thoughts. "We set arbitrary deadlines to arbitrary events, and then rush to fulfill them. The world before you just *is*. It was yesterday, and will be tomorrow. And it is the same for all life, including you and me."

"But we grow old and die. We know that yesterday is gone, and tomorrow might not be."

"True. But by aligning ourselves with our world, we can slow time and exist in accordance with natural law. Only then can we influence events in a natural way. That is the first step in healing."

"I'm afraid I don't understand."

"All living beings are designed to grow, to remain in balanced health for their natural lifetimes. When illness or disease interferes with this natural process, the shaman must know what to do to restore the harmony, the balance. To be effective, we must understand the basic principle, and be in harmony ourselves. Otherwise, we make much activity but gain no effectiveness."

"Rituals, in other words."

"Yes, rituals. Rituals are essential to creating the climate for healing, but rituals in and of themselves do not heal. Healing comes from the power of the life force, which must be channeled and nurtured carefully, and plants are uniquely suited to aid us in that endeavor. Come, it is time for examples."

Chinto got up and led along the edge of the alpine meadow. Morning glories twined among the low foliage. "If you pluck the seeds and dry them, and then grind them into a paste and ingest them, they will lead you into the world of nonordinary reality, as does peyote. They are often used by curanderos, medicine men, for healing. The castor beans we cultivate in our gardens have many medicinal uses, yet the seed itself is lethal. It contains a substance more deadly than rattlesnake venom."

Chinto continued walking and pointing out the various plants and discussing their uses. Caleb grew concerned. "How will I remember all that you are teaching me?" he replied.

Chinto stopped and turned to Caleb with a serious expression. "How did you find the answer to escaping the Guardian? Did you remember how?"

"No. I just did it; I still don't know how."

"That's the way it is with plants. Once you know them, and that they are sentient beings, they will help you."

"But how do I communicate with a plant?"

"You must learn to be receptive. Plants communicate with each other through their roots, and through aromas. The aromas are also utilized to communicate with insects that help the plant to propagate. Once you learn to be receptive, you will understand them without knowing how you understand."

Caleb shook his head. Maybe he would not be a shaman after all. He would get the Huastecs to safety and then return with Shanni to his ranch. All this would fade like a nightmare into his past. But he did not wish to appear ungrateful to Chinto. After all Chinto had saved his life and felt this was important to his understanding.

"All knowledge comes from inside. The basis of the spirit quest is to learn that. When you learn to truly trust yourself, all things are possible."

"But how can I recall something I have never learned?"

"Learning and teaching are artificial constructs of humans. It is something we invented. And as we proceed to pursue our learning we lose touch with all that we are born with, that we already know. Does the hawk learn to hunt? It already knows what to do to survive."

"So I don't have to remember what we've discussed today?"

"No. Our purpose is to reacquaint you with your natural perception of the living beings that share our planet that we call plants. Once you can communicate with them at will, they will teach you what you need to know. That is how our ancestors learned of our sacred plants."

"Then I can return to the Huastecs and continue to learn?"

"Now that your awareness is heightened, when there is a need you will know what to do."

Caleb gazed along the meadow and out across the long valley. The landscape glittered with auras, casting bright rainbows of color across the surreal landscape. Was he back in the world of nonordinary reality? He reached to check his pulse, and felt his heart beating.

Chinto noticed the gesture and nodded. "One of the great gifts of the spirit quest is that we learn to move back and forth at will between the worlds of ordinary and nonordinary reality. The effects of Tonah's potion are wearing off, but now you don't need it. Now you can alter your state with your intent alone. Now we can go back. There is no more I can show you."

Chinto started back down the meadow and across the ravines leading back to the Huichol village. Dusk was falling and Caleb marveled. Where had the time gone? He felt they had only left a few hours ago. And then he recalled Chinto's comment. Time was an artificial constraint that became elastic in the sorcerer's world. He had become engrossed in Chinto's explanations and lost all track of time.

Fireflies flickered as they neared camp. Chinto reached out to catch one in his hand. He apologized quietly and thanked the firefly for its life, and then he gently pressed the firefly's body with his thumb. A liquid fluorescence streaked his hand. "Every thing that man uses was invented by nature. Many things that we utilize we cannot explain. The firefly can make light without heat."

Caleb caught a firefly and replicated Chinto's action. The liquid glowed without heat and slowly dimmed to go out.

"Everything can be utilized for good or evil," Chinto continued. "The liquid from three fireflies, if ingested, is fatal to man. Evil sorcerers sometimes use it to poison their enemies. But now that you are introduced to sentient beings, you will know how to avoid it."

"How will I know?"

"If it is put in your food, it will glow for your eyes only."

"No one else will see it?"

"No. Only you."

Caleb remained silent, thinking, as he followed Chinto back into camp. What a strange day! They had spent the whole day on the mountain and he didn't know what he had learned. It all seemed too sketchy, too fragmented. Chinto had thought it important, but Caleb had the feeling he had missed Chinto's point.

Goyathlay was waiting when they returned to camp and joined him in the evening meal. Goyathlay hardly spoke, and his fierce visage was unreadable, but Caleb perceived a sharp intelligence and indomitable will behind those piercing black eyes. Caleb knew that the man he knew as Geronimo was capable of great brutality, and his hatred of Anglos was legend along the border. Yet he had carried Caleb more than fifty miles to save his life. Why? Caleb continued eating silently, not knowing what to say.

"The introduction to the sentient beings is complete?" Goyathlay spoke suddenly.

"Yes. It is finished."

"Then tomorrow I will show the Anglo the way back to his people."

"Why did you help me?" Caleb asked.

"I did not help you. I helped Power. When it calls I must respond."

"Why?"

"It is the way of Power. One resists at his peril."

"Why do you hate the Anglos so?"

"Hate? A sorcerer does not hate. A sorcerer remains detached. I used to hate but I learned better."

"So you no longer wish to kill?"

"The Apache lived here for a thousand generations. The land was hard and unforgiving but we learned to live in harmony with it. And then the Mexican troops came and murdered our people. My mother, my wife and our children were slaughtered at camp while I was out hunting. Later, the Anglos came and talked of treaties. They invited my people to a feast and they shot us like animals. Many died. At first I hated, but no longer. Now I am detached. The Mexicans and the Anglos kill us, and I kill them. It is the reality they chose and forced upon me."

"Why didn't you kill me?"

"You were already dying, killed by the panther."

"And yet you saved my life."

"I saw the power marks on your arm and realized that you were apprenticed to Power. You were no longer an Anglo."

"And now?"

"You can never go back to what you were. Power has claimed you."

A cold chill went through Caleb at Goyathlay's words. What if he couldn't control this new perception? He only wanted to return to his ranch with Shanni to settle down and raise their children. What would his life be like in he couldn't shut off this nonordinary perception? Could he lose control and descend into madness?

"Well, for what it is worth, you saved my life and for that I am grateful. I am obliged to you and hope that someday I can help you in return."

Goyathlay looked up, a flicker of surprise in his eyes, his impassive face otherwise unreadable. His black eyes glimmered a moment and then he returned his gaze to the fire. Caleb felt a great sadness as he realized that Goyathlay had not yet achieved complete detachment. Goyathlay could never rise above pain of his loss. Caleb rose and sought his bed. They would leave early the next morning.

They had walked miles down out of the mountains when Goyathlay stopped at a promontory and pointed at the desert spread out below, extending to the western horizon. Caleb glanced back at the silent hills covered with evergreens and realized he could never find the valley of the Huichols in the hidden fastness. Already it seemed like a dream. Maybe it did not exist in ordinary reality.

"Continue west," Goyathlay said. "You will cross the trail of the Huastecs, and turn south to catch up."

"How far?"

"A day, maybe more. They proceed slowly. Now I must go."

Instinctively, without thinking, Caleb extended his hand in farewell.

Goyathlay stared into his eyes and Caleb stood, returning the gaze. Slowly Goyathlay reached out and took his hand in a strong grasp. Goyathlay formed his left hand into a fist and touched it to his chest in a silent salute. And then he released Caleb's hand and turned to trot down the slope and disappear into the ravine.

Caleb hoisted the water gourd and the leather carry bag and stepped out into the desert. His heart lifted as he thought of Shanni. His spirit quest was completed. Now there was nothing to separate them again.

Chapter 26

AT DUSK, SHANNI walked to the edge of camp and looked up at the stars beginning to twinkle in the clear desert sky. The warriors were preparing to continue the journey south, and tomorrow they must leave. She had wanted to go on seeking Caleb, but there were too few horses to spare. But she could not bear the thought of leaving him behind, for he would be returning on foot, his horse long since gone in the desert. Was he out there somewhere, gazing up at these same stars, and wondering if he could find his way back? She recalled how simple and complete their love had been in Mesa Verde, before the outside world had intervened. There they had known the love and intimacy of the innocent, of children still believing that the world cared for them and wished their happiness. How their lives had changed!

Once the Huastecs were forced from Mesa Verde, they found a world they did not understand, and a world that sought to harm them. Only Caleb had understood, and tried to intercede. And he had paid a price, for dangers had surfaced that he would not have faced had he remained in his world, rebuilding his range. And she was no longer the person who had naively trusted the world to protect her. She had learned to fight and to kill. There was a hardness to her, an edge, that rose to meet the world on its own terms. It was the hardness she had sensed in Caleb, the edge that she had not understood. Caleb had shown the way, and the Huastecs had learned. They could fight and survive in the physical world now.

But there was more to life than survival. There was love, and warmth, and the desire to be together and raise their children. How long could they postpone their own lives without coming apart, split by the danger, the upheavals, the burdens that seemingly never ended? What did she really want? And what did Caleb want?

She found a quiet place and sat down on a low boulder. The moon was rising in the east, lighting the desert with eerie shadows that stretched out into lines, crisscrossing the low hills and dry washes. It could be the surface of the moon, she thought, dry, lifeless, unchanging. Shanni closed her eyes and centered herself, slowing her breathing and reaching out with her perception. Dreamlike, she felt her awareness spreading like a mist across the landscape, listening, perceiving.

She felt a ripple of emotion, of surprise. And then she felt a warmth, a caring, a feeling of well-being and belonging in the cool desert night.

I am here, she felt the presence. *Caleb, is it you?.*

I am here, and I am coming to you. Do not be concerned.

So many questions ran through her mind. Was he all right? How far away was he, when would he reach camp? But the questions interfered with her centeredness, and broke the link. She quickly composed herself and shut off her internal dialogue. She entered the trance-like state that perceived, and again she felt the contact with Caleb. This time there was no voice, only a feeling, the feeling of love and of caring. Caleb sent his love across the desert night, and she wrapped herself in its warmth. How could she have doubted that he would still love her? She gave herself to it, realizing that love was what bound their world together, giving it meaning. Love created the magic, that filled every moment of life with meaning. He was out there somewhere, and he was finding his way home.

Shanni opened her eyes and saw the shadow making its way slowly toward her across the desert floor, and she leapt to her feet, her heart racing. She started to run, her feet scarcely touching the sand as she flew toward the shadow that was becoming flesh. She leapt into Caleb's arms and felt his strong body lift her up, enveloping her, and she was lost in the love of him.

Walpi was propped against his bedroll near the campfire when Caleb joined him in the bright sun of early morning. Caleb sensed a quiet serenity surrounding Walpi, a sense he had not felt before. The spirit quest had changed him; he sensed things at a new level, indeed on many levels. Now he knew things without asking. Walpi had changed; he was a different person.

"It is good to see you recovering. Aurel said you came very close to death."

"Yes. I faced the threshold, and saw the tunnel of light. Aurel brought me back to the world of the living. I owe him my life."

"What will you do now?"

"When I am able, I will return to my home with the Navaho, and live out my days. I have grandchildren, and will make myself a warm lodge. I will be at peace."

"You could have done that before. We owe you much for coming along and teaching the Huastecs how to fight, and leading them in combat."

"It was my wish. I discussed it with Manuelito, who understood. All my life I have been a warrior. My joy was in the doing, the fighting for a good cause. All that has changed for the Navaho. I realized the Huastecs offered me one last hunt, one last chance to be a warrior. Manuelito understood, and allowed me to go with his blessing, although he could have used me there. I think deep in his heart, Manuelito also would like a last hunt, the opportunity to be a real Navaho, but of course he realizes his duty to his people."

Caleb was silent, thinking back to those times when he had risked his own life, fighting for something he believed in. Sometimes his own life was at stake, or the lives of his friends. Later he fought to avenge his father and to reclaim the range that was rightfully his. He understood why Walpi had come, and had risked his life. A man was at his best when he dedicated himself to a worthy cause and committed his all to it.

Shanni, Tonah and Aurel exchanged greetings and joined them. "We've finished eating, and the supplies are packed, such as they are," Aurel said. "We'll be leaving soon." Aurel continued, briefing Caleb on the events that had nearly destroyed the caravan in his absence.

Caleb nodded. Necessity drove them now, his questions could wait. They must find food and water.

"What about you, Walpi?" Aurel continued. "Will you be able to ride?"

"Yes, I'll go along. After we find supplies and a horse of my own, I'll return home to the Navaho."

"What's our plan?" Caleb asked, turning to Aurel.

"Matal is leading us away from the desert and into the mountains. It's dangerous, but we can find water and game there. We'll likely run into replacements brought in to run the mine, but we'll find horses. With fresh supplies, we can head south and leave them behind."

"It's as good a plan as any," Caleb replied. "We'll live better away from this desert."

Matal led out on foot, followed by warriors leading the horses loaded with packs, and one bearing Walpi. They walked steadily until the sun was high in the noon sky, when they sought shade and shelter from the heat. In midafternoon, they continued. By dusk they could see the dim outline of the western Sierra Madres, reminding Shanni of the evil they had encountered there at the hands of Alvarez and his men. With Alvarez's death, they would be dispersed now, having gone back to their villages. But soon others would come, driven by their greed for silver, and the mine would start up again, and the marauding to capture workers would resume.

With the coolness of evening, Matal elected to keep traveling, getting as close to the mountains as they could before stopping for the night. They would need daylight in order to navigate the ravines and canyons once they left the desert.

Hours later, Matal called a halt and the warriors began making camp for the night. Sentries were posted, and food was passed out. There would be no fires to alert an enemy to their presence. Four people were sent out to scout for water. Shanni felt better, despite her fatigue. They had made progress today, and were back in charge. They would find what they needed to resupply and carry on. And once they all had horses, they would travel swiftly.

A Warrior's Heart

Heart, what keeps you beating so?
What drives you on, I'd like to know.
No one could blame you if you chose to stop.

I remember long nights filled with pain,
When you lunged and surged, and surged again
Pumping blood and forcing life
Upon my failing body.

Pushed by potions too strong for me,
I look but cannot see
How you stood up and rode it out unyielding.

Perhaps once in a distant land,
You pumped blood in a different man
A gladiator perhaps who drove you hard
without a thought.

How disappointed you must have been
To find yourself in my poor frame,
But you've done well by me
And I am grateful.

Sometimes in the still of night
I wonder if, suddenly, you might
fail me.

But like an old friend tried and true
I'm confident that you
Will carry on without complaining.

Until that time when you are told
It's time I left this earthly mold.
Your job is done,
And you can cease your labor.

Let me say before we go,
That I am grateful, even so
Next time you deserve
To drive a better man.

(Walpi's chant, during his slow recovery.)

Chapter 27

THEY REACHED THE foothills in midmorning, feeling the cool breeze that wafted down from the mountain, bearing the fresh scent of evergreens. Scouts were far out front on foot, seeking a way through the broken country and on the lookout for potential enemies. Nothing stirred in the stillness as the silent mountains beckoned, with promise of cooler air and plentiful water. Where there was water, there would be grass and game, and they desperately needed to replenish their supplies.

They entered the tree line and climbed ever higher, winding among the pinions that led up to pines and spruce on the higher slopes. Caleb drew in deep breaths, savoring the air after the dry dustiness of the desert.

Shanni walked silently beside him, smiling at his glances, and pointing out flowers and scenes of particular beauty. She loves the mountains as I do, he thought. She will love my ranch high on the slopes of the Uncompahgre Plateau. With the thought, his mood sobered. When would they ever return to his land and settle down to make their life together? Now they were in a strange land, with only the unknown in front of them. When would it all end?

Shanni sensed his change in mood, and whispered quietly, "We are together. That is enough."

"Yes," he answered. "We should not spoil today in anticipation of tomorrow."

"Why, that sounds like something Tonah would say. You've changed since returning from the spirit quest."

"I suppose so," Caleb nodded. "Somehow, after the spirit quest, I take a longer view, seeing things from a different perspective."

"Is that a good thing or a bad thing?"

"I think it is a good thing. Somehow I'm more trusting that the universe is on our side. While it does not actively intervene, it cares for its beings and wants their lives to be happy. Does that make sense?"

"It is better than to focus on the evil in the world and become paranoid."

"The spirit quest is very intense. One is changed after experiencing it. You will see. Both you and Aurel will see."

"We were preparing to make our spirit quests when the bandits raided our camp and everything changed. We haven't had time to bring it up with Tonah. We should see what he has in mind."

"Time enough when we get supplies and plan a new course of action"

Shanni nodded agreement and continued beside him in silence.

They reached a glade covered with lush grass, sheltered by spruce and fir trees. Jack rabbits scurried for cover, as birds flitted among the trees. They saw signs of deer that had been grazing until their sensitive ears detected the approach of the Huastecs. The scouts returned, reporting no sign of human presence, and settled down to eat. Matal posted sentries well out from the glade as a precaution, and then he and the other Huastecs scattered out along the meadow to rest and eat. They were soon engaged in conversation, planning the remainder of the day and sharing ideas for the next day's journey.

Tonah seemed preoccupied and moved off to himself, eating slowly, seeming distracted. He looked tired, and Shanni eased over to check on him. "Do you wish solitude?" She asked.

"Why, we already have that," Tonah answered, raising his eyebrows. "I was absorbing the beauty of this place."

"I thought maybe you wished to be alone with your thoughts."

"No, I am fine. Please join me, and invite Aurel and Caleb. This is a good place, a power spot. Here we can talk."

Shanni beckoned Aurel and Caleb, who left the group with Matal and strolled over. Caleb settled back gratefully against a saddle roll and continued chewing on his cold meal of dried meat and corn meal. Tonah ate silently, seeming distracted, his mind elsewhere, while Aurel ate with relish, his body absorbing strength wherever it could find it.

Shanni sat down next to Caleb. Never again would she take his nearness for granted. They had been torn apart too much since leaving Mesa Verde. She had trained as a warrior and now wherever life took Caleb she would go with him.

Aurel finished eating, and as usual, he was transparent with what he was thinking. "Tonah, we are traveling further into the unknown, and I still haven't completed my spirit quest. How can I complete it and find my way back in this wilderness?"

"I have the same problem," Shanni nodded. "We do not know this land, and you dare not leave a trail for us to follow."

"But you have already completed your spirit quests," Tonah answered. "Power has already interceded."

"How?" Aurel looked surprised.

"When you healed Walpi. That was your spirit quest."

"But I thought I had to go into the wilderness, see visions, and find a power animal."

"That is one way, but not the only way. The essence of the spirit quest is to face death, and know viscerally that you are going to die if you do not take the appropriate action. When you realized you might have to die yourself to save Walpi, what did you do?"

Aurel's brow furled in thought. The whole experience was surrealistic, disjointed, like a nightmare that fades with the light. "I searched for what to do."

"And where did you find it?"

"I asked you to help me, but you were unable."

"So where did you turn?"

"To myself. I had no other choice."

"Precisely. You trusted yourself and found your answer. You were forced to get in touch with your true self, and for the remainder of your life, you are changed. When faced with life or death decisions, you will know to look within for the answer."

"That's what Chinto was trying to tell me when he introduced me to the plants as sentient beings." Caleb interjected.

"Yes," Tonah agreed. "Once you accept that you can communicate with them, plants can teach you what you need to know at the time you need it. That is far superior to trying to memorize the recipes for various potions that may or may not be effective on different human bodies."

"What about my vision quest?" Shanni asked.

"Yours was in the world of ordinary reality. You grew up accepting the world of nonordinary reality, and can move freely in it, just as Caleb grew up in the world of ordinary reality and has survived successfully in it. Each of you had to face your mortality in the other world. Only when we face the primordial terror of our own death do we realize our connectedness with the universal consciousness. Then we accept that all the knowledge of the universe is available to us if we know how to access it."

"And we access it by trusting ourselves," Caleb answered.

"Precisely, but it cannot be an intellectual exercise. Your core being, the sea of life itself, can only be accessed by the intuitive side of your mind, and only if you have complete faith and trust that the universe will respond to your need when you call."

"I experienced parts of myself that I did not know existed," Caleb said.

"And you felt yourself in a state of acceptance, where neither fear nor panic exists. A state of calm poise, where you acted with deliberation, never questioning that it was precisely the right action at the right time."

"Yes," Caleb said. "The fear that I was about to die stopped, and I entered a state where the only thing that mattered was that I take the right action."

"That is the moment of detachment from your individual self, and your reconnecting with the sentience of the universe, of which you are an inseparable part. That is when you realize that your individual death is only a transition, a raindrop returning to the lake. You no longer fear death, and you trust yourself to take the right action to avoid it."

"But if we don't fear death, why do we take action to avoid it?"

"Our programming. An animal is born, and as it matures, it moves outside into the world. It hears a sudden noise, and it instinctively reacts, running away or seeking shelter. We are the same. Our bodies exist in a world of danger. We are programmed to avoid death long enough to grow strong, enjoy life in this dimension, and have offspring to carry on our species. Our success speaks for itself."

"So my spirit quest was in the physical world," Shanni interjected. "When I fought for my life with Alvarez."

"Yes. You knew what to do in the worlds of nonordinary reality, but did not know terror until you faced Alvarez and his men. You had to detach from your fear and revulsion to take the appropriate action to save yourself. And you risked your life again by choosing to return and rescue the other prisoners. The most powerful spirit quest is when one faces death to save others."

"I'm afraid I missed that part," Caleb observed. "I fought in the spirit world to save myself."

"But the spirit quest became necessary for you only because you had committed yourself to our cause, which awakened the evil forces against you. You were already risking your life to aid us."

Everyone remained silent, absorbing the meaning of Tonah's words. So much had happened that they had not had time to absorb what they had learned.

Tonah took a deep breath and smiled. "All is as it should be," he said. "My work here is done at last. Now I can rest."

"What do you mean," Shanni asked, alarmed at his demeanor.

"Each of you is now a full shaman in your own right. I have led you to the abyss, and you have crossed over. There is no more I can teach you."

"So what happens now?" Aurel asked.

"You will go forth, and you will utilize your skills to find the Center, and then you will know what to do to protect the Huastecs."

"You mean 'we', don't you?" Aurel asked, picking up on Tonah's strange tone of voice.

"In a way, yes. I will always be a part of you, just as my mentors were always a part of me. But my body is old, held together by my will until I finished my task here on earth. Now I am freed of it, and already my spirit is looking forward to the next dimension of existence."

"You mean you're dying?"

"There is much work for me to do at the next level. I must go to it and proceed."

"But we need you here! How can we succeed without your knowledge to guide us?" Aurel's voice registered his concern.

"When you call, I will answer. But once you connected with the universal consciousness, you know everything I know. It is all there, for each of us, always."

Tears welled in Shanni's eyes. "Please don't speak of leaving us. You are all the family I have left. We must finish the journey together. Now is no time to talk of death, after we have suffered so much!"

"We shamans take a different view of death. To us, death is only moving from one phase of life into another. We view the transition with detachment, as we go to an active existence in the next dimension. We choose our time and we go. We simply disappear from the earth. You will know when your time has come and do the same."

"How can there be closure if you just disappear? What about last respects, and ...burial?" Aurel stumbled over the last word.

"Now that we all understand that death is only a transition, a moving to a new existence, we no longer feel the need for sorrow," Tonah replied softly.

Tears welled in Shanni's eyes. "You have been my only family for so long, I cannot imagine life without you. The very thought terrifies me; I can already feel the *aloneness*!"

"We humans know love; we need our rituals, our way of letting go and getting past the loss of a loved one," Aurel added. "You have meant so much to all of us."

"As you wish. But is it not unusual for one to attend his own 'funeral'?"

"Please!" Shanni pleaded. "No more of this. I simply cannot deal with this so coldly. We are human beings. We love, and we feel loss. Let's have no more talk of your leaving us, Grandfather."

Tonah stood up. "We must go now." He had planted the seed, preparing them for what was to come. He would need to prepare the others tonight. His time on the earth had run out, and soon he must go.

Tonah called the group together around the campfire as darkness fell. The group stood expectantly, as his discussion earlier in the day had been passed around quietly as they traveled. A pale moon had risen, casting a faint shadow over the mountains splitting the horizon. The setting was surreal, as if time had stood still, Caleb thought. The scene before him burned into his retina, for he realized that from this moment on, his life, and that of the Huastecs would be forever changed. Tonah would be lost to them, and already Caleb felt the enormity of that loss. Like the Huastecs, he had come to lean on Tonah's strength, his certainty and confidence in dealing with life's problems. Now Caleb, Shanni, and Aurel must take up his mantle and go forth without Tonah. It was a sobering responsibility.

Tonah stood before them, calm and strong. He emanated a kind of timeless affection, Caleb perceived, a caring for each individual and strength of character that caused all who knew him to trust him. With his heightened powers, Caleb saw Tonah's core being as an inner radiance of timeless good will and peace.

Tonah drew himself up to his full height, drawing a deep breath. His dark eyes softened as he gazed across the group.

"My friends," he began. "You are more than friends, you are like my children, for I remember the special times when each of you were born. I watched you play as children, and grow into the fine men and women you are today. I acknowledge and thank you for the gift your lives are to me.

"But there is much that you must do. You are the hope for the future of the Huastecs. Only you can carry the banner forward and re-establish our race. The others have lost heart and gone back. They have chosen the path of security with its unfortunate lose of identity, while you have chosen the path of freedom. You carry a heavy responsibility, and you will prevail. With the risks come the rewards and one day you will be remembered for rebuilding the nation of the Huastecs. The way will be hard and fraught with danger, but do not falter. Your cause is just. Go with my blessing."

"Now I must leave you. My work on this plane is done, and there is much waiting for me to do in the next world. Do not grieve for me; instead, join me in celebrating the gift of life on this earth, for my joys are many and my regrets are few. Shanni, Caleb and Aurel have completed their spirit quests and now they will lead in my place. Through them, I will be in touch with you and following with pride your progress. Now I will embrace each of you one last time with this earthly body that has served me so well. But like the moth that must leave its cocoon, I have outgrown this body and must leave it now."

Shanni blinked back tears as Tonah hugged her and Caleb, one in each arm, and then gently pulled them together as he stepped back and walked around the silent circle, embracing each of the Huastecs in turn. He walked to the edge of the light cast by the fire, turned and waved and stepped into the darkness.

The Huastecs stood in stunned silence, gazing after his departed form. Stars twinkled overhead in the clear dark sky. Each lost in his thoughts, they were unaware of the time passing until a faint glow formed halfway up the forested slope of the mountain. The glow grew stronger, seeming to hang like a blue mist over the tops of the pines. The mist coalesced suddenly and then exploded into a blinding flash of light. From the core emanated a single beam of blue-white light that beamed skyward and disappeared. The blue mist fragmented and dissipated like sparks from a fire, and there remained only the darkness and the silence. Tonah was gone.

Their eyes readjusted to the night sky as Matal turned to the campfire and spoke. "Tonah has shown us the way. We must finish our work in this world and then follow him. Tomorrow we will continue south, with faith that we will find the Center, the promised land of the Huastecs. We will build, and when the time is right, we will send for the others. Together we will rebuild the nation of the Huastecs."

Murmurs of approval greeted Matal's words, but soon their thoughts returned to the present. They were strangers in a hostile land, and they were tired. Each lost to his own thoughts, they began preparation to retire for the night, for tomorrow would come soon, and with it new challenges for survival. For now, being alive was enough.

Caleb reached out and drew Shanni into his arms. Life had taken them far from home, but they were together as man and wife. With each other, they could go forth and face the unknown. For now it was enough.

COMING SOON:

ANASAZI DESOLATION, fourth in the ANASAZI PRINCESS series of novels continues the saga of the Huastecs, forced out of their home in Mesa Verde, Territory of Colorado, during the 1870s. Their perilous journey has carried the Anglo gunfighter Caleb Stone, the Huastec princess Shanni, and the band of Huastecs deep into Mexico in search of the fabled "Center", homeland of the Huastec nation. Enemies are arrayed against them in the physical world, as anarchy reigns during the turbulent time of the Mexican revolution. Additional danger comes from the spirit world, as evil sorcerers use paranormal powers against them in the world of nonordinary reality. Caleb and the Huastecs must utilize their strength and newfound skills in both worlds to survive the onslaught and reach their destination. Only then can Caleb and Shanni return to his ranch in western Colorado and build their life together.

The following pages are a preview of the fourth novel in the ANASAZI PRINCESS series.

ANASAZI DESOLATION,
A Novel:

PROLOGUE

"*There is a river whose streams make glad the city of God...*" (Psalms 46:4, Bible. NIV)

❖

THE HAWK GLIDED silently to a perch high in the pines lining the slope of the mountains. Its keen eyes scanned the forest, looking for prey. It detected movement, far in the distance, black specks lost in the vastness that fell away league after league to the horizon. It blinked, and then lifted off hurriedly on strong wings, for the forms were men, and where there were men, there was death.

Matal raised his hand, halting the small band of Huastecs. They dropped their packs gratefully and sat down, for they had walked briskly without pause all morning. Caleb Stone glanced across the faces of his companions, thinking back to the strange turn of events that had brought him here to the Sierra Madre mountains of northern Mexico, helping the Huastecs in their dangerous journey to find their ancient Mayan homeland to the south.

His gaze settled on Shanni, the Huastec princess who had saved his life and captured his heart. His love for her had led him far from his ranch in western Colorado, and engaged him in the desperate quest to find a homeland for the Huastecs before they were captured or killed in the turbulent times of the Anglos' settling of the west. How his world had changed! Hardly a year had passed since he had returned to Mancos, Colorado to find his father's killers and reclaim his ranch. His enemies had ambushed him, and only the rescue by Shanni and her grandfather, Tonah, the shaman, had saved his life.

When the Huastecs were forced out of their hidden enclave in Mesa Verde, Caleb's love for Shanni had pulled him into the quest to return to their fabled homeland far to the south.

And now he was here, with less than two dozen remnants of the nearly one hundred families who had started the journey. Many had perished and others had turned back, and their quest was hardly begun.

But now he was with Shanni and he was committed to their cause. When the journey was complete, and the Huastecs settled in their new home, he and Shanni would return to his ranch, raise their children, and live out their days in peace.

Shanni felt his gaze and smiled, wiping perspiration from her brow. She was a tall woman, with flashing black eyes and glistening hair that hung long, braided for travel, down her back. She had trained with the others for weeks under Walpi's tutelage, becoming expert in the use of the Anglos' weapons: revolvers and rifles. She had become strong and tanned by the weeks of hand-to-hand combat training.

Matal, their leader, turned to confer with the group. Matal was stock and strong, his even features serious as he spoke. "Soon we'll reach the timberline, and the forest will no longer shelter us. Without horses we will be vulnerable to attack. Caleb, do you know this country?"

"Only generally. My travels never brought me this far south. There are two mountain ranges, east and west, called the Sierra Madres. The desert we came through separates them. I believe we are on the eastern slope of the western, or Occidental, range. The two converge further south as the land narrows. We will enter the highlands then."

"Should we continue on foot, or seek to capture horses?"

"Horses would only be in our way until we enter more open country. Soon we'll approach populate areas, even cities. Then we may be able to travel swiftly by train."

"What is a train?" Matal looked puzzled, glancing around at the others as they gazed expectantly at Caleb.

"An Anglo machine large enough to transport many people, their horses and supplies."

Matal shook his head in wonder. "That must be something to see!"

"And something to ride," Caleb agreed. "But more importantly, it covers great distances very quickly. Some go more than forty miles in an hour."

Caleb saw disbelief in the faces of the Huastecs gathered about him. "Don't worry," he smiled, "You'll see for yourselves before long, and I suspect many other 'wonders' before we're done."

"Already we've seen many wonders since we left Mesa Verde," Matal agreed. "We had no concept that the outside world was so big!"

"And so dangerous!" Mala interjected. Like all the Huastec women, Mala's hair was black, glistening in the sun. She had completed the combat training along with the other women and had elected to continue south when many of the Huastec families, devastated by the bandits' attacks, had elected to turn back. Now the future of the Huastecs rested on the small band's quest to reach the Mayan "Center", known to them only in legend.

"These are turbulent times," Caleb answered. "Driven by political upheaval and lawless men. A time will come when the rule of law will replace guns and knives, and people will be able to raise their families in peace."

"As we lived at Mesa Verde," Aurel added, nodding. Aurel was Tonah's apprentice, who like Caleb and Shanni, had completed his spirit quest during the journey. Tonah had passed on into the spirit world, and as shamans, they carried on his legacy to guide and protect the Huastecs.

"In small communities, people know one another and few laws are needed. But there are countries where the people are many in number, in the thousands and tens of thousands. Many laws are needed to govern behavior."

"So we have only touched the world so far in our journey?" Matal observed.

"Only touched it," Caleb agreed. "There is much, much more to experience; too much complexity to explain."

"Then we will learn as we go," Matal returned, lifting his pack. "Where others have gone, we can go."

"Yes," Caleb agreed as the Huastecs gathered up their packs to continue. "That is how we all learn. As much as one might like to, you cannot stop the world. It goes on continuously changing."

ANASAZI DESOLATION, fourth in the ANASAZI PRINCESS series, is targeted for publication in November, 2003. Check our web site for details at "www.pentaclespress.com".

BOOKS BY JAMES GIBSON

at

www.pentaclespress.com

ANASAZI PRINCESS: A Fable of the Old West. *Anasazi Princess* combines traditional Western romance with Native American shamanism to create a "New Age" Western in which Caleb Stone returns to Mancos, Colorado to avenge his father's murder and reclaim his family's land. After he is ambushed, the Huastecs Tonah and his granddaughter, Shanni rescue Caleb and take him away to their hidden enclave in Mesa Verde where Tonah uses his shamanistic powers to save Caleb's life. As he recovers, Caleb falls in love with Shanni and becomes caught up in the Huastecs' quest to return to the Mayan "Center" of their civilization. (Published 2001; 193 pages.)

ANASAZI JOURNEY: A Novel: The *Anasazi Princess* saga continues...Anasazi princess Shanni and her people, the Huastecs are lost and suffering in the desert of New Mexico as they journey south in an attempt to reach the "Center" of their ancient Mayan homeland. Seeking help to find food and water, they fall into the hands of renegade leader Kaibito, who takes them prisoner. The Huastec shaman, Tonah, realizes that a more sinister force in the spirit world threatens the Huastecs and the life of Caleb Stone, the Anglo who has joined the band to help Shanni and the Huastecs complete their journey. The sorcerer Jorge Tupac utilizes ancient Mayan occult arts in an attempt to murder Shanni, forcing Caleb and Tonah to risk their lives to rescue her and deliver the Huastec nation from a strange and perilous world. (Published 2002; 178 pages.)

ANASAZI QUEST: A Novel: As the *Anasazi Princess* saga continues, the Huastec nation escapes from the clutches of renegades and forges southward from the Territory of New Mexico to enter Mexico during the turbulent times of the revolution of the 1870s. Despite their peaceful intent to return to the mythical "Center" of their ancient Mayan civilization, the Huastecs are attacked, and princess Shanni and her women warriors are carried off into captivity. At the same time, a sinister force of Mayan sorcerers attempts to attack, forcing Tonah, the Huastec shaman, to send the Anglo Caleb Stone on a spirit quest to learn how to save his own life and that of Shanni. As they face their individual crises, both Caleb and Shanni learn to use the latent powers of the human mind to survive in strange and hostile worlds. (Published, 2003; 224 pages.)

ANASAZI DESOLATION: A Novel: The fourth novel in the *Anasazi Princess* saga carries a small remnant of Huastec warriors deep into Mexico in the search for their homeland centered in the ancient Mayan civilization in the Yucatan. With the loss of her grandfather, the shaman Tonah, the Huastec princess Shanni is forced to deal with the strange and sinister attacks by sorcerers in the spirit world who threaten her life and that of her husband, the Anglo Caleb Stone. As the attacks intensify, Shanni is forced to probe the depths of the human psyche, and fight an imposed paranoia that threatens to destroy her sanity and her love for Caleb. (Publication planned for November, 2003; approximately 200 pages.)

ANASAZI TRIUMPH: A Novel: The final novel in the *Anasazi Princess* saga brings the Huastec warriors into the Yucatan, and face to face with their tormentors, the Mayan sorcerers who have made repeated attempts to kill Caleb and Shanni and prevent them from uncovering the horrible secret of the Mayas hidden for a thousand years. (Publication planned for June, 2004; approximately 175 pages.)

GLOSSARY OF TERMS

Anasazi (AH-NAH-sah-zi): Modern Navaho word for the "Ancient Ones", the Basket Weaver-Puebla culture of Native Americans who inhabited the region of what is now northern Arizona-western Colorado from CE 100-1300. They are noted for their elaborate pueblo and cliff dwellings (e.g., Chaco Canyon, Mesa Verde.)

Caleb (KAY-leb): Biblical name, representing "courage". In Numbers 14:24, Caleb is allowed to enter Canaan, the "Promised Land" because of his faithfulness in spite of great adversity and threats from his own people.

Goyathlay (Goy-AHTH-LAY): Bedonkohe Apache name, "One who yawns", for the Apache warrior (1829?-1909) believed to have mystical powers. After his mother, wife, and two small children were murdered by Mexican troops, Goyathlay became a vengeful killer of Mexican nationals, which struck such terror that they are said to have prayed to Saint Jerome for protection, hence the source of the Mexican name under which he became famous: "Geronimo".

Huastecs (Hu-AZ-teks): Descendants of the Mayas living in the Yucatan region of southern Mexico. The term is used fictionally in the *Anasazi Princess* series of books to surmise a connection between the Anasazi of western Colorado and the Maya, which becomes the motivation for Shanni and her people to attempt the journey back to their mythical "Center".

Shaman (SHAH-mon): From the Tungusic word 'saman' in Siberia; one who actively enters into an altered state of consciousness ("nonordinary reality") in order to gain knowledge, harness power, and develop extraordinary abilities to solve problems and to heal sickness in the ordinary world.

Shanni (SHAH-nee): Princess of the Huastecs, a fictional sect of the Anasazi, who possesses paranormal powers.

Sorcerer (SOR-SIR-er): In the *Anasazi Princess* series context, a shaman who goes beyond healing to use paranormal powers in states of nonordinary reality to gain knowledge, increase power, and fight battles. In Mexico, sorcerers are referred to as "brujos" (male) and "brujerias" (female), and "healers" are sometimes referred to as "curanderos".

Tonah (TONE-ah): Shaman, sorcerer, and spiritual leader of the fictional Huastecs of Mesa Verde; despite his age, Shanni considers him her "grandfather".

Vision Quest (VEZ-YON KWEST), also called 'Spirit Quest': A rite of passage common to many aboriginal and/or shamanistic societies in which the initiate goes into the wilderness alone and faces physical death. The belief is that the danger taps into latent survival abilities and mystical knowledge deep within the psyche that is only activated to save the person's life when death is imminent.

SELECTED BIBLIOGRAPHY

Biblical:

Books of *Deuteronomy, Exodus, Numbers, Psalms*: Old Testament; *Matthew:* New Testament. (Bible, New International Version);

Medicinal/Psychedelic Plants:

Pinchbeck, Daniel. *Breaking Open the Head: A Psychedelic Journey into the Heart of Contemporary Shamanism*. (Berkley Books, Random House, New York, NY. 2002).

Plotkin, Mark J., Ph.D. *Medicine Quest: In Search of Nature's Healing Secrets*. (Penguin Putnam, Inc. New York, NY. 2000).

Sacks, Oliver. *Oaxaca Journal*. (National Geographic Directions, National Geographic, Washington, D.C., 2002).

Paranormal/Psychic Phenomena:

Dong, Paul & Thomas E. Raffill. *China's Super Psychics*. (Marlowe and Company, New York, NY. 1997).

Hughes, James. *Altered States*. (Watson-Guptill Publications, Division of BPI Communications, New York, NY. 1999).

McCrumb, Sharyn. *She Walks These Hills* (fiction). (Signet, Division of Penguin Putnam, New York, NY. 1994).

Sugrue, Thomas. *The Story of Edgar Cayce: There is a River*. (A.R.E. Press, Association for Research and Enlightenment, Inc., Virginia Beach, Virginia. 1990).

<u>*Shamanism:*</u>

Drury, Nevill. *Shamanism: An Introductory Guide to Living in Harmony with Nature.* (Element Books, Inc., Boston, Massachusetts. 2000).

Harner, Michael. *The Way of the Shaman.* (Harper & Row, HarperCollins Publishers, New York, NY. 1990).

Wolfe, Amber. *The Truth About Shamanism.* (Llewellyn Publications, St. Paul, Minnesota. 1988).

Books by James Gibson:
at
www.pentaclespress.com

Anasazi Princess
Anasazi Journey
Anasazi Quest

Order Form

To order additional copies, fill out this form and send it along with your check or money order to: James N. Gibson LLC, P.O. Box 51, Novi, MI 48376.
Or order online: www.pentaclespress.com

Cost per copy $9.95 plus $2.50 P&H. (MI residents add 6% sales tax)

Ship _______ copies of *Anasazi Quest* to:

Name_____________________________

Address:__________________________

City:_________________________

State/Zip:__________________________

☐ Check box for signed copy

Please tell us how you found out about this book.

☐ Friend ☐ Internet
☐ Book Store ☐ Radio
☐ Newspaper ☐ Magazine
☐ Other _________________________